THE FAR SIDE OF THE WILD WEST

Lyn McConchie

Hadrosaur Productions, Mesilla Park, NM

The Far Side of the Wild West
Hadrosaur Productions
First Edition: September 2024

ISBN-13: 979-8-9851120-8-5

Hadrosaur Productions
P.O. Box 2194
Mesilla Park, NM 88047-2194
www.hadrosaur.com

Portions of this book have appeared previously as follows:

"The Taxidermist" published as "The Guy Who Stuffed Chooks" in *Write Now* (NZ) May '99.

"Ernest" appeared in *Roar 6* anthology, June 2015.

"On the Road to Bodie" appeared in *Six-Guns Straight from Hell* 2010

"Great-Aunt Edna" appeared in *Strange Summer Fun* anthology July 2014.

"Lone-Star Jackson – Outlaw" appeared in *Steampunk Trails* issue 1. Sept 2013.

A Steam-Powered Camera" appeared in *Steampunk Trails*. August 2014.

"Doing the Right Thing" appeared in *A Fistful of Hollers* anthology 2010, USA.

"A Friend of Granny Jarni" appeared in *Myriad Lands* Vol. 1 antho Aug 2016. substantially different version.

"Bath Salts and Bedlam" appeared in *Tales of the Talisman,* Spring 2015.

"The Wheel" appeared in *Myriad Lands* Vol. 1 antho Aug 2016.

"Life in Stages" appeared in *A Fistful of Hollers* anthology 2010.

CONTENTS

THE
FAR SIDE
OF THE
WILD
WEST
W

THE TAXIDERMIST

I never liked Jason Aldmire. Of course, he was a year older than me. He didn't work too hard in school and last year the teachers kept him back a class. He hated that and he was a bully. Maybe that was why he took up the hobby he did. His granddad used to be a taxidermist. That's a bloke who skins things. He makes a wire frame then puts the skin back over it. After that they sort of fill the skin out with stuffing. Then they put in glass eyes. And before you know it, there's the trout you caught looking back at you just like it was alive again.

Jase's granddad did that for years. But my dad says the bottom fell out of the market. I asked him why and all he could say was that the Comanche caused trouble, and a lot of them as were rich stopped their hunting parties around our way. Jase's granddad died and for years all of his gear just sat in the back of the shed where he'd worked, stashed in big black tin trunks that were moth-proof and watertight, until Jase decided to take it up. I don't know why. But the first we knew of it was Jase coming into school and showing off this hen.

To tell the truth it made me feel a bit sick. I mean, there it was looking at you. Just as if it was alive, when its guts were sawdust or something, and its eyes were glass. You knew all that. But it still looked as if the chook was going to sit down, cackle and lay an egg. I've never liked chickens; they have beady little eyes that always have a sort of hungry look in them. The teacher made quite a fuss of Jason. Said he'd done a wonderful job and he just wished his old dog looked half as good as the chicken did – and he was still alive.

Of course that was asking for it. The dog died a few weeks later. Jase was around at the teacher's place next day asking if he could have the body. Maybe Mr. Davies didn't like to say no after what he'd said in class in front of us all, so Jase went home carrying the dog. My best mate, Joe, was disgusted.

3

"Funny the way the dog died right after Mr. Davies said that."

"Ah, come on," I said. "How'd Jase kill him? And anyway, it wasn't right after. It was more than a month."

Joe snorted. "Yeah, and Mr. Davies gave Jase low marks in math just before that. I heard Jase got into real trouble with his dad about it."

I could believe that. Jase's dad thinks education is important and I won't say he's wrong. But no guy likes to have the whole street hear his dad yelling about how stupid he is when he brings home a bad report.

Joe was still thinking. "I reckon it's gruesome too."

"What is? Stuffing animals?" I laughed a bit at what I'd said and so did Joe, then he went serious.

"Yeah. You've got to take out all their guts and get the skin off. My brother says it isn't like just skinning a rabbit. To do the job properly you've got to sort of peel the skin. All around the eyes and face and everything."

"So why take the guts out?"

"So, you don't get mess all over the skin and spoil it, I suppose." We both thought about that for a while.

"Makes sense," I told him. "If the animal had just had a big meal the guts could burst and get that all over you and the skin too."

I went home about then and when I didn't feel much like dinner, mum was annoyed.

Jase got a lot of interest over the dog but then it all died down. Who can stay pumped up over a dead dog? Even a stuffed one that looks sort of alive. So, Jase went looking. Over the next few months, he showed us a couple of racoons, a cat, and a rabbit. The rabbit had belonged to Jase's kid sister. He said he'd found it dead. That wasn't what she said, until he talked to her in a corner and after that she didn't say much about anything at all. The cat had belonged to Jase's neighbor. The neighbor said that last time he'd seen his cat it was alive. Jase said it was dead when he found it. And Jase's dad got mad and asked the neighbor if he was saying that Jase had killed it. The neighbor backed off about then. But Joe who lives in the same street in our township said there were some nasty looks going around. Then he looked at me sort of meaningfully. I giggled a bit nervously.

"What? You think he really did?"

"Maybe. I'm not saying anything but it was funny." I knew he was dying to tell me something, so I asked.

"I saw that cat alive too. It was around the back of the Aldmire place and Jase was feeding it."

I looked at Joe and he looked at me. I dropped my voice. "Did you see what it was eating?"

"No, and I'm not going to ask."

Nor was I.

Things went on like that a while. The new school year started and Joe and I were in the same class with Jase again. Pets kept disappearing and showing up stuffed. Jase kept swearing that he'd found them dead. The owners just kept swearing.

No one was going to start anything with no proof and Mr. Aldmire, a lawyer, does stuff for some of the big ranchers. It stayed like that until we got something new to talk about. Flying saucers. My dad said the town was crazy. A few odd clouds, one of those small whirlwinds, and everyone was seeing weird stuff that'd never existed.

I didn't argue. But Joe and I had been out one night. I couldn't tell dad. I'd sneaked out to go night-fishing with Joe and dad would have been hopping. We'd been down at the pond, which was where the stream had washed out a wider deeper place when it floods, and a funny looking light went right over us. I looked up. I couldn't really see much, just something shaped sort of like a pear-shaped plate. (Mrs. Chauncy's got one to put fruit in in her parlour.)

Joe swore he could see a light in front like a window. I don't remember that. Maybe he saw it. Joe doesn't lie, or not often anyhow. So, between gossiping about UFOs, and Jase finding dead animals everywhere, the township was busy.

So was Jase. I think he didn't like losing the attention. He started to find animals more often. The neighbors were getting noisy about it. Jase's dad was hanging in there and telling them what he'd do if anyone made claims they couldn't back up. Joe said there were some great arguments going on around his place these days.

"What do you think, Joe?"

He gave me a sideways stare. Then he dug his toe into the

ground. "Dunno. But it's funny how it's always Jase who finds dead animals. How come the rest of us never see them first. We all get around the same places. I live right near their house and *I've* never seen any of them."

That made a *lot* of sense. So much so that I said it to Billy Mulleen when I saw him later on. He said it to someone else and the next time Mr. Aldmire defended Jase, that was what someone said to *him*. Joe said Jase's father went quiet. He marched inside and slammed the door so's you could hear it all down the street. Everyone went back inside their own places then. And the whole place got awfully quiet.

That night the light went over again. It was Halloween so almost everyone was outside and saw it, I mean, you couldn't miss it and most of the town was talking about what it could be, between going from house-to-house trick or treating It made things even spookier an' while most of us kids loved it, our parents weren't so sure.

The town marshal saw it too although he said he hadn't. I guess marshals aren't allowed to see UFOs. That night Jase must have sneaked out after most people had gone home. He didn't come back and by next day half the town was looking for him. Someone saw a boy walking along the road that evening. The marshal thought Jase had run away and started checking places where a kid could hide.

All us kids were supposed to stay in at night just in case. But Joe and I sneaked out again taking a little bucket of our candy with us. Moonlit nights are good for fishing, talking, and eating seven different types of Halloween candy – Mrs. Mulleen makes really great peppermint taffy.

"You got the bait?" Joe asked me.

I nodded.

"I dug worms this afternoon after school."

We went down to the pond. It was surrounded by trees and shrubs as well on the side nearest town, and once you were there even quite a bright lamp wouldn't show past those. I stood my lantern on the ground while we baited hooks. We had a peaceful hour before that darn light showed up above the pond. This time it was slanting lower and looked as if it whatever it was might be landing.

"Run! It's right behind the rocks." That was Joe. He'd be in a hurry to his hanging my dad says.

I followed Joe. We came out of the trees and there was something there. It was big and dark and solid. I couldn't see much but Joe was sneaking closer. I kept on his heels. I wasn't going to have anyone say I'd left him to the what-ever-that-was. We could hear a funny sound as we got near the shape, like a low hum.

It landed, the hum stopped, and a ramp came rolling out like a giant tongue, then a dim reddish light came on. It was enough for us to see something standing by where the end of the ramp had stopped. It was sort of like a dog but it had six legs and spines down its back. It stood there stiffly. I looked harder, and darned if the thing didn't look stuffed. Then something else came down the ramp. It wasn't little, it wasn't green, and it probably wasn't any kind of a man either. But I think that it was what people meant when they talked about little green men.

It picked up the dog thing and carried it up the ramp. Then we both saw Jase. He was standing there by the ramp too. Like the dog thing, he didn't move and his eyes kind of shone. Joe was hissing at me.

"You think he stuffed their dog?"

"I guess so." What's more, I guessed that maybe it hadn't been dead when he found it. The way he'd 'found' the neighbors' pets. It looked as if the dog's owner hadn't liked it any more than the neighbors had. He could just deal with Jase a lot better.

The dog thing's owner came back and carried Jase up the ramp. We kept watching and a few minutes later the ramp rolled up into the ship again, there was a whoosh, a rising hum, and the whatever-it-was left. Joe and I didn't say anything. We dived back into the trees, grabbed everything and ran for home. No one ever found Jase, and his family left town a while later. I had a lot of questions but I knew better than to ask them in case it came back to dad.

Even Joe and I didn't talk about it much, just once about six months afterwards. Joe was off at his grandmother's for a visit and when he got back, we went fishing again. "My grandma's got a coat stand," he said out of the blue, and I stared at him wondering what he was on about.

He looked at me. "Grandpa shot a bear when he was only twenty. It was a really big bear, so he had it stuffed. Grandma uses it to hang her overcoat on. It stands there halfway down their hall all day. With a coat over its head an' a coupl'a umbrellas hooked over its paw." His voice trailed off.

Now I knew what he meant. "Yeah," I said softly. "Wonder what sort of coats an' umbrellas people like that thing have?" I said nothing more and Joe left that to lie.

The whole business happened a long time ago now, a good two years before the north started trouble, our south fought back, a lot of people died, and a fair few things changed and never came back to what they'd been. Joe and me, we never talked about it since. But I still wonder about the coat question – and a few other things, like if somewhere out there Jase stands in someone's hall and what *their* kids say about *him*.

FAR TO GO

I have never liked people much. My parents died in 1843 when I was eleven, and two distant relatives took over. They were members of a sect that specialized in narrow mindedness and for ten years they beat the love of God into me with mental cruelty and physical savagery. Once I was old enough to leave, I went with the velocity of a flung spear and never looked back. I had carefully waited until I was legally allowed to depart under certain provisions – even as a female – and I made certain I fulfilled every one, so they were unable to force my return. They were furious of course, since the work I did paid for part of their lifestyle, and with me gone they would have to retrench considerably. But since I was adamant, so was the law and my lawyer saw to it they were told pretty sharply to leave me alone once I complained.

I stayed at the dead-end job they had found me for another year, saving every penny. I wasn't pretty but men seem to like me well enough. It was me that was the trouble. I couldn't seem to be interested. Eventually I had enough money saved and I withdrew it all and took a coach to a bigger town. I got a part-time job as a waitress in a small hotel, lived there, and started to write. The job paid mostly in bed and board, but it did give me something, and I had my savings to fall back on for extras and for two years I did what I had always wanted to do, I wrote during every hour I wasn't working or sleeping.

Slowly stories, mostly under males' names, began to sell and by the end of the two years I was selling a steady trickle to various magazines and newspapers around the country, I spent my days off calculating. Should I try a book? When could I afford to stop working as a waitress or should I stay on as yet? I decided to stay one more year. I'd be twenty-four and by then I'd have saved a decent amount and I'd gamble on going somewhere quiet for six months pure writing.

I worked harder. It paid off and by the time I had almost reached my deadline I was selling as many short stories as I could write. I gave my notice and was surprised to discover that my co-workers seemed sorry to lose me from their midst. Coach after coach took me and my savings across-country while I changed to new coach-lines regularly. I slept nights in shabby hotels, and watched as the towns became smaller and further west.

Finally, my current coach stopped towards late afternoon, and I glanced out. We were well into the fringe of a mountain range and as I looked, the sun lit the peaks with sunset. I stared and a story slipped into my mind. Without thinking, I scrambled off the coach and demanded my trunk, The driver protested. I had a ticket that took me much further, but I was firm, The coach pulled out and I watched it leave, the story bubbling in my brain.

"Help you, lady?"

I whirled; it was one of the men who had been sitting on the porch in front of the store.

"Is there a place I could stay?"

"Nothin' fancy."

"Clean and quiet is all I want."

"Miz Brower' d likely take you in."

He placed my trunk in a barrow and began to walk. I gathered up my handbag, coat, portable writing bureau, and followed.

The house was clean and big. Miss Brower was clean and small. The room she showed me to was huge, sited up in the top of the house, it ran as an immense attic over the entire top of the place. It must have been sixty feet long and wide, but it pleased me. The tiny windows looked towards the mountains and a clean scent flowed in when I opened one. I politely haggled and Miss Brower graciously agreed to the terms.

As soon as she had gone, I dropped coat and bag to reach for the inkpot and pens. The story flowed faster than ever before until hours later I wrote the final words and sat back to realize I was starving.

There was a tap at the half-open door. "Miss Underwood, would you like to eat now?"

I beamed, exactly the words I needed to hear. I joined the old lady at her meal and ate heartily.

"Have you any idea how long you may be staying, dear?"

"At least six months if that's all right?"

"Certainly, dear, that will be very nice."

I detected a gleam in her eye and my mind sharpened. I glanced casually around and noted the shabbiness of furniture and furnishings. Everything was spotless but worn almost to shreds and I guessed the reason. Little Miss Brower was poor, the house would have been from her parents, with her perhaps as the only child. There'd be no suitable work for her here, she probably lived on a small income they'd had, I'd be a godsend so long as I behaved myself and didn't lower her standing in this small community.

After the meal – an excellent one – I excused myself and walked upstairs quickly. The best thing I could do would be to make her my confident and champion. Finding my list of stories published to date was the work of a moment and then I was back in her dining room again,

"Miss Brower?"

"Yes, dear?"

"I should tell you why I'm here."

"That isn't necessary but if you wish to—" Her eyes were alight with interest and I hid a smile.

"I'm a writer, I decided to take time to work at writing full time in a place where I wouldn't be bothered by people trying to sell me something or friends dropping in just when the work was flowing well." I stopped and glanced at her. The faded eyes were shining, and she smiled happily.

"A writer, dear? How exciting, and have you had anything published?"

I grinned back and handed her the list.

"Yes."

She read down it, making small sounds of interest and suddenly recognition.

"You wrote 'Days of Sorrow'?"

I blinked. Of all the list I had hardly expected her to have read that one. It had appeared in a woman's magazine, under a version of my own name. Not that it wasn't good, but the tale of love between a vampire and a human with the bitterness and final death was not quite the sort of thing I thought she'd be reading.

"Ah, yes, I did. Did you like it?"

"My dear, I *loved* it. So beautiful at the end when they chose to die together rather than live apart."

A smile slowly spread inside me as I nodded recognition of her praise, she'd simply seen it as a love story, and skipped over all the horror. Still, I was in, and the whole place would hear about it. I'd be left alone as I wanted, any small eccentricities would be put down to my occupation, and no one would blame my landlady for anything I did.

"May I show your list to my friends?"

"Of course."

I remained politely to drink a cup of tea and then ran for my attic. Her conversation had given me another idea and I wanted to catch it before it vanished. I found I'd been right about Miss Brower and the town. Clearly, she'd told everyone, and the list must have been well circulated, but no one bothered me unduly. If I shopped at the store and showed myself prepared to chat, the good people would be happy to ask questions and discuss stories of mine they had read. If I kept my head down and moved briskly, I was left strictly alone and I reveled in it. My work flowed like a torrent. I began the book I wanted to write, breaking off at intervals to produce short stories which always seemed to sell. This place was lucky for me.

I decided after the initial three months, I'd stay as long as I could afford to and if my work continued to sell as well as it had been, that could be a considerably longer time than the six months planned.

I finished my second book, a dime novel featuring a brother and sister who owned a ranch on the edge of Indian territory, walked in the early morning to the mail office and sent it to an editor. Restlessness descended and I wandered out along the street. The mountains were clear and beautiful in the soft air, and without thought I made for them. In two hours, I was into the foothills and climbing among trees. I followed a deer path, crossed a tiny stream, and clambered up the side of a gully. I sat and enjoyed the solitude for a couple of hours before wending my way back down the slopes to home.

There, a bulky parcel awaited me. The editor liked the first book sent, *Mountains of Blood, Valleys of Pain* and wished to see a rewrite bearing in mind certain points – and if I had a second novel, they would evaluate that at the same time.

I dropped everything and wrote furiously. Miss Brower took a proprietary interest and kept me going with strong tea and hot meals brought up to my room, where she stood over me until I stopped writing long enough to gulp down food and drink, before returning to work. I finished in a record six weeks. Exhausted I parceled the edited manuscript and the completed second, and sent them off with a covering letter. Then I fell into bed and slept.

The old lady had the sense to allow me my sleep-out and I woke starving. The food was delectable, and I smiled to myself as I realized I couldn't actually remember the composition of any meal since I'd begun the rewrite and second book.

"What are you going to do now, dear?"

I considered. What was I going to do? For the moment I felt written out, perhaps I should take a break? I communicated this and we sat in silence,

"Mr. Webster has a very nice horse." I blinked. Was I supposed to write a story about Mr. Webster's horse?

"It's gray and used to the mountains, very sure-footed, and he has pack-horses too." Slowly, her idea seeped into my mind. A trip into the mountains for a couple of weeks, hard physical work, and nothing for the mind to do would make a new woman out of me. I'd return refreshed, overflowing with new plots, to write my heart out again. I grinned happily into the gentle eyes.

"Could you arrange it with Mr. Webster?"

"Of course, dear."

She was as good as her word and in two mornings I was setting off on a smallish gray horse, a larger bay following loose.

"Now don't you worry about a thing, Miss. The horses know the hills they'll see you right."

I smiled politely down. "Thank you, Mr. Webster."

He nodded and I kicked my mount into movement. I made camp high in the mountains, the tiny township below looking like a group of children's playhouses, I slept soundly and woke to eat, pack, and kill the small fire. I saddled the horses and set out again. I had no idea where I was going but I was going there anyway. We walked the hours down until late afternoon. By now I was deep into the mountains and there was a twinge of fear as I looked back and saw nothing but slopes, tree-covered and dark. Still Mr. Webster had assured me, that given their heads, the horses would take me home, so I quelled my twitches and made camp.

I ate and slept, to come awake with a jump as something howled. I listened. A coyote? No: There was something about the sound, like the sorrow of a world. It came again and there was a wild beauty to it that thrilled me as I shivered. A wolf? It had to be. On impulse I sat back on my haunches and howled back, trying to make my cries sound the same.

A pause and the beast howled in answer. I howled back once more and then snuggled down in my sleeping bag. I knew about wolves. From a human deep in these mountains and far from help I might have been in danger. Not from a wolf. They were the gentlest of beasts, loving to their mates and cubs, slow to anger, naturally peaceful and it was a time of the year when there was ample food for them.

In the morning, I mounted again. At a whim I sent the horses in the direction of the cries I had heard. We traveled all day, and the horses were tired when I finally made camp. So was I and I slept without disturbance. We moved on again late next morning and just after noon I found the place to stay a while.

Below the ridge where we stood was a small lake cupped in vegetation's green hands. A flight of ducks floated at one end, and I guessed that it might hold fish as well, I heeled my mount into motion, and we picked our way down the trails until we came out on the small flat behind the ridge. The lake spread before me while indignant ducks departed in a crack of ascending wings. I glanced guiltily around and slid from my mount. I was hot, sticky and tired. The water called me, and I decided not to resist. My clothes landed in a heap, and I was into the water with a yelp. It was cold – snow water I'd bet – but better than any water I'd ever swum in before.

I looked up and saw that the horses waited patiently. Damn, not fair to them, I climbed out and unsaddled them, fitting hobbles and letting them wander off to graze in peace. Then I returned to my lovely lake. I was just executing a plunge when out of the corner of my eye I caught movement. I opened my mouth to call out just as gravity returned me to the depths and I choked. Staggering up from the watery grave I seemed intent on consigning myself into, I stared at the gray bushy-tailed figure that laughed tongue-lollingly at my confusion.

I couldn't help it; I began to laugh back, and it was several minutes before I could speak.

"Hello to you."

A tiny whine answered me and then, turning away, he vanished into the trees. I dressed, musing on the fact that there were wolves in these mountains. That certainly had been a wolf, but equally clearly, a non-hostile one. I carried a gun, but I would never have used it on the wolf without real signs of aggression. Perhaps if I showed myself friendly, he'd come back? I busied myself setting up the camp on a site chosen back and to one side of the lake. I didn't want to make it hard for the wildlife to drink, they had as much right to the water as I had. More, since they were the original owners.

That night l lit my fire and gathered a heap of dry wood to feed it. I lay comfortably in the warmth of my bedroll, watching pictures in the flames and singing softly. An old song my mother always sang, until into the chorus broke a long singing cry.

I chuckled; my wolf was in good voice tonight. I waited until he howled again and howled back. For several minutes we made the mountain ring in turn until I decided enough was enough and rolled over to sleep. The ducks were back at dawn, and I wondered if an Indian trick I had once read of would work. I could always use the gun, but somehow, I didn't want to. I gathered water debris and made a small floating heap. Slipping into the water, I poked my head up into it and allowed it to drift towards the center of the lake.

Seeing no sign of me, the ducks circled the water and returned to settle back on the surface again. I chose two plump males that seemed to have no mates and drifted closer. The water was chill, and I must be starting to turn blue.

Mentally, I shrugged, I had survived cold before, it had been a common punishment by those who'd taken me in when I was young, I set my teeth and waited. The ducks dived for the lake bounty, and I slid nearer, nearer. Then together my prey dived and without a ripple, failed to surface. The deep breath I had taken ran out and I surfaced back into my floating camouflage, a drowned duck held securely in each hand. I guided my island along the lake to where tree roots dipped into the water. Unobtrusively I dragged myself out, ducks in hand, and vanished into the trees without having unduly alarmed the prey. I returned to my tent with an ear-to-ear grin at my success.

Cross legged in the sun I sat and began to pluck. I felt eyes on me and looked up with a start. My wolf sat at the clearing edge. I smiled, carefully keeping my mouth closed. I didn't want him to think I was showing teeth aggressively. He stood and moved closer, eyes on a duck. I giggled and he glanced at me.

"Oi! I worked for that."

He bowed front legs and bounced, something I'd seen in dogs as an invitation to play, or as a gesture of friendship. I picked up the still-feathered duck and looked at him.

"You want this?"

Again, the bow and bounce. His amber eyes were alight with humor I was being teased. I tossed the duck slowly over, letting him see the coming movement. It landed in front of him, and he paced forward to take it up.

"I hope you enjoy it, just don't expect one every day."

Duck firmly held, he stared at me a moment and padded away. I grinned after him. It looked as if the book I had read and the tales of the naturalist who'd been my parents' acquaintance, were true. The only danger I might be in as far as my wolf was concerned, was being eaten out of house and home.

The next night, I made a stew out of dried meat and dried vegetables plus duck leftovers. Just in case I was visited, I made extra and dug out a spare tin plate. It was as well I did. Glowing green eyes studied me in the firelight and the wolf drifted out of the shadows to seat himself on the other side of the fire just as I began to eat, I reached for the plate, dumping the remainder of the stew onto it, keeping my movements slow and easily identified.

"Now, I'd like to offer you this, how do I do it?"

His ears drifted backwards.

"It worries you? What about me?"

He rose and did the bow and bounce. I laughed softly, "All right, I'll believe you. Just back off a bit will you."

I pushed my hand at him and to my surprise, he backed. I walked slowly around the fire, laid the plate on the ground, and stepped away.

"Okay, it's all yours." I moved slowly back to my position and sat again to continue my own meal. The wolf ate quickly but neatly and then stretched out to gaze into the flames.

"What do you see there, I wonder?" I asked softly. He looked up and whined. "Do you see wolf stories? What kind of fairy tales would your people have?"

I suddenly laughed and the wolf jumped. "I wonder if you tell each other werewolf stories on dark nights?" His ears pricked forward, and his forehead smoothed out. "Ah ha, ring a bell, does it? You know, I never understood that werewolf stuff. If wolves are all as nice as you, why should werewolves be so different? Maybe they get the worst of both heritages or something."

The wolf's tongue lolled out and he smiled at the sound of my voice. "I see, the subject interests you, I can see that it might." I reached for a can of peaches and opened it, studying them thoughtfully. "How do you feel about peaches?"

I held up the can and his eyes focused on it, I tilted the edge to display the contents and watched him scent the fruit. "If you want some, you can have them.". I walked slowly around the fire and he backed up. Half a can on his plate and we returned to our seats to eat peacefully, He did like peaches I observed, probably because they were sweet.

The next few days passed quietly. I picked off a few more ducks and shared them with my friend. I was considerably startled to be brought a rabbit a week into my vacation.

"A rabbit? For me?" I received the bow and bounce to assure me the gift was indeed mine. I knew animals did bring presents to favored human friends. I had a friend as a child whose cat stole anything portable to offer her.

"Thank you but you must share it."

Cleaned, skinned, and cut into halves I proffered one portion back uncooked. My half I roasted on a stick over the fire. He was finished long before me and lay watching the fire as I chewed. A thought crossed my mind and I looked over at him.

"You know, this is what I wanted in a man and never found. The ability to share in silence, to just *be*." He crinkled an eyebrow and went back to the flames. I considered; it was quite true. Because of my distant relatives' cruelty, I had never seen men as anything but fearsome. And as I grew older, I disliked the continual chatter of humanity with its petty bickering and gossip.

Half of our town must have known of the treatment I'd received but all were unwilling to be involved. So for ten years, I'd been brutalized until I could escape. I had been lucky once I'd done so to send stories to a new magazine starting out. The editor had seen potential and returned them with comments. Rewrites were purchased. I had never looked back, I had never met him, and my tales sold under three different names. But then, initially I hadn't wanted to risk being known as a female, so I'd used male names. I still did for all but a quarter of what I sold; those to women's magazines.

I had only once had a woman friend, then her father divorced her mother for adultery and suddenly I was forbidden to speak to her. Shortly after that, they moved away. Not that either of us had been women then – female though. Perhaps I could make a female friend here? I crawled into my bedding and settled down, On the other side of the fire, eyes gleamed.

"Goodnight, friend. Maybe you could find me a nice human female friend too." His eyes flickered in the firelight until I fell asleep.

Far too quickly it was twelve days gone and I packed up. I should have said I'd stay away longer but the food was almost gone and somehow, I didn't want to use the gun here and disturb the lake's peace. The wolf watched me go in silence.

"I'll be back, I promise. Just give me time to write a few more stories and make some money." I stopped the horse as we crested the ridge. The little lake below was blue shading green where it shallowed. There was no longer any sign of my wolf.

Back in the township, I was swept into my writing again. An editor at the publisher where I'd offered my books wrote two weeks later that both was accepted and would appear next spring. Contracts arrived and I signed them, to receive in return more money than I had hoped for. My head was abuzz with tales still though and I sat up late for a month writing like a madwoman, producing a stack of short stories which I could send. Then, once the contracts were signed, the money in the bank, I purchased envelopes and placed a completed short story in each. I had the postage marked on them and left for Miss Brower's house.

"Would Mr. Webster have two pack horses?"

"Yes, of course dear why? Do you plan to have another vacation?"

"I thought a sort of working break, I could take my portable bureau."

"I 'm sure that would be very nice for you, dear."

"If I left these stories with you, could you mail one every week?"

"I'd be happy to."

"I was thinking of being away for a month or two. I'd pay for my room of course."

Miss Brower nodded, I knew that my room was making the difference for her between poverty and living in comfort. I paid well since as I explained to her, she should be compensated for my odd hours and comings and goings. Besides, now I could afford to and I liked the old lady. It pleased me to know that my money helped her.

"Your room will be waiting for you when you get back, dear." I smiled at her and wandered off to talk to Mr. Webster.

"Two pack horses, Missy? Ayup, I can do that."

"Good, I thought of going tomorrow morning?"

"Have them waiting for you at six?"

"That would be fine. Thank you, Mr. Webster."

"Could I ask whereabouts you're heading?"

"There's a lake… "

He looked surprised. " A small one? Three days to the east?"

"Yes."

"See anyone?" I shook my head. I would not betray my wolf; I had no idea how the township might feel about him. And Heaven forbid they should hunt him. "There' s people up there, family called Lucus. They wouldn't hurt you or nothing, but they aren't much for strangers."

"I won't bother them. Anyway, I never saw anybody."

I rode away early next morning. No one was around but Mr. Webster had left the horses in the lean-to. The food and other supplies, he had packed neatly and loaded onto the pack-horses for me. I doubted he had done that the night before so he must have been up very early but now there was no sign of him,

I chirruped to the animals and we vanished into the foothills at a steady walk. This time there was no hesitation or delay. I headed for the lake and settled in. As soon as my bedding was laid out and water on the fire, I sat back and scanned the area. No sign of my wolf. Perhaps he wouldn't come this time. Could something have happened to him? I made myself shrug. No use in fussing. He'd be here, or he wouldn't. I drank the hot tea I'd brewed, ate and laid down to doze. It was moonlight when I woke and I lay watching the occasional cloud drift across her brightness.

Something moved in the darkness, and I peered. "Who's there?" A shadow, a faint glint of green.

"Wolf, is that you?" I tossed a couple of sticks on the coals and the fire flared up.

"Ah ha, nice to see you. I promised I'd be back, didn't I?" A tiny whine. "I keep my promises. See you in the morning."

The shadow melted into the trees, and I slept again, secure in the knowledge my friend was back. I was right about that; a rabbit awaited my rising in morning light.

I grinned as I worked on it. Later if the ducks were back, I'd take a couple of them to share back. There was the sound of something moving lightly through the brush and I looked up expecting to see the wolf.

"Ulp." opening my mouth to greet my friend I was confronted by a girl instead and involuntarily I shied back.

"Um, I'm sorry. Were you expecting someone?"

"No, I thought you were a raccoon or something." Not for worlds would I give my wolf away.

Her eyes flickered over my face."Are you here alone?"

"Yes. Do you live around here?"

She looked at me thoughtfully. "Yes, my family lives in the mountains near here."

I nodded – the Lucus people Webster had spoken of. I had expected a degenerate type, but she was fine-boned, her every movement graceful, her hair was a thick mass of wavy black and her eyes a clear hazel.

"My name's Nan?"

"I'm Murna."

"That's lovely," I said sincerely. "Where does it come from?"

She shrugged, "An old family name. We were English originally. Why are you here?"

I explained about my writing, and she was awed to find I had written and sold two books. We talked and suddenly we were friends. She came back the next day and the next. Sometimes we talked and sometimes I wrote while she sat and watched, yet somehow, she never felt intrusive.

She was shy but her intelligence was sparkling as was her wit. I began to feel I was leading a double life. She never appeared before mid-morning and was usually gone by late afternoon. My wolf tended to show up as soon as she vanished into the trees and I teased him about it asking if he was really her in disguise, I received a look of deep disgust in reply and I giggled.

"Sorry, but maybe you change sex as well as shape" That gave me an idea for my next story and I grabbed for pen and ink. Murna was back mid-morning and I handed it over for her to read.

"I like it."

"Why?"

"They're real people."

I beamed. "Thank you. I've never seen that vampires should be anything else."

"Do you believe in them?

I shook my head. "Not really"

"What about werewolves?"

"Not like the books."

"Why?"

"Well, an acquaintance of my parents was a naturalist, and talked about them. I read one of his books too. Wolves seem to be gentle, affectionate, loving with their family and sensible, as well as intelligent."

Murna looked at me surprised. "You really think so?"

"Yes," I said firmly and there was a small silence before she began to discuss something else. Perhaps she thought I was stupid. Maybe she believed in the type of wolf that many stories talked about – a ravening beast that killed for pleasure. She left early that day and my wolf was there almost as her footsteps faded.

"Hello fella." I offered the duck I had saved and it was taken. On impulse as he reached for it, I brushed my fingers along the thick fur. I had never touched him before not wishing to intrude, but my touch was clearly acceptable, and he made no objection. He took the duck to the far side of the fire, and I continued to write. I was deep in a complicated bit when I felt him move. I glanced down at him as he settled beside me.

"You think I won't mind huh? Well, you're right, Nice to have you there."

I returned to my work, and he lay comfortably against my thigh. Heavy fur warm as he leaned gently and gazed into the flames in front of us.

After that, he often joined me on my side of the fire. I made no moves to entice him but sometimes I permitted myself to lay a hand against his fur when I spoke to him. It should have felt dangerous or strange but somehow it was familiar. Murna and I were fast friends now but for some reason I never spoke to her of the wolf. I think I was afraid that she might fear him or set her family to hunting my friend. I had been in the mountains six weeks. Soon I would have to consider returning.

"Must you go?"

"I don't want to, but I've a whole batch of stories to post and my supplies will run out in a few more days."

"You could post the stories and get more supplies, then come back at once, couldn't you?"

"Yes, suppose I could." I scanned the sky. It was still only mid-Summer. There was no reason why I couldn't return.

"Please?"

"Okay, but I'll have to be back in town soon." I stayed another five days and then left, Murna waving to me from the lakeside as I rode over the ridge above.

* * *

"Have a good trip, little lady?"

"Very good, Mr. Webster. So good that I'd like to go right back as soon as I've restocked."

"Fine by me. Would you want the same horses?"

"If that's all right?"

"Yup, and I could restock the packsaddles for you if 'n you want to leave in the morning."

"Thank you, thank you very much."

He smiled comfortably at me. Then I'll get it done. Meet any of the Lucases up there?"

"Yes, a girl called Murna."

He nodded, "Figures. She's the only daughter. There's a twin boy too, but they're much younger than the rest. I'd guess she's mebbe lonely for a woman her own age to talk to."

I walked off towards Miss Brower's home. That made sense. No wonder Murna was so keen for me to come back. I left another pile of mail ready for my landlady to post, paid my rent and opened my letters. Money, lots of it from my publisher and a request. Could I do a third book with the same brother and sister characters? I added more paper to my pack-sack.

I'd had an idea while chatting to Murna one day. Perhaps that would make another book, I could try anyhow. I bid an affectionate goodbye to Miss Brower who insisted on seeing me off next morning.

"Another long trip? Will you be gone that long again?"

"Longer."

"But you will be back before fall?"

I smiled down at her small figure. "Well before winter anyway."

This time Murna was at the lake to help me set up camp. I handed her the small gift I had brought and watched her surprised delight.

"It's beautiful, what is it?"

"Scrimshaw. I found it right in the back of a shop when I took a coach into the bigger town last time."

"It's ivory?"

"Uh huh. See, there's a wolf chasing a deer, then a hunter shooting the deer and him and the wolf sharing the meat." Murna gazed at it entranced, then looked up at me.

"Thank you so much, Nan, I love it."

I patted her shoulder. "Good. Now, I'm starving. Let's find something we can eat that doesn't take time to cook."

"There's berries up there." She pointed to a bush growing out of the cliff above the water.

"They'll be staying there for all of me." I informed her. "I'm not a monkey."

She laughed, a soft chime that echoed across the water. "I can get them."

Before I could stop her, she was along the shore and partway up the cliff. She reached for the bush and began to pick, while I stood nervously at the bottom. I didn't like that cliff. The rock had always looked rotten to me and that was why I'd never attempted the climb. Murna had my kettle full, and I tossed up a ball of string. She lowered the booty carefully and I put them on one side to watch her climb down.

She transferred her handhold, and the rock broke away. I cried in terror for her as she fell and ran to drop down beside her. "Murna, Murna are you hurt?"

"My leg." She tried to move and fainted.

I looked – a break. I looked again and muttered furiously. Two breaks in the right leg, both clean but there was no way she could walk. I'd have to get help from her family. I sat and studied the situation, mustn't panic and run in circles. Soon it would be dark. If I got her into my bedding, she could rest there until morning and I could go for help then. I have always been strong. The years of heavy work for my relatives saw to that. Murna was slender and I managed to lift her and carry the limp form into shelter, placing her in my bedding.

"Now, let me get something hot on for tea and we're set. I'll look for help in the morning." There was an odd sound from Murna then, echoed by a whine from outside the tent.

I looked out. "Wolf, hi." He paced forward and standing beside me looked down at Murna who had begun to whimper in pain. "I know. She's hurt. I wish you could help. I need to get her to her family. I'm worried about her."

He looked up at me and then padded out silently. I returned to sponging the white face.

"Do you need help?"

I spun so fast I almost fell. Behind me a young man stood, all wire and whipcord, about my age I noted and barely two inches taller. His resemblance to Murna was stunning.

"You're her twin?"

"Yes." He knelt down beside her and took her hand.

"Do you have anything for fever?"

"No."

"Bring me water and bark from that tree then." He pointed. I moved to obey and took up a bag. "No, use the enamel plate and mug."

I blinked. How did he know I had any? They were tucked away, still unpacked. He glanced up impatiently and my breath caught. His gaze sharpened as he saw I realized.

"Does she die for it?"

I scrambled to obey. We worked over Murna all night. By morning, her leg was set, the short fever gone, I walked outside with him and turned to look into green eyes.

"Change!" I demanded. He hesitated. "Change!"

His lean strength blurred into heavy fur and green eyes in a powerful muzzle. I knelt and held out my arms to him, "I believe that wolves are gentle, affectionate and loving to their friends and family. I do not believe that your subspecies is different."

If I was wrong, I was going to be the prototype of every horror story. With a soft whine, he flung his body in.to my arms and I held on hard. "Wolf, friend."

He writhed and I was holding a male human, I let go at once and he grinned.

"I can see I'll have to win you all over again as a human."

I smiled back as we walked in to tend Murna. She was his sister, but maybe one day, she would be mine as well. Until then, I had two friends. I was content to wait.

ERNEST

Ernest was a rooster and he was twenty feet up a tree when it happened. He reeled, crowed angrily and considered his options after that feeling of spatial dislocation. It was as if his surroundings had whirled about him and he didn't like it. In fact, he disliked it so much that he spent the remainder of the night only half asleep and at first light he headed home again. *Home was where,* he thought to himself, *when you had to go there, they had to take you in.* Unfortunately home was no longer where it had been.

Ernest could fly well, it was moderately unusual for a domestic fowl, but he'd been bred on a small farm where they advertised that their chickens were excellent layers, sensible and mild-tempered – and mostly capable of surviving as free-range birds.

To this end, Ernest, like the rest of his kin, was only three-quarters domestic breed, the other quarter was gamecock. It gave the huge rooster the fountain of bronze tail-feathers, and the collar of red-gold feathers around his neck. It had also given him the ability to fly well – left out at night his kind roosted high up in a tree, on light branches that put him out of predator reach. His breeding also gave him a passionate sense of territory, and the aggression to defend it at need. As a final gesture, the mix had endowed him with hybrid vigor and a size larger even than his main breed. The rest was as advertised down to the usually mild temper – with humans whom he liked.

Except that the previous day even a mild-tempered bird might have revolted against events. At six months of age Ernest had been sold to a small farm. There for a year and a half, he'd ruled the roost, produced a positive fountain of magnificent pullets and young roosters, and been just gentle as advertised.

I rule! I rule. This place, this land, my wives and these humans are mine!

He was right, until someone came to visit for a weekend, with a small fluffy yapping dog that persistently chased the hens, culminating, one afternoon when everyone was away for a couple of hours, with a dastardly attack on a pullet.

Ernest, help, save me! She had squawked, and Ernest had provided the assistance any good rooster owed.

Dog, enemy, my land, my wife, run or die. The dog, an idiot, had not run and, Ernest's gamecock ancestry well to the fore, he'd attacked and the yapping bundle of fur, only half the size of the big rooster – one that was well armed with a formidable beak and razor-like fighting spurs – had succumbed while Ernest stood on the body clapping his wings and announcing raucous victory.

I won, I vanquished the enemy, I am Ernest, Lord, King!

The owner of the dog hadn't seen the outcome as amusing, or even justified. They'd threatened and Ernest's owners had pronounced sentence – to be carried out in the morning. That would have been that except that their daughter, nine, blonde, and the one that mainly cared for their poultry had been devoted to Ernest. While accepting that her parents would not alter their decision, she reasoned that if her friend weren't around, it would be hard to do anything to him. At dusk she'd sneaked out and released him.

Where are we going? Oh, yes, all right, I'll allow it, but I hope there's food at the end of this wandervogel?

She'd carried him half a mile down an old deer track, waited until he'd flapped his way up a tree, put a handful of wheat in a hollow where one branch met another and gone home. She would never know what happened to him but half-mile in that particular direction had been crucial.

A rare and random portal had opened right across the upper branches of the tree in which Ernest spent that night. And at first light he ate his wheat and began to make his way home. Except that home was no longer there, and his sense of direction was utterly confused.

That tree faced the sun. If I go this way home should only be ... but, but, where is my home?

He flew from tree to tree, pausing now and then to descend warily to eat from the banquet of bugs and greenery. There was something wrong about this whole scenario but precisely what that was, Ernest was unable to determine. He could only keep heading for home and hope all would be well once he reached it.

Towards evening he roosted in another tree, weary but well-fed. He must surely be close to home by now. Just a little further in the morning and he'd be there. At first light he roused, dropped to the ground and began to eat bugs in a small clearing where the earth was turned in a short narrow strip. He heard the sow coming first and ignored her. He was familiar with pigs.

Behind her came a small, blond girl and Ernest halted his scratching. He stood in the shaft of sunlight that lit the clearing, clapped his wings, rose to his full height, and posed at the head of the turned earth. Sun struck bronze-green and brown-gold lights from his tail-feathers and a red-gold from the circle of feathers around his neck.

To Leesha he was a creature from myth – almost half her size, dominant, proud, and lit to glory by sunlight. He stood poised at the head of her brother's grave, the brother she had idolized, who had adored and protected his baby sister, the brother, murdered by outlaws from out of the mountains. The brother she missed with all her five-year-old heart. It was Year's End Day when presents were given to mark the coming of a new year and her brother would never have forgotten her. There had been little of fairy tales in her life, and less of beauty, but in one flashing moment she believed, that somehow, someway, he had sent this wondrous gift, this miracle of beauty to her.

"Vernest?" she asked in her tongue, it meant defender, and had been her brother's name but the big rooster didn't know that.

She knows me. I must be near my home, and see how like my own little human she is.

He relaxed at his familiar name. The child's posture shouted admiration, awe and respect. He pranced up making the small sound in his throat that was his greeting to that other child – now far ahead in a more civilized time. Leesha considered. The sow would stay where she was for a while even if untended. This miracle must be led home for the scrutiny of her grandfather. She found a few crumbs in her pocket from the single thick slice of dry bread that had been her breakfast, offering them to Ernest and was delighted by the gentle way he accepted her tribute.

"Vernest, come."

She feeds me. She speaks my name. She treats me with respect. All is as it should be.

The rooster followed until they reached the tiny cabin deep in the mountain foothills that Leesha shared with her grandfather and at nights, with the sow and five small scruffy hens. It was the hens on which Ernest immediately focused. He clapped his wings, stretched his neck and crowed as Leesha scurried in to fetch her grandfather. The hens gaped and clustered about him. Never in all their lives had they seen anything so magnificent, so stunningly, awesomely, *virile.*

I am Ernest, your new Lord. Let all know that I am here now, your lord and master of this place.

"Leesha, ist da?" Johan was surprised to see his granddaughter back so soon, and babbling about a miracle? He stepped outside and in turn became transfixed. A farmer all his life until he'd come to this new land, he was under no apprehension that Ernest was a miracle, or not exactly, but the size, the quality and the sheer *majesty* of the rooster stunned him. The bird must have escaped from some lord's flock. Although – in this new land he'd been told they had no lords. Nonetheless, the bird could have only come from the property of someone fabulously wealthy. Never in all his life had Johan seen a bird so fine – or one so swift to take charge. A small grin curved his lips. If someone came looking in a couple of days it would be too late. The bird would have fertilized every egg laid, and – Johan's eyes narrowed – if the creature bred true?

He turned back and scrabbled in a bag. There was a meager amount of grain still left there intended to help the hens survive winter. If it would bind this bird to the place so that it stayed, the grain would be better spent now. In a series of jumps, his mind had leapt to a vision. Chicks sired by this rooster would be finer than anything he'd ever seen, even chicks from his own poor hens. Before winter, they would be old enough to sell, and they would fetch – by his standards – a very fair price indeed. Ernest had temporarily finished with the hens and was approaching Leesha hopefully again.

Johan thrust a half-handful of grain at her. "Give him this, just a pinch at a time."

He watched as the huge bird took the food carefully from the child's palm. Gentle too, but those spurs were not for show, Johan suspected. A bird that size, if he became enraged, would not be a pushover. Leesha laughed as Ernest's beak explored her hand.

A good little human, yes, and the man too gave me respect. I might stay here for a while, just until my own humans find me. Besides, new wives were not to be overlooked.

"Vernest, mi Vernest." Ernest settled down beside her, enjoying the small stroking hand. Involuntarily Johan smiled.

God knew there'd been nothing to smile about this past year. His son and his son's wife murdered by outlaws, their home looted then burned, his grandchildren left with almost nothing. Johan had managed to get the children away before they were found, and, thanks be to a merciful God, he'd managed to snatch food, a few small items and their tiny hoard of coins as he went. His son died fighting, Merri his wife – the daughter-in-law old Johan had never much liked – had died too, at some stage, but in silence. He'd give her that. She had to have, since no one had come after them seeking Johan, the children, or the family's handful of saved coppers and silver coins.

Johan sighed as he watched Ernest and Leesha. They'd come to this new land on the promise of land and a future. All they'd had so far was death and destruction. After the attack they'd made for the seven-house hamlet where his wife's youngest sister still lived. There was no room in her home for three more. She had sold him an elderly sow in pig for half the coins, the rest to be paid when the piglets could be brought to the monthly market attended by those from scattered farms about. The other half of the coins had gone on essentials.

His sister-in-law had, looking about her to make sure no one overheard, told him of the old cabin up here, the owner dead almost two years. If no one knew where he and her grandniece and nephew were, no one could protest his use of it. But ten-year-old Vernest had been careless, walked into a trio of outlaws who'd shot in fear he would talk, so now it was one old man with a small girl – and he feared desperately for Leesha and her future.

But from God had come a chance, a hope. If only all went well for a while it might yet be that Leesha could have a decent future. It seemed to Johan as the months passed that God was indeed good.

My land, my wives, my humans, I am Lord, Master, let no enemy come against me! Ernest was assiduous in his duties. His wives hatched chicks of marvelous size and looks and most survived. Twice Ernest attacked a marauding raccoon – that, faced with a bird of such size and temper, fled with spur-gashed face.

Before the start of winter, Johan left to walk all day to the market. With him went the carcasses of a dozen fat capons, all killed, plucked and gutted only the night before. By village quality, they were magnificent birds. They sold for a price surprising even to Johan so that he was able to buy supplies for the winter that were generous by his standards.

He and Leesha ate better that year. Twice more in the next moon, he walked down to the market, the second time to sell piglets as well as chickens, and to pay off his debt to his sister-in-law. He managed a third trip before the worst of winter set in, that third time to breed the elderly sow to a boar, paying with two fine capons. He returned to settle in for winter. No one knew exactly where they were. They should be safe, and who traveled when the snows began? The answer to that, unfortunately, was no one except those who must. It was a traveling bandit dodging the trouble he'd raised elsewhere, who came upon Leesha before the snow was too deep and as she watched the foraging sow. Johan had gone the other way to gather kindling, and cut more wood for their fire.

No brat would be far from home at this time of year, the bandit thought, dismounting silently from his mule. Her cabin would mean food and drink, perhaps something of value – if there were no strong men to drive him off – and, a woman perhaps? His tongue slid across his lips. He stalked the child with care and on foot. The mule was trained to stand and would wait until he could return for it.

When Leesha returned to her home, he was behind her, silent and cautious. It had snowed lightly soon after dawn, he studied the doorway and saw no tracks but hers. The brat was alone, her kin probably at market or visiting friends while she was left to tend the pig. He could wring from her the hiding place of any coins, wait for those who would return, and ambush them.

He waited until she passed near him, stepped out, and seized her by one wrist. Leesha shrieked. It was foolish, futile, but in her terror, she called for her defender, the one sent by her brother.

"Vernest, Vernest!"

The big rooster had been scratching under a tree, unseen by the fighter. He knew that note of terror, his hens called like that when a predator threatened them. And – this was his territory.

Mine! My little human! My land! You show yourself as an enemy and I am Ernest! I fight as I stand. Release what is mine.

Outraged, goaded by the small thin cries of his name, and without hesitation, he attacked. So great was his momentum aided by flapping wings that when he reached the outlaw, he literally ran up the man's body and clung, claws fastened in the open top of the leather jerkin, wings beating the man about the ears, beak striking savagely at the startled eyes. In the following melee Leesha wrenched free and fled screaming.

Ernest hung on grimly. *You do not run? I shall show you why you should, human intruder. I shall show you until your blood runs at least.*

The outlaw knew chickens, but those he knew were the small scrawny birds of the western lands. Ernest was four times that size and to the confused man it was more like being attacked by an eagle. He was blinded by the savagely beating wings and his grabs at the bird missed. Nor did they go unpunished as Ernest lifted each foot in turn, striking viciously with his spurs at the man's face and clutching fingers.

In those moments, he was all gamecock. The small English bird bred for a thousand generations for one thing, to fight to the death, never backing down, never surrendering. This predator had invaded Ernest's territory and it should die. The fight could end only that way, of course, and would have, except for another who entered the scene. There was a dull thump that resounded in the clear crisp air. Ernest rode his enemy down to the ground, standing, claws sunk into the invader's neck as he clapped his wings above the sprawled body and screamed his triumph.

I am Ernest. My enemy is dead. I killed him. Let my enemies beware! Then he stepped down and went to check over his territory, crooning reassuringly to Leesha as she reached out to stroke him in passing.

Johan buried the intruder, after stripping him of everything usable. He hauled him far into the brush – finding the mule and the bandit's pack when he did so. He sought out a small deep depression between two slabs of rock and entombed the bandit there. But the booty the man provided would be incredibly valuable. A fine rifle and a handgun, a good knife, many other small items he could use or sell, including a purse of coins, two of which were gold eagles. He would buy a generous bag of good grain for the bird with some of it, Johan resolved. As a farmer he'd known that roosters could be belligerent, but who could have known a bird would fight like that – and for a child?

At the first spring market, he sold his booty cautiously, an item here, another there, spending coppers to buy the promised grain. He also visited his sister-in-law to assure her that he and Leesha had survived the winter. As a gift, he brought for her a live daughter of Ernest. The pullet was half Ernest's size but she was still far larger and of much greater quality in comparison to any other hen in the township or surrounding area. Alva was delighted with her gift.

"I won't ask questions about her. But there are those who'd value such a fine bird. If you have others to bring to market next time, could some be alive like this one?"

Old Johan smiled. "Perhaps I might bring one or two."

Flooding the market would bring prices down, but if he brought only hens to sell, their offspring would be one quarter of Ernst's blood. He alone would retain the best of the line. It worked as he'd hoped. In two years in that tiny settlement, and in others nearby, Ernest's daughters were known for their quality. In four years, there was enough money saved – adding the two gold eagles to it – to pay for the building of a cabin of their own, a woodcutting saw, and two younger sows. Moved to their new small cabin on the edge of the village, Ernest thrived.

Ah, yes, admire me. I hear the words my small human uses. My name, and such sounds as 'bad man' and 'many chicks', yes, respect me, I am Ernest, warrior and lover, and I hold my territory against all.

In two more years, Ernest was an admired and established part of the village and Johan with his flock and his relationship to Alva, had status among them – sufficient status that no one ever asked where he had obtained his magnificent flock leader. Why should they? Ernest's offspring in a quiet, modest way, were providing a higher level of prosperity for them all.

Over those years since Ernest arrived, Johan bred his chickens with great care. He might know little about genetics, but he knew farming practice. Breed the best to the best and hope for the best. His flock was the finest in the area and local farmers brought from him in preference to any other. Over those years too, Johan had never heard of any, even a rich ranch-holder, with a rooster that matched Ernest's description and he wondered. *What* he wondered however, he kept to himself in true peasant fashion. Ernest died quietly in Leesha's arms one fine cool day in early summer.

I am weary. Let me sleep a while and then I'll get up and call my wives again. I am Ernest, warrior, lover, Lord of my territory, always your friend, my human, but for now, let me sleep a while...

Leesha wept, and Johan comforted her.

"He lived long, very long for a chicken. We had him for almost ten years. He was an adult when he came – and he knew you loved him."

"You won't...?"

Johan covered his brief hesitation. No, it would not be seemly since the bird had saved the life of Johan's granddaughter. His old country's customs against waste or not, it would be akin to cannibalism.

"Of course not. He'll be buried as he should be. We'll take him up and bury him by Vernest."

Leesha nodded. "Yes, my brother sent him, it's right he should go back."

They went alone, carrying the body of the bird unobtrusively. It wouldn't do for the village to gossip. They buried Ernest at the foot of the grave, and Leesha patted the earth down very gently. She tossed leaves over it until no one would know that the grave had been disturbed.

"He saved me."

"Yes."

"I'm sure Vernest sent him to me."

"Perhaps so."

"I loved him."

"Yes, and he loved you," and involuntarily, "what a fighter he was. I'll never forget that man waving his arms all over the place, his face torn and bleeding, trying so hard to get Vernest off him. An outlaw, a killer, beaten by a rooster."

Johan laughed, Leesha's giggle harmonizing. There'd never be another bird like Vernest, Leesha would miss him, and oddly enough, thought the unsentimental old migrant, so would he. He didn't know if God or even his grandson had sent the bird to them or not, but next time he was near a church he'd give thanks anyway. Thanks for a feathered, fighting, Year's End miracle that had given Leesha a future.

DEAD

In 1893 my husband and I had a small ranch near the town of Bodie. We'd settled in four years earlier and our joy at having our own home was increased by the advent of a daughter a year later. We had a son six years after her. but it is of my daughter I tell this tale. She was seven and adored horses. But a reasonable child's pony costs money as does its saddle, bridle and halter – which come dearer than the standard tack for a horse – neither of us would have considered buying her one of the too-powerful wild-eyed half-broken mustangs we were offered now and then. My parents had purchased me a good mare, fifteen hands, two inches, with some Morgan blood, but she was far too large for a small, light-boned seven-year-old to ride.

I mentioned this to a woman at our sewing circle and she nodded. "My dear, I may be able to help. My children are all grown-up and gone. We have the pony they learned to ride on. Strictly speaking, he belongs to our eldest daughter, but I'll ask her."

The eldest daughter, written to, replied that she didn't mind my daughter riding her pony, but he must stay at the ranch. I thought that a bit mean, it would mean Miranda – known as Miri – walking three miles there and back any time she wanted to ride, but I had no right to look a gift – pony – in the mouth. I smiled at that thought, from other things said, I suspected that the pony was old, and with that in mind I mentioned to Miri that she shouldn't gallop him too much, that Rodney – named after the pony's giver, (an uncle) wasn't young anymore. It's possible I shouldn't have said that, but I was worried about it not being our animal.

Miri adored Rodney. He was a sturdy, nondescript dun of just above thirteen hands. He was kind, sensible, sure-footed, and knew his way home from any place he'd been before. He adored apples – we'd planted three different types of apple trees by the house, so Miri could always find a windfall, and it

36

took only a few days before he was at the fence waiting when he saw her plodding towards his paddock. They adventured together he and Miri, sometimes in her imagination, and other times as she grew a little older and the Swensons saw she was a sensible rider and adored the pony, Miri was permitted to take him further afield.

Somewhere over the three years she rode Rodney, she discovered that he was eighteen. Now it was true that mustangs, ridden hard as most were, tend not to live beyond twenty, but a loved and cared-for pony may live longer – even a lot longer, and Miri was careful never to over-tax her beloved friend. Until the day when she rode further than usual, then hurried to get back before dusk. She rubbed Rodney down lovingly, said she'd see him in the morning, and walked home.

Morning came. Miri enjoyed a hearty breakfast then headed for Rodney's paddock as usual, to find no pony waiting by the fence. Instead, when she scanned the paddock, she could see him lying motionless some distance away. She looked, spoke his name, and he remained in what became to her a terrifying stillness. Miri backed away, a step at a time, her face whitening, as she came to the realization of what must have happened. She'd overworked Rodney. He was old, he'd given her all he had because they were friends, but during the night … during the night…

Miri fled for home. She stumbled into our yard crying hysterically. It so happened that there'd been a robbery in Bodie a couple of hours ago and both the sheriff and his deputy were at our ranch asking if we'd seen anything. Miri arrived, tearstained, wailing like something out of a Greek Tragedy. "Dead, he's dead. Mommy, he's dead. Right by Swenson's fence. He's d … d … d … dead."

If you don't know what someone is talking about, you tend to relate it to your own concerns. The sheriff's head came up, and before I could demand to know who was dead, he was ahorse and galloping towards the Swenson ranch. My mare was conveniently saddled and bridled, tied to the fence, since I'd planned to go into town. I paused only to ask who was dead, and receive a one-word reply. When I saw the deputy tear off after his boss, realised they'd be furious when they discovered *who* was deceased, and I followed. My husband, who'd just come from the barn, took off after us on foot, as did two of the ranch hands from the ranch between us and the Swensons', who'd been on their horses checking the fence, and who weren't going to be left out of any excitement.

Five riders strong, we thundered down the road, hurled our mounts around the bend just before Swenson's boundary – and discovered a young hard-faced man, leading a limping horse. Before any of us could react, he'd produced a gun and the shooting started. The deputy got off a single shot, before taking a bullet himself. The sheriff shot twice, missed both times, the ranch hands, firing wildly and no marksmen, also missed, while I under cover of the excitement, and mostly hidden by plunging horses and shouting riders, quietly produced the saddle-gun I carried in case of necessity, and shot once.

The furor died down. My husband caught up to us with Miri in tow, and the deputy, all of eighteen, sat cursing and holding a shoulder. "*Blank* got me in the blank arm. Who the *blank blank was* this *blank?*" I eyed him severely and realising ten-year-old Miri was staring round-eyed at him he blushed and fell silent.

The sheriff was checking the dead man and then his bulging saddlebags. He looked up. "He was the man that robbed Peterson's store," he said slowly. "He fits Peterson's description, and Peterson said the man stole a silk bandanna as well as the cash." He held up a bandanna of a lovely crimson silk. "That's here and so's the money. Reckon Peterson will be relieved, and then too, I know this face, had a poster on him just the other month. That's Joe Watford. Bounty on him's three hundred dollars. Reckon you'll come in for that, Mrs. Ward."

A whole line of thoughts flicked through my mind, and I shook my head. "No, I'd like enough out of that to buy Miri a decent pony and whatever gear it needs, the rest should go to you, sheriff, your deputy, and these hands who risked their lives to bring an outlaw to justice."

Everyone beamed. A decent pony, even a good one with saddle, bride, and a halter too maybe, wouldn't be more than sixty dollars. Whereas my offer meant that the four men would each receive over two months' wages as their share. They heaved the body onto the sheriff's horse, and with him leading that and the lame mount limping behind, they all started for town. Once we reached the ranch gates, I took Miri in, while my husband stayed behind briefly with the sheriff.

When he re-joined us, he was leading the limping mount and I raised an eyebrow. "Sheriff says it's for us. If Miri hadn't given the alarm, he'd never have got back everything Watford stole. He's right happy about it." He glanced at Miri who was crying again. "What's wrong anyhow? She said someone was dead. They may be now, but I never saw anyone dead before you shot that man."

I turned to Miri. "Get up behind me, and we'll go and check Rodney."

"He's dead. I saw him. It's my fault, I took him too far yesterday then I hurried him home." The small heart-broken face looked up at me as I reached down to haul her up behind me.

"Then let's go and see, shall we. If he's dead, we can give him a funeral. On the way you can tell me why you think he's dead." Jack walked beside us listening to the sad tale of how Miri had found Rodney stretched out,

"He always hears me coming and he's there for his apple. He was just lying there, sort of flat, he never moved." She wept again. "It's my fault, he was my best friend and I killed him!"

The last words were a pitiful wail – which stopped abruptly – as we reached the Swenson fence line, and Rodney came cantering to meet us, demanding his apple. Miri was late, where was his treat? Since in all the excitement, she still had it, Rodney received his due while my daughter watched him. Finally, she looked up. "He wasn't dead?"

It was Jack who answered that. "No. he was asleep."

"But he's never slept lying down before?"

"You said that yesterday you went further than usual, and you hurried back?" Miri nodded. "So yesterday he was more tired than usual, and he slept laying down and he slept more deeply than usual too."

"Oh. So, he's fine?"

"Yes, but it's a good thing mommy's going to get you a new pony, that way you can have Rodney for your friend still, and he can rest more."

Miri saw the sense in that. I found her a pony that suited her to a T, although often she rode to where Rodney lived, and she always had two apples, one for him, and one for her new pony to chomp while she talked to her older friend and scratched around his ears. The lame horse found a home with us, Jack found him an excellent animal, and well-trained. No one ever claimed him, so we came to the conclusion Joe Watford must have bought him. And the sheriff, a smart man, never asked who it was that Miri had claimed to be dead. Why ask when the answer may make you look silly?

Whereas what actually happened made him look a hero to the whole of Bodie and particularly to Mr. Peterson who could have been ruined, and when you collect money from it into the bargain. It didn't hurt, that in the interim the bounty on Watford's head had gone up, and all four men did very well out of it. I wasn't bothered, I considered we'd done well too. Miri had a pony, Jack had a fine go-to-town mount, and I had the satisfaction of seeing Rodney canter to meet us for many more years, while Miri laughed and fed him apples. But she never forgot the truth she'd learned, that sometime a tired mount sleeps lying down – happily it doesn't always mean they're dead.

ON THE ROAD TO BODIE

T he stories of the West tend to be those of great events, the tales of gunslingers, outlaws, and gold strikes, Indian attacks and range wars. Mostly the stories told are of those who made a name and of them, it is the men who are remembered. But do not forget that in that time there were ordinary people, also that a majority of those were women and children.

When Manny McGovern died in the cave-in of his worthless mine soon after the gold rush in Bodie, California, there was little choice for his Mexican widow and his daughter. Maria went to work at the Bodie laundry for old Wang Ling, while his daughter Ines went to work for Willie Smyth on his ranch seven miles out of town.

That was a hard life for a girl of thirteen. Willie worked her day and night, or if not night, then late into the evening until the child was dropping from exhaustion. Her food was simple, basic – and there was never quite enough of it for a girl growing up. He never laid a hand on her for he was one of those iron-fisted, righteous Christians who would have scorned to use a servant that way. But Ines feared him more than the devil despite that forbearance.

Once a month she took her day off, walking early into town to spend a half-day with her mother, before walking home again in the cool of the evening. And an eleven-mile walk was no less tiring than her work. Always her mother fed her, held her against her heart and mourned that she could do no better for her daughter.

"Once we had land, a land grant given before Texas was a state, but the deed was lost when my grandfather was murdered. Our family became poor when we could no longer prove what was ours. Once I could have given you clothes to shame any woman in this town even those women whose men found gold. You could have gone to a good school with the nuns then married well. Now we have

41

nothing and who will you marry?"

"No one, mamacita," A glimmer of fun stirred. "I will search the tailings and find a golden nugget, I will buy you a house and stay with you always, we will be two old ladies together. We will find a good cat for the mice and wear purple dresses on Sundays."

Maria was betrayed into a small laugh. "Ah, si, a good dream. Well, it is true that now and again I find a pinch of gold dust in the pockets of the shirts I wash, never enough to free us from this place though. But what I find I save and it may be that one day I will have sufficient to take us back to Texas."

"Texas?" Ines knew the dream but it was always pleasant to hear her mother tell it again.

"Texas, yes. To the land we owned until the deed was lost. No one farms that land yet. If we came with the deed, we could take it up. Be landholders and hire kin from beyond the border to work it for us."

"We would need money to stock the ranch," Ines said practically.

"Si, but the lands were great, we could take a loan from the bank for that. Or we could sell a portion of the land to buy what we need and owe nothing to anyone."

"I think that would be better." The girl's voice was thoughtful. "I have seen here how people hate those who have too much. It makes them a target for thieves. Better to sell half the land and buy what is needed in cattle and gear. Hire men who are recommended as trustworthy, owe nothing to the bank, and make friends nearby, go to church, and speak politely to all. That way if any come against us there are those who will speak for us and come to our aid."

Maria looked at her almost respectfully. "You have an old head on those young shoulders. Si, that is a good plan. When the deed is found that is what we should do."

"Mama? Why did my papa's family not assist you when he died? And how was the deed lost?"

Maria sighed. "Ah, my Manny was a fine man, a loving husband, a good father. But his family did not like that he married a woman of Mexico, nor were they pleased when he said he was coming here to find gold and be rich."

"Did you write to them that he had died?"

"I did – and heard nothing. I sold his claim for what I could. I have the money still. One day it will be yours so that you have some choice in what you will do."

That part Ines knew, and knew too that the claim had not proved out, it had been all but valueless. What her mother had received would be barely enough to take them back to Texas on the stage. And what would be the use of returning to a family that had no interest in them, or to land they could not prove was theirs?

That evening she walked back to the ranch, slept deeply, and rose to work again. Willie was gone and his foreman was in the house. John Garton was as Ines was, by basic breeding, in his case the son of an American and his half-Mexican wife. Thus, he was three-quarters American and proud of that, despising his mother's mother's people. But Ines he did not despise, she was growing into her dresses, filling out and John had begun to notice. She was young, but she'd make a wife – if she was well schooled to respect her husband and obedient in following his orders.

He made advances while Willie wasn't there to say differently and was denied. He went away smoldering that she dared to reject him. But he could bide his time, Willie Smyth would not be always at home. A year later, Willie was gone briefly and John moved into the house again. He sent at once for Ines.

"Why do you send me away, girl? I have a good job, I earn well, I would marry you before the priest if that is what you want?"

"I do not want to marry you."

"You are a child. You do not know what you want," John said contemptuously.

"And do you wish to marry a child?" Ines's tone cut with the implications.

"I will marry you. You have the folly of a child, the mind that does not see what is good for it. But you are a woman in body – or so says American law. And I will have you. I'll speak to Willie on his return and he will give you to me."

"He is not my father. He can give me to no one."

John smiled then. "Can he not, pretty Ines? Remember the girl who had your job before you came here? You'd have heard, she lay with a cow-puncher and the boss fired her as soon as he heard. He said he wasn't having a whore on the place. How if I tell him that you've lain with me and that I wish to wed. He is a church-going man. He will command that you marry me or leave. And if you leave the ranch branded a whore, who will have you in Bodie? Who will give employment to Garton's whore?"

What he said was true. But the thought of taking him as her man sickened her. And – if she could hold him off for long enough another might take his fancy. She might even speak privately to Mr. Smyth and have him order Garton to leave her alone. She summoned courage.

"That may be so, all of it, but I want time to consider. My mother must hear of your offer, if she bids me accept you then it may be that I shall. And my father's relations should know, they have a large ranch in Texas and would surely wish to come to a wedding." None of the latter was true, but she was fighting with what weapons she had.

John Garton guessed at her desperation, believed in his eventual success – and his smile was ugly. "Very well, I shall wait until you have written to your father's family and until you have discussed this with your mother. I give you three months. After that, look for me. I shall be your husband yet."

Ines walked steadily along the road to Bodie a month later. She had written the letter to the McGovern family and would post it in town to catch the stage that evening as it came through. Willie Smyth would be home in two more weeks as well. She had two strings to her bow of hope and she prayed that one or the other would save her.

The letter went as she'd planned. She'd written carefully, in her best handwriting, a plea that her father's family should come or send for her and her mother. Even if they only gave the two of them the same work as they did now but in Texas, it would be far better than what John Garton planned.

Maria held out no false hope. "You could not bear to marry him?"

Ines shuddered. "To the center of my bones he disgusts me."

Maria nodded. "We have sufficient money saved. We would take the stage to Texas perhaps. It might be that if we were standing before them, your father's kin might help us?"

"And if they still will not?" Ines asked quietly. "Then we have spent all we have. We are stranded in another place and without work. What do we do then and where would we go?"

Maria nodded slowly. "Yet there is this. At least we would still be together and – John Garton would not be with us."

It was desperation and Ines felt it, that her mother would willingly throw away all they had to save her daughter. But there were still the other possibilities. They waited, but no letter came nor any rider from Texas. Three months passed and it seemed clear that no one else would save them. What could be done they must do themselves. Ines gathered her courage and asked for a private word with her employer.

"Mr. Smyth, I ask that you give me your advice."

Willie leaned back in his chair. That was the sort of thing he liked to hear. He could tell his fellow church-goers how his employees came to him for aid, even the least of them. He knew what the problem was. John Garton had an eye for a pretty girl and wanted to marry this one. No doubt she was humble at her good fortune and wished to be sure that her employer agreed. Garton had hinted that he'd had his way with her – and *that* Willie Smith most strongly disapproved. But so long as he married the girl there was no harm done.

He listened to Ines' faltering words and was stunned into silence. Far from wishing to marry the man who had most likely already dishonored her, she wanted her employer to send him away. Or at the least it seemed, to order John Garton to leave her be.

"He raped you?" That was the only thing he could think of.

Ines was stunned in turn before understanding came to her. Her head lifted proudly. "No, sir. He has laid no hand on me ever. But he wishes to marry me, by force he has said, if I come not willing. I want none of him. I would not wed John Garton even if he *had* raped me."

Willie Smyth looked at her and was angered by this folly. John Garton was a good foreman. If he had his mind set on the girl, why should he not wed her? And if she would not, then he'd have a foreman who did not have his mind on his work while the girl was nearby. Worse still, if Garton did as the girl claimed he'd threatened then it would be a scandal – and

Willie Smyth went to church each Sunday. There they would ask perhaps, why he had not prevented it. He made up his mind.

"I will give you the advice you asked for, Ines. Marry John and be a good wife to him. Or if you are so set against that, take this." He dug into his pocket and spilled three gold eagles into her hand. "Here, two months wages for a cowhand. You and your mother catch the stage for another place before tomorrow night, because you no longer have a job here unless you are marrying John. Marry him and the money is yours anyway."

It was worth it to him to have her gone – or wed – and his good foreman with his mind back on the ranch's prosperity again. Or at the least, the girl would be gone without a scandal that would tarnish Willie's reputation.

Ines stood staring, her fingers clasped around the coins. She saw from her employer's face that there was no appeal. Very well then, it must be Texas. She had little here, she could pack it all into a sack and be gone in an hour and walking into her mother's room in town in two more. It would be dark when she arrived and dusk for the last part of the journey but she was not afraid, she'd walked the road to Bodie often enough to know every foot of it.

She had packed her meager belongings and was halfway home when John Garton rode back from where he and his men had been gathering the cattle. He went quietly to her room – to find the girl and all that she owned were gone. He went to Willie and heard with increasing rage of the talk his boss had had with the girl.

So, she would not wed him of her free will. Well, then, she would wed him anyhow and once she was in his hands he would know how to tame her. He took his best mount, a bay that liked to run, and followed the road at a speed that would bring him up with her long before she reached town – even if she didn't stop on the way to rest a while.

Ines *had* stopped. It was a warm night. Little though her belongings weighed, they seemed heavy after she had walked past halfway, and there was a convenient boulder when she could sit a while. But as she approached, she could see a man already sat there. Nearby a roan grazed. A fine beast, wearing a very old-fashioned saddle. The man was of middle-age and medium size – a Mexican lithe as a cat with an old cap and ball gun on one hip and a sheathed knife at the other.

Ines slowed and he smiled at her. "Ay, chiquita, come and sit and do not be afraid. I had a wife and a daughter once and, in their name and for the love I had for them, no harm shall come to you. Tell me, your face seems known to me. Where do you go so late and who are your kin?"

"I am Ines McGovern. My mother is Maria McGovern who was Ines Mendoza."

He nodded. "Ines Mendoza of the land that borders the river, and of the family of Juan Cuchillo?"

"Yes, you knew her?"

"Not her, but her mother and her father before her." He moved abruptly, his hand going into his shirt. "I came on a long road to bring her something."

Ines would have feared but for the kindness she saw in his eyes. She waited, watching him as he removed a small roll of white buckskin tied close, from inside his shirt. She noticed a small scar down his left cheek, a thin white wandering line. At his throat was an Indian medallion made of beads, a circle of white with a black center. He saw her looking at it.

"A gift from a friend." His voice was quiet. "From one who was a ga'an dancer in his time, given me to bring a blessing, a warding off of evil." He smiled at her. "My heart tells me that evil follows you and that a blessing and a ward would aid you this night." He lifted the medallion from about his neck and beckoned her close. "Take it!" The words were gentle, but an order, and without thinking she obeyed, dropping it on the thong over her head so that it nestled below her throat.

"That is well." He handed her the buckskin roll and pointed to the road. "Now, child, take this to your mother, and walk quickly."

Ines took the roll in her hand and thrust it into her pack. She had guessed who the man might be, she thought. He had to be one of her father's kin, sent to bring an offer of refuge to Ines and her mother.

She smiled up at him, deep gratitude in her eyes. "I thank you for your gifts, señor."

"Vaya con dios, Ines McGovern."

"And you, señor. May I know your name before we part?"

"Juan. Go now and do not pause until you are safe."

"Gracias, Juan, I will do as you bid me."

She started walking and when she looked back some ten minutes later there was no sign of Juan or his mount. Ines walked on, ahead she could see the outskirts of Bodie in the distance, it was almost dark, but the lights glowed to show her the way home. She reached the start of the main street and paused as she heard hoof-beats that pounded nearer on the dry ground. She swung about already knowing what she would see.

John Garton, his face twisted in fury, rode towards her, people on the boardwalk were starting to look up but Ines despaired. He would seize her, carry her away, no one would stop him who was a respected man offering marriage to a part-Mexican girl too stupid to know her good fortune. Her hand closed on the medallion and she prayed. "Ward off this evil as Juan said you were made to do."

The bay reared then, screaming, and people scattered. John Garton yelled in almost insane rage, beat his mount and forced it forward. It reared again, higher and higher until gravity took toll and it fell backwards – onto the rider who had not moved quickly enough to leap clear. There was a cry cut-off, a cracking sound, and the bay rolled to his hooves and stood trembling. In the dust of Bodie's main street John Garton lay still.

Ines slipped away. Garton had said nothing to her, no one knew that it had been her he'd been hunting. She found her mother in the small dark room, handed her the scroll and spoke softly as the lamp was lit.

"Willie Smyth said that if I would not marry John Garton I must leave. He gave me money and said that we should seek another town." She placed the three gold coins on the table. "I chose to leave. I would have rested at the boulder by the turnoff but another was already there. He said he knew our kin and that I was to give you this." She handed her mother the tied roll of buckskin. "The gold will get us back to Texas without the need to touch your savings or the price of my father's mine. We have been given a choice. And – John Garton is dead."

Her mother looked up from the buckskin. "He gave us more choice than you know. But what happened to John and where did you get this?"

"John followed me. I thought he would stay with the herd all night but he must have come back to the ranch and been told I was gone. He caught up with me at the edge of town. I was afraid. But the man I met on the road to Bodie gave me a medallion he said warded off evil. I held it and prayed and John's horse went mad. It reared, and fell back on him, I think he is dead, or if not dead, then so injured it will be very long before he seeks me again."

"And the man who met you, who gave you this?" Maria was staring at the medallion.

Ines remembered the kind eyes, the gentle voice. "He said he had not known you but he'd known your mother and her father. He said he had come to bring you this," her finger pointed at the buckskin. "He was perhaps forty, he had a thin scar on his cheek, wavering, as if from wire. Oh, and he said that his name was Juan." She looked at the buckskin. "Mama, what is that?"

Maria smiled, a wide joyous smile such as Ines had not seen since her father's death. "Thus, my daughter, are our choices returned to us. That is the deed my grandfather hid before he was slain, and that we could not find. With this in our hands I can take back our heritage, the bank will grant us money at my asking, and you shall marry only where you will."

"But where would my father's family find that?"

Maria looked at her, knowing what the girl had thought. "Your father's family sent nothing," she said quietly. "It was my grandfather who brought us this, and his medallion, given him by an Apache warrior, that warded off the evil that followed you."

Ines stared. "My great-grandfather has been dead since before you were born."

"That I know. But before my mother died, I saw the drawing she had of her father wearing the medallion, the scar down his cheek. And I – I remember that it was always the boast of Juan Cuchillo that he took care of his own. Tonight, he met you on the road to Bodie, my daughter, and proved that dead or living he *is* a man of his word."

THE LIONS' SHADOW

"**W**here'd you come from?"
"Far enough away from here that my stepfather won't look for me, I hope." She shivered as he looked at her.

"Like that, was he?"

This time she only nodded. That was all the confirmation that he needed to understand though, it was often the story for kids on the old city streets in eighteen-eighty-nine. Abuse until the abused one could bear it no longer and ran – from the blows, the drunken shouting, or the quiet opening of a bedroom door after dark.

"What about your mother?" The line moved up and he walked with it indicating that she should follow. He saw her hesitation and shook his head. "Nothing to worry about. The Fathers' of St. James feed you and they won't ask questions."

"Do they have a place for us to sleep?"

"You don't want that. The ones who feed us don't ask for anything, but if you go to a shelter the Father Superior will be nosy."

He saw her fear and guessed it to be twofold; that her stepfather could find her here if she was known or that she might be handed over to some official. They'd start by giving her back too, unless she told why she'd run, then there would be all the fuss probably ending in a belief that she was a liar and she'd be handed back anyhow. She'd been smart enough to wear her hair chopped short, boy's clothes, her grimy feet were bare, and she has an old canvas carrysack over one thin shoulder.

Life on the streets wasn't anything wonderful, but if you were smart and learned to work the system you survived, and at least you were free. He'd been free almost two years. His father had thrown him out after the scandal when the school had expelled him.

He was sorry for the teacher Mike had been caught with, but the man had pressured him. Not that Mike had been that unwilling. But after that everything had come crashing down on their heads.

The teacher was sacked very quietly by his superiors and Mike was expelled. His father, a rich rancher, hadn't cared originally when he'd thought it was for some sort of ordinary misbehavior. It had been "a chip off the old block" and "I wasn't any good at school either, and it doesn't stop me owning a ranch now." Then his dad found out exactly why Mike had been expelled and the whole atmosphere changed.

"You filthy … you were caught with a man! The headmaster told me today; he thought I should know the real reason. He said that the Board only put that you were being slung out for inappropriate actions. I thought you'd been caught with a girl, instead you're a…" he used a vicious epithet. "I've bred a dirty little…! That's it; I'm not having you here for people to talk about. I make my living in this town. You can go stay with your aunt down in south Texas."

Except that his aunt in Austin hadn't wanted him either and, in the end, Mike had come down to the city where he'd found a living of sorts on the streets. He looked at the kid in front of him. She wouldn't last on her own. Some guy would pick her up, give her a place to stay and expect her to pay for it the only way she could.

He touched her shoulder. "How old are you?"

"Sixteen."

He grinned at her, a broad cheerful smile that accepted the lie while showing that he knew it for what it was and she dropped her gaze, digging the toe of one bare foot into the dirt. "Okay, okay, I'm fourteen. Well, I will be in another couple of months. How old are you?"

"Fifteen, I've been here almost two years."

"What's it like?"

"Not bad if you're careful and you know what you're doing." He saw her sudden fear. "When did you get in?"

"This morning. A girl I met told me to come here for a free meal."

"Have you got any money?"

She looked at him. "A bit, not much, I thought I could maybe get a room for the night then look for a job."

He groaned quietly. "Girl, you're out of luck there. Any employer will take one look at you and either he won't hire you or he'll expect you to pay him to keep quiet."

"How..." he saw her understand what he hadn't put into words and she cringed. "I won't. My stepfather – I won't – that was why I ran away."

"Yeah, I know."

"You too?"

"Sort of. Look, don't worry. Once we've eaten you can come with me. I know where there's a safe place to sleep and I won't let anyone hassle you." He saw the doubt in her gaze as she studied him, and his smile was wry. "It's okay, I don't fancy girls." He wondered if she was too naive to understand that, but after a moment she nodded.

"Okay." She remembered his earlier question. "My Dad died when I was three, Mum married my stepfather when I was almost twelve. He started touching me right after the wedding. I told her but she said that I was lying, that I was jealous because she was happy. So long as she was there, he didn't go too far, but then she got sick. She died a couple of months ago and he started coming into my bedroom at night. I locked the door and he took the lock off. I started staying outside at night and he'd lock the door so I couldn't get in again until he let me back. I knew he'd get tired of trying to persuade me soon and..." she stopped.

"So, you got out in time." Mike's voice was matter of fact. She nodded. "Smart." he approved. "What's your name?"

"Jackie, call me Jack. What's yours?"

"Mike." By now they had reached the table where the food was given out and he passed her one of the plates, speaking quietly. "Don't take your carrysack off ever." when she went to shrug it from her shoulder. "Now, eat everything they give you and go back for seconds if they'll let you." He overrode what she was about to say. "Look, I know you aren't that hungry, but trust me."

Jackie decided he must know what he was doing; he'd survived here for two years. Obediently she accepted her filled plate and followed him to a seat, moving her carrysack to one shoulder but keeping it with her as he'd said. He ate quickly, eyes on the food, then he went up with her, shuffling her in front.

"Uh, Father Henry. This kid's new here, an' he's still hungry; can he have a bit more? Just some bread and butter?"

The man behind the table eyed him, and then considered Jackie. "Yes, I see. All right, are you looking after him, Mike?"

"Guess so."

"Then make sure he gets this. Don't let one of the others take it off him." He piled several slices of buttered bread onto an old tin plate and passed the plate over. "Here."

"Thanks." Mike let her take the plate then steered her for the doorway.

"Aren't we going to eat here?"

"Nope. Let's get out quickly before anyone else notices you got seconds."

Once out in the street he whisked her down an alleyway and took the plate from her. Producing a moderately clean handkerchief from his pocket he bundled the food up and passed it to her. "Stick that in your bag. That's your breakfast, see?" Jackie saw.

"What about you?"

"I'll be okay. I can beg awhile. You can come with me on that but we have to be careful. If the town officers see you, they'll want to know who you are. Your stepfather could have reported you missing."

Jackie flinched. "He could have, I don't know. Would he risk it?"

"Maybe, maybe not. But if anyone where you've come from realizes that you aren't with him anymore, they'll ask questions. If people start wondering about where you've got to, he might have to tell the authorities to keep himself out of trouble."

Her mouth set grimly. "If they pick me up and try to make me go back, I'll have to say why I won't."

He looked at her. At the small slender figure, the short light-brown hair and oval face with her eyes a warm hazel in grime-darkened skin. He studied the face. There was a determined set to the chin and a steady look in the hazel eyes. She'd talk – and take her chances if she were recaptured. Her stepfather would know that.

"It's likely he'll try to cover up that you've gone," Mike said, thinking it out. "He'll know you'd talk if you get picked up and someone tries to send you back. Haven't you got any other relatives you could go to?"

"My mother's cousin, she's older'n me, she's a dressmaker an' she's got a place in Austin."

"Okay, then here's what you do. You know her address?" She nodded. "Good. Write it down and keep it in your pocket. If the marshals pick you up, you say you live with her there. You had an argument and ran away, and you give her address. There's a good chance they'll just give you a lecture and let you go, tell you to go home, and if they see you again next time, they'll put you on the stage with someone to make sure you get back to her. To get away with that you have to stay clean and tidy and they have to think you're a boy. You got spare clothes in that bag?"

Jackie nodded.

"Good, then you keep them washed, and you have regular baths in one of the streams."

All the time they talked he was leading her through narrow streets, down alleyways that serviced shops, and across broken-down back fences. They came out in a clean-enough street and he slumped to the ground, his back against a wall. Pulling Jackie down to sit with him on the warm pavement, he took a mouth harp from his pocket, laid out a bandanna by his legs, and began to play a jaunty version of Polly Wolly Doodle.

Jackie listened. She'd sneaked a day-long ride on a loaded wagon to get here and she was tiring. Her stomach was full, and somehow, she trusted Mike. She leaned against the wall, and her eyes closed slowly. He finished the song, started another and glanced at her. She was asleep. He reached over, pulling her gently so that she leaned against him and moved into a slow rendition of "Dear Little Brother of Mine."

As he'd expected, the pace of coins dropping into his plate promptly sped up. People loved anything cute. Jackie made a young-looking boy and her being asleep on his shoulder while he played made an attractive picture. Big brother looking after his trusting kid brother. All the same he kept an eye open for any law officer. They wouldn't be so touched by the picture.

But after a couple of hours there'd been no sign of the

town marshal or his deputies. Jackie still slept, and he figured that it was time he packed up. He'd been scooping any of the larger coins from the plate as he played, just in case he had to run or someone else made a grab at the coins. He'd made almost three dollars, which was quite a lot better than usual.

It'd be worth keeping Jackie, teaching her the tricks of survival and besides – although he'd never have admitted to either feeling – he was lonely, and her sleeping so trustingly on his shoulder was kind of nice. He woke her gently, packed up his mouth harp, his bandanna, and hauled her to her feet.

"We're on our way."

"Where?"

"A place I know where we can sleep. Just keep up and don't talk too loud."

Jackie followed him again as they wove through back alleys and past derelict buildings. Mike slipped though yet another broken fence, holding a board aside for her to follow. He halted her with one hand on her arm while he listened. Jackie could hear nothing, but waited patiently. Mike signaled her to follow after him as he sidled around the adobe wall of a building, approached a massive plank door, and fiddled briefly with the old-fashioned lock. The door opened silently and he waved her inside.

"This is home. What do you think of it?"

Jackie stared about. In the half-light, she could see the place had likely been some sort of warehouse … once. She couldn't see any holes in the ceiling above her, and while outside temperatures had been dropping for the last hour, inside the old adobe walls it was quite warm.

"It's great. How'd you find it and how come you've got a key?"

Mike grinned. "I heard about it from a friend. He worked for someone who used to use it when it was still a business and he made a copy of the old key for me." In fact, the guy had been an occasional lover who'd paid Mike off with the key — but he didn't tell her that.

"Won't people come to look at it?"

"Nope. It belonged to some guy who died. His kids started a court case against his second wife that's been going for years. Looks like they'll be doing that for ages yet. So long as they're on about it, no one comes here at all."

"Not even the marshal?"

"Nope. Whoever was in charge of the place left the roof tanks alone so there's water." He reckoned he had a right to be proud of himself. Very few with no money out there would ever have a place as good as this. He felt smug that he could share it with Jackie, but he had to impress something on her first.

"You can't ever let anyone know about this. That's real important. If some of the others knew, they'd come in and take over. You never come straight here, always dodge about. I'll show you the different ways so you can manage on your own if you have to. I've got a real safe place deeper in here too, where even if someone does come looking, they won't find you. I'll show you that too but right now I've got to do a few things. You can find the wash tub and wash out your gear on your own, can't you?"

Jackie nodded and plodded off with her carrysack drooping from one arm, her footsteps heavy with weariness. It had been a long day.

He should count his evening's takings to begin with, Mike thought. After that he'd heat soup on the tiny stove upstairs in his safe room. He'd share the soup with Jackie and he should have enough bedding to split it so they could both have their own bed. She'd be more comfortable with that. They might be able to find more bedding in the next day or two though, and they'd need it. In another couple of months, it would be getting into winter and life on the streets would become a lot harder.

He dug coins out of his pockets, counted, and beamed. Wow, almost five dollars in total. Jack had brought him luck. This city, it took with one hand but sometimes it gave back with the other. There were strange tales about the city. He'd been around long enough to hear some of them from Mexican kids, and every now and again something happened that made a man wonder. Mike shrugged as he stowed the cash into a bag that he trotted silently upstairs to conceal.

Jimenez had told him once that the city ate people. It was true that there were always kids who went missing, no one knew where they went but there were weird tales. Mike thought that probably those who'd gone missing had just left town, but he knew that half of one of Patti Jackson' best stories was true – and it could be the other half was as well.

Jackie was back. "I've washed out my things and hung them on some string I had. Is that safe?"

"Should be now it's getting dark. Nobody much comes around then. Come upstairs, I'll show you where you can bed down and we'll have hot soup."

"How?"

"I've got a sort of stove – just a couple a' sheets of iron and a trivet over them. Works pretty well. Come with me and I'll start the soup then we can sort out the blankets and stuff while it heats up." He saw her sidelong glance and added, "We'll have to keep an eye out for more blankets or something, I've got a fair bit, but giving you half is going to cut down on that." He produced a candle-lantern from a niche in the wall.

Her shoulders relaxed, as she understood what he was telling her. "I can look for more bed stuff if you tell me what to watch for."

He explained briefly and she nodded.

"You won't be cold if you give me half?"

"Not too bad."

Jackie took a deep breath. "I read once where some who came west shared a bed to stay warm and put a blanket between them. You know, sort of one blanket over one person and under the other. We could do that until we can find more blankets. The bed's yours and it wouldn't be fair for you to be cold."

"If you're okay with that?"

"Yes – yes." She wavered initially, and then her voice became decided. She'd learned from her stepfather the sort of look a guy gave you if he was interested. Mike looked at her like a big brother and he'd said that he liked other boys. She knew about that from a friend she'd had, so if he liked other boys, he wouldn't want to touch a girl.

He opened the door, walked across the room, reached up to pull out an unobtrusive panel and unfolded a ladder attached to the ceiling.

"Up here." Jackie climbed the rungs after him, balancing on the beam to watch as Mike hauled the ladder up again. "This way." He walked along the beam, stopped and tugged open a second panel. "Down here. The ladder lets down as soon as you put your weight on the top rung." It did and Jackie descended into a small room. She moved aside to let Mike join her as she stared about.

The room was good-sized, almost ten-foot square she estimated. There were no windows, maybe it has been some type of store room. She asked.

Mike nodded. "I dunno exactly. I think maybe a long time ago when the place was built, it was used for valuables – furs and such. After a time, no one remembered this room was here."

"But the door, there must be a door." Jackie stared about. "There." She pointed. "That's a door to the rest of the place. How come no one's ever noticed that?"

Mike looked pleased with himself. "'Cos it doesn't show as a door on the other side. I don't know why, but I guess it was meant that way."

"How did you find it then?"

"I'll tell you, but let's get the soup on and sort out the bed. It'll have to be spread out a bit. I like space to sleep."

They worked on that, sipped their hot soup, then Mike began to talk about the room, his room. It was a story he'd never told anyone before, just as no one else knew about his room, but there was something about this kid. He felt sort of protective, and it felt good to share the story, seeing her wide eyes in the candlelight.

"Brian got me the key to this place after I was hassled. They don't like my sort," he was matter-of-fact about that. It was just life. Nothing anyone could do about it, but some of the Mex guys had beaten him up before Brian gave him a key. "I moved in and started exploring until I found I could get up into the rafters. I climbed all over up there." He pointed upwards, remembering the ladders, ropes, and odd items that may have once been used as hoists to move heavier stuff.

"I spotted a loose panel in the ceiling up there. The room was what I wanted, but I was scared it would be too easy to find – so I went looking around on the other side of the wall in the theater. That's how I know no one knows about the room being here."

"How?"

"The dust and some of the junk. There's dust all over. I'd say it's been years and years since the door there was opened. And I squirmed into some of the stuff stacked in front; there are things there that were dumped maybe twenty-thirty years back. And look here." He picked up the lantern and took her over to the doorway. "See, the nails are rusted in. The crack around the door's filled with dirt 'n' dust. I'd say it's been so long since this old door was open, you'd have to use a pry-bar to get it open again."

"And we'd hear them if they tried." Jackie said with satisfaction.

"That's right. We'd go up the ladder and along the beams then and they'd never catch us if we were quiet enough."

"What about your gear?"

"It's only bedding. Most times when I go out, I stick it in that big cupboard over there, and put the camp stove underneath it. If anyone managed to get into the room while I was out, they probably wouldn't bother to open the cupboard, and if they did, they'd just think it was more rubbish stacked away. I keep a few things in other hiding places around the building. No one's gonna find all of them."

They settled themselves to sleep, Jackie leaving on most of her clothes, and seeing that, Mike did the same.

"The bed's really comfortable," Jackie praised.

"Yeah."

"Goo'ni'" she was asleep. Mike stayed awake a few minutes longer, thinking that the company was nice. She seemed like a good kid. He'd teach her all the ways to survive. He hadn't done so badly. He had regulars, guys who liked a boy, who paid well, and didn't ill-treat him. He made extra money when he needed it by begging. The gangs were the only real problem. One Mexican bunch had hated him ever since they found out he was making it with one of their guys.

They'd caught him twice, given him a going-over the second time and suggested he leave. The leader had made it clear what they'd do if they caught him still around for a third time. Oh, well. He'd just have to be careful and teach Jackie to watch out for them too. There were places they hung out, and he knew them all.

He drifted into sleep so gently he never knew it when he began to dream. Perhaps it was the child beside him, her warmth comforting. But he dreamed a dream of safety, friends all about him, support, love, a family who cared and Jackie was there too, basking in the sunshine, pausing in their game to drink the cool clear water. In sleep his face relaxed into a child's look, innocent and trusting, and his lips curved into a small happy smile.

The days after that were a month of finding bedding and scrounging food. Jackie visited the little public library quite often; they'd faked an identity for her using the address of someone with the same surname.

"Be careful you take the books back on time." Mike cautioned. "If they go looking for you because the books are late back, they'll find you're a fraud and you won't be able to take out books again."

Jackie was very careful about that, knowing that he was right. She also did her share of begging and helping with the chores in their room, and Mike was proud of the way she learned. Luckily, she didn't panic easily either, as he found the day the deputy marshal picked her up.

"All right young man, what are you doing here?" The deputy was tall and skinny, but he had her cornered and he looked as if he could run if he had to. Mike had faded away as soon as he saw her stopped. She knew he wouldn't have gone far and he'd help if he could – but it wouldn't be a good idea to try to run.

Bob Olsen looked down at the kid. He had an idea he might have seen him before, busking with that boy, Mike. The kid was clean, though, and his clothes smelled as if they'd been recently washed. "Well, who are you?"

"Jack Drew. Just been to the library."

The deputy glanced at the offered card, and nodded. That looked legit, and any boy who read, even if it was at the charity library of St. James had to be fairly well educated.

He supposed it was all right to let the kid go. It wasn't as if he had no work to do. He nodded. "Behave yourself and take care."

Jack smiled at him. He said the last words as if he meant them. "I will. You too, sir."

She walked away, careful not to hurry. Mike had impressed on her never to run from a marshal. If they saw you running, they wondered why. But she made sure to be around the nearest corner without wasting time. Once she was out of the marshal's sight she dodged between two of the shops, down the service alley, and along a dead-end street before stepping through a broken board in the fence. Mike found her ten minutes later.

"That was close. We'd better stay out of sight for a week or two though. He'll look out for you for a while now, just in case."

"We could dye my hair."

"Yeah, one of the girls I know uses a rinse. It washes out after a couple of times but that'd be better. If he sees you in the distance with dark hair, then lighter again, he won't think it's the same person."

"And I could have a red rinse as well."

"Good idea. I'll talk to Val about it."

They found the big woman with a friend, a small old lady with bright dark eyes, still-black hair, and a scrawny upright figure. She nodded to Mike.

"Who's your friend?"

"Jackie, she's with me. Jackie, meet Val, and Granny Jarni, she's from elsewhere but she comes here now and again. Granny tells great stories – some could even be true."

The old woman chuckled softly. "Eh, he's right. I tell good stories and you can make up your own mind. But I'm guessing you aren't here for a story."

"Nope. Marshall Olsen stopped Jackie today. She gave him a tale. He didn't see he's a girl, an' he let her walk – but I'm thinking it'd be better if he doesn't recognize her for a while. We'll stay away but in case he sees her in the distance it'd be good if she doesn't look like she does now."

When they left, Jackie was a redhead, that being the rinse Val had available. Granny Jarni looked after them. Winter was almost here and it was always a hard time for those who lived on the streets. She'd tell the girl a story or two next time she saw them. A good tale might not fill your stomach or warm you up, but it took your mind off needing those things.

A week later she was about when the two came by. She

waved them to join her, bought them a cup of coffee each and began to talk.

"Anyone ever told you the city's stories?"

"Some," Jackie said, remembering. "The man at the coffee-cart says the city eats people, and Patti says there's a spirit that lives in the harbor. Mr. Aronson at the fruit shop says that the memorial they put up after the war is haunted and Paul that plays squeeze-box told me that sometimes on a dark night you can see old buildings that aren't there anymore."

Granny Jarni chuckled softly. "The city doesn't eat people, but sometimes people vanish – if they really want to. The spirit, I'll say nothing about. But the civil war memorial's haunted right enough, a good haunting. If you sleep in the shadow of the lions there's nothing bad can touch you. As for the stuff about old buildings, that's true too here and there."

"How?"

"There's all of times and places in a city. Every time since it began, every building that ever stood here and some of the spirits of the people who lived or worked in them. There's dark corners here, places where things change."

"Change how?"

"That you have to see for yourself. Maybe you will. Don't be afraid if it happens. The city will look after you. It's real people you have to fear, not the city."

"And the lions' shadows will protect me?" Jackie liked that idea. She knew the two lions that guarded the memorial. She'd heard a British rancher who'd lost a son to that war over twenty years back had paid for it and said it was to have the lions. One night she'd sat on one while Mike sat on the other. She'd dreamed the lions would carry the two of them away, somewhere where they'd be safe forever. Where Mike wouldn't have to do the things he did for money and she would never have to be scared her stepfather would find her.

"They protect the good in heart."

Mike snorted, "That lets me out."

Granny Jarni raised an eyebrow at him. "I said the good in heart, boy, not pure. I know what you do, but you took in Jackie here. You looked after her, and you see no one hurts her. In my book that makes you good enough." Mike blushed and changed the subject.

They saw the old woman regularly that winter. She told them stories, Jackie often ran errands for her, or helped with her shopping, and Mike fixed the loose hinge on her door. Jackie spent many of the short cold and wet days reading. She liked animal books, reading about lions and other big cats, bears, and elephants. It was the elephants she *really* loved to read about. Mike wanted to know why.

"Because they're too big and strong for anything to hurt them, but they don't kill other animals either, except in self-defense. They have families like we do, and they take care of each other." She sighed. "I bet they don't feel the cold as much as we do either and anyway, it's warm where they live."

"And they have to eat all day because they need lots of food," Mike said, having read some of the same book one afternoon when he was bored. "And they aren't too big and strong to be killed, people do it all the time."

"I know. Well, I wish that the elephants lived in a place where there were no people. They could be safe there and have families and plenty to eat, and no one would bother them."

Mike thought that she really meant that wish for herself, and it wasn't a bad one. He wouldn't mind being somewhere where there was plenty of food, a family that loved you, and nothing to be scared of. He stood up.

"Yeah, you got a point, Jackie, but we need to eat. Let's go down to the Parrot. In an hour they'll be shutting up and throwing out the food that's been cooked too many times an' didn't sell."

"I know."

"Okay, let's go."

They were on the way home, already eating, and arguing about something Jackie had read, when out of the corner of her eye she saw him. It was dusk, but he knew all the same and cringed. Automatically she ducked her head, silenced in mid-word, her small face turning white. Mike looked around but saw nothing.

"Jackie, what's the matter?"

"My stepfather."

"Nah, he can't be here. How would he know you'd come here? And anyhow, if he sets the marshal on you, it'll be him they'll be after once you tell them."

Jackie shivered. "Maybe they won't believe me." Her face reddened as she forced the words out. "He didn't like, you know ... I ran before he could. The doctor would say an' maybe the marshal would think I was lying?"

Mike considered that and nodded slowly. "Look, I'll talk to a few people, see if anyone's been asking around for a kid of your description. If they have, then maybe we could get out of the city for a while. There's other cities."

"None we know as well."

"We'd manage."

"Would you mind?"

"Nope, better than having him grab you one night, or you having to go with Bob Olson. Just hang on a while and I'll find out if he's been around asking, that's all."

Val told him what she knew. "Some bloke, not very tall, but wide, like. Gave a good description of the kid. Said she'd run away from home and her Mum was frantic. Said he just wanted to find her, get her back. No trouble for anyone an' maybe some cash if we could tell him anything."

Mike snarled. "Her Mum's dead. He's her step Dad an' he fancies her. That's why she ran. Pass it around, Val. Granny Jarni likes her and no one knows anything."

Val looked at him. "Kid, someone will talk. None of your friends will and we like her too, but his kind can always find someone even if he has to pay them."

"We're getting out in a couple of days, but I've got to talk to my clients, make arrangements if I want them around still when I come back. Takes money to get gone."

"I've got a few bucks," Val offered.

"Thanks, but we'll be right. It isn't the money I need, it's the time."

"Don't take too much of it. He's looking hard and offering a good price. Sooner or later, someone will take him up on it and I'd say it'll be sooner."

Mike went back to the theater and said nothing. In the morning, he went looking and where he found people he talked quietly. He'd see his clients one last time, then they could go to a pal of his who traded off with him when they needed a break. This one final time though, he had to take the risk and have the cash. Jackie went with him part of the way.

She'd hide herself in the library or around back of the church then get food, they'd meet up again where he'd be. His last appointment was near Davis Street – they could go home after that to pack what they'd take in a couple of carrysacks.

By midnight, Mike was tired out and, on the way back to meet Jackie, ahead he could see her waiting on the corner of one of the streets by the station. It was mostly dark, though the gas streetlight by the memorial made a small pool of radiance and he was happy he was done for the night. He and Jackie could go north once they'd slept and spend some time in a city up there; her stepfather could go to hell.

A hand came down on his shoulder and he was flung sideways into the dark of an alley, ending sprawled against the fence

"You didn't leave when you should have, niño. Now you're gonna learn why you should do what you're told. And before that, we gotta a question for you. Where's that kid you hang out with? There's a man who'll pay good money to know, and you're gonna tell us."

Mike twisted slightly in the hard grip. Johnny Suarez and some of his dogs. They'd kill him this time for sure. He hoped Jackie had seen what happened and be smart enough to clear out. A fist thudded into his ribs with a force that left him doubled over. A foot came up and slammed him against a wall.

"Talk, kid!"

"You mean Jack? He's gone. He saw the guy who's looking for 'im and ran."

"Ran where?" A fist emphasized the question. Mike felt something tear loose in his chest.

"I dunno. Just away, anywhere he isn't. Had money from begging. Maybe he's gone up the line." Suarez shook him savagely then hit him twice in the ribs. The second blow left a blinding trail of pain all down his chest.

"And maybe *she* hasn't. Yeah, guy looking told us a lot. Maybe you're lying an' that isn't good, Mikey boy."

From the street he heard a voice, it was female, loud, and angry. It sounded like Jackie but older, more strident and rougher.

"I tell you, Officer, they're in the rail yard. They snatched my purse, then took off that way." The voice lifted to a pitch that must have had everyone in the street listening. "Look, I can see one of them. Well, what are you standing there for? You're a deputy marshal, aren't you? That guy stole my bag."

A male voice bellowed, raised so as to be heard all over the yards. "You there, this is a deputy, come out!" The small tableau was frozen as Johnny Suarez cursed softly. If he didn't come out or leave via a different way, the deputy would dig them out, and that could cause problems. Mike picked that moment to crumple to the the ground. His mouth was filled with blood and his chest was on fire. Suarez cursed again and bolted with his friends behind him. They could find the boy any time and there'd been no sign of the damn girl anyhow.

Footsteps pounded towards the bridge, a lantern shone on him, "You all right?"

Mike swallowed and held his voice steady with a massive effort. "I'm fine, sir, they just knocked me over. You get them, sir, and get back the lady's purse."

He heard a grunt of approval and agreement. The footsteps receded the way Suarez had gone and Mike found himself briefly alone. Jackie came running quietly down the alley towards him.

"Get me out of here, that deputy will be back soon. We have to be away."

"You're hurt."

"I'll be a damn sight more hurt if Suarez gets me again. It's late, there's not enough people on the street to hide us and he'll will be looking for me again the minute they shake that deputy. You were right. Your stepfather's in town looking for you, an' he's paying."

Jackie paused, then spoke softly. "Lean on me and try to look drunk. Can you sing a bit?"

"Nope, can't get my breath. Suarez really pasted me. Just get me home."

Jackie took his weight and began to walk. It was a long way to the old warehouse, she was afraid Mike wouldn't make it, but she remembered what Granny Jarni had told her. If she could just get Mike to the memorial, the lions would protect them. She wasn't sure she believed, but it was all she had and it was only half the distance.

Mike's strength was running out with every step. Jackie was taking more and more of his weight and time was blurred for him. When they stopped and he was eased to the ground, he was confused. Surely home was further away still? But it hurt less when he wasn't moving. The fire in his chest was bad but the stabbing agony was gone. His mouth was filled with blood and he spat, seeing the blood black in the radiance of the gaslight.

More blood filled his mouth. Weakness was slipping through his body. That Suarez must have done more damage than Mike had thought, but it was okay, Jackie was here. He'd just rest for a little while then they'd go home. The pain was leaving him. He felt cold, but it was a late winter night an' him with no coat. What could a guy expect?

Jackie dragged Mike into the shadow of the nearest lion and crouched beside him. Mike had wanted to go home but they'd been too slow. She had seen Johnny Suarez and his friends coming down the street looking around them. The area was almost deserted, and no one would go against Suarez's guys, not to rescue kids they didn't know.

She huddled closer to Mike, pulling them both into the deepest part of the shadow, whispering to the lions, as all the time her fear ran like mice over her body. Her hand stretched up imploringly to touch the cold metal.

"Let us be safe. Please, lions, protect us like Granny Jarni said you would. Mike's good at heart. He's taken care of me for months. He doesn't hurt people. Please lions, help us, give us somewhere to be safe!"

It seemed to her then that the metal beast turned, opened fierce golden eyes to look at her. A question formed in her mind. Somewhere safe? There was a place like that, a home, but she could not go there, not as she was.

At her side, Mike moaned quietly. Pulled from her waking dream, Jackie scrabbled for the matches she carried, shielding the light from the street with her body. She was untrained in any medical area, but something told her what she saw. Mike was dying. She didn't question the knowledge as it came to her. She knew it for truth, and she quailed. He was her friend, her protector, her brother, and her whole heart.

There was no time to call for help – if there was anyone

within earshot who'd even answer; she could only hold him against her while the slow tears fell on his blood-smeared face. Her hand reached up again to touch chill metal.

"Anything, anywhere, anyhow at all so long as he lives and we're safe for always." She remembered, "And Mike wants a family. If there's one going." Amusement lit the wild golden gaze that turned to her. Light glowed about them, and two humans were gone – somewhere.

In another place where humans had never walked and never would, two young elephants plodded across grasslands to rejoin the herd. Their family was waiting for them. They were strong, free, and for each, their best friend walked beside them. As they paced through the shallow river, memories of another place slid away and wounds healed. While on the memorial, in another world and time, two metal lions sat proudly, guardians, protectors, as they had always been. As they had been cast to be.

Granny Jarni had a new story after that. She says that the lions on that memorial occasionally dream of their true home, and if you're near when they dream, you can smell grass and trees, and hear the faint sound of elephants trumpeting as they wade in river shallows and toss the water in silver arcs. But if she is asked what happened to two of her young friends no one sees any more, she only shrugs. Maybe they went somewhere else, who knows? But if Granny Jarni knows, she tells nothing, and no one else can say.

YOU KNOW BEST

It wasn't that he was a bad man by his own lights. But his parents had died in an accident when he was very young, and he'd been raised by a grandfather who believed a woman's place was in the home. Raising her children, cooking and cleaning for her man. When we got married the year after World War Two ended, my parents weren't happy about it. They said he was older than I was, and more set in his ways. They didn't believe he'd make me happy. I was young. I saw his certainty about life as strength. So, I married him – and found out soon enough that they'd been right.

I grew up as an only child on a large prosperous dairy farm. I was helping my father with the cows by the time I was five. I like animals and I understand them. That was part of the trouble. To my husband, John, a beast was something which obeyed, or it was useless. So was a wife I discovered eventually. Oh, not that he ever struck me. He would have regarded that as failure. His grandfather had taught him no decent man raises a hand to a woman. He doesn't need to. Instead, I was trained with a quiet, deadly, etching of criticism. I leaned to nod.

"You know best, darling." I would say. And John would smile smugly, quite certain I was right. He said I was ignorant. A country girl who didn't understand the city. I would have liked to. I'd have enjoyed exploring it, finding out of the way places, interesting buildings – and new friends. John disapproved of women who went off on their own though, so I didn't. It was his place to work, mine to stay home. Mine to prepare beautiful meals from basic ingredients and keep the house spotless. Mine to have his son. He said I failed in that last but he made allowances. It wasn't my fault if I was barren.

That was the way he put it. Barren. I suggested once that we see a doctor and he was incredulous. It wasn't him of course. It was me, and he had no intention of subjecting himself to medical busy-bodying. I was the failure in his eyes.

He was polite about it, not mentioning it more than once a day. But his eyes would go to a proud father taking his small son out in the park. Then he'd look at me and his look would be meaningful.

I didn't do so badly with the cooking and cleaning. I wasn't a bad cook and I did keep the house shining. But I was bored. I'd have liked a pet but John loathed cats, which don't take orders well. As for dogs, he'd had a dog when he was a boy. He'd punished it once too often and it had turned on him. It was from that I knew he'd have liked to hit me as well sometimes. But his early training held. You could beat an animal all you wished, that was lawful, but not a wife. There were other ways to discipline them. I'd have gone out on my own save that John disapproved as I said. To be sure I obeyed, he had a retired friend who lived nearby check on me. Through Davis, he also left me instructions. Orders mostly, disguised as requests. In any case I was busy. When that sour old man who'd raised him had died, he'd left John the family home. It was a big five-bedroomed house on half an acre of grounds on the edge of an old-established suburb. I hated the place. It was chill, damp, and gloomy with its surrounding trees. John was horrified when I suggested we could sell it and find somewhere more pleasant.

"My dear Elizabeth, one does not sell a home like this. One passes it on." His look was openly critical of my failure to produce a son to whom he could do just that. "In any case, to live here makes one known for what one is."

It certainly did that. The suburb was known to others as 'diehards ditch.' It was where all the old sticklers for a way of life fast disappearing, clung to the glorious past. Most of the houses here were like ours. Except that most of those who lived in them had a man who came in every week to do the grounds. Many also had a woman who came in every day to do the house. But they had children as John always reminded me when I mentioned it. Children who must be cared for and took up their mother's time. I didn't. So, I was free to spend my life mowing the extensive lawns, tending the garden and coming back inside again to cook and clean. I grew to hate the house and every blade of grass around it. There were too many times when all I wanted to do was march out, toss something poisonous all over the lawn and flower-beds, then set a fire and stand there as the land shrivelled and the house burned. But John wouldn't have approved.

It wasn't as if we didn't have money. John was partner in a firm which looked after properties for absentee landlords. He was meticulous, which meant the firm was highly regarded. No landlord placing his property in the hands of Taggert and Masterton has ever regretted it. At least, the landlords hadn't. Tenants were less happy but as John always said, "They signed a lease. They read it. I always insist on that. I have an additional form they sign which agrees they did read and understand the lease. But people are so casual." He sighed. "They seem to think conditions don't apply to them."

"Mrs. Armstrong can't help needing to care for her mother."

"Naturally, my dear Elizabeth. However, she should put the woman in a home. I'm responsible to the building's owners. I am not employed to overlook infractions, and worse still, damage!" He drew himself up. "The old lady is senile. Mrs. Armstrong can make no assurances her mother will not draw on the walls again. The lease clearly states also that there may be only two people in the apartment on a permanent basis."

"Mrs Armstrong's mother won't live forever," I offered.

John remained polite. "No, my dear, of course not. However, the lease states that twelve weeks is the term. After which the additional tenant must leave." There was a smugness in his tones. "I envisioned tenants who would take a mile if offered an inch. Therefore, when we wrote the lease I listed a time limit. Twelve weeks is sufficient. It allows for an older child home from boarding school or university. relatives visiting, or perhaps needing to care for a family member recovering from an illness. It is a fair time, even generous. I will not have advantage taken beyond it."

"You know best." I saw that poor Mrs. Armstrong was either moving out or placing her mother in a home and that was that.

Life dragged on. I cooked, cleaned, listened to John's criticism of tenants and his triumphs in persuading yet another wealthy landlord to sign with Taggert and Masterton. Our sex life was just what one could expect. Once a week for several minutes – and he thanked me politely afterwards.

We went to see my parents two or three times a year for the day. I wouldn't have subjected my mother to him any longer. Her cooking lived up to John's standards but her cleaning didn't. After all, it was a dairy farm, mud in winter is a quality impossible to lose. As is dust in summer. Nor did mother see any reason why she should wipe the floors six times a day just to please my husband. The first time he made one of his delicate comments suggesting she should, he was quietly told to mind his own business. Not quite that crudely – but for once he did get the message.

I daresay John did try. But the way he did was guaranteed to annoy anyone. With my father he suggested they stop running the bull with the cows as we'd always done. It was dangerous, John said, bulls were also undesirable for insurance reasons. My father patiently explained that with artificial insemination, fertility rates were lower. John was incredulous. He argued briefly then ceased with the air of a man who is tolerantly accepting of an older man's foolish ignorance. It annoyed everyone. What my father said was true, we had the farm statistics to prove it, and anyhow, any long-time competent dairy farmer knows that.

I stayed silent though. John wouldn't have listened if I had said anything and I didn't want to start his quiet asides to me again. There'd been a row over that two years ago and we hadn't visited for one miserable year. I'd been deep in discussion with my father about a new cow he'd bought from a recent clearance sale. I'd laughed.

"Well, if she doesn't like standing at that end of the shed when she's being milked, you'll just have to let her be at the other end."

My father had nodded. "I know, still, it's a nuisance."

John overheard and snorted. "What you need is a firm hand. The animal must be taught she does as you require."

My father spoke quietly. "It doesn't work like that with cows. If I try that, her milk yield will drop badly."

My husband was openly incredulous. "She's a cow. How can she do that?" His smile was condescending. "You farmers."

Mt father stood. "Yes, us farmers. I've been a farmer all my life as my father was before me. I know animals. If I need advice, I can get it from men who know stock, not from a pompous little city slicker who can't even breed a calf of his own."

My husband went white. "To use your own metaphor, sir. Even a top bull couldn't get a calf on a barren cow. Now if you'll excuse me, we must be going. It's a long drive home." He ignored my father's words, flung after us.

"Aye, had this top bull tested, have you? Know it's the cow who's barren for a fact, do you?"

The next time we would have gone to the farm John had an excuse. Then the next. The third time a year later I made it very clear I was going and that was that. Alone if necessary. It was the only time since our first year of married life I'd been stubborn over something and John unwillingly caved in. But it was never the same after that. Everyone was polite, saying almost nothing but commonplaces and my parents took pains to see none of the neighbours visited that day.

I knew they did. I'd heard mother putting off a friend from a couple of farms away who'd rung to say she might visit. I knew why. Afterwards mother came into the hall and saw me standing there. I said nothing, nor did she, instead she asked me something it was clear had been preying on her mind.

"Why don't you have children, Beth? I know John says it's your fault but have you ever had that checked?"

"John won't agree."

"Beth, you had a perfectly good brain before you married. Have yourself checked without him. You know how that goes. If you're fertile then it has to be John's problem." She put her hands on my shoulders, looking into my face.

"I've had a good life with your father. We're a team. I don't say a woman has to have children but she should have a life. You don't even have that."

I looked into her eyes and knew she was right. I could leave my husband I supposed, but what then. I didn't know what to do. In the end.

I did nothing. Perhaps life with John had drained most of the initiative from me.

It was five years after that, I'd been married almost ten years when my mother became ill. It was a shock to us all. My parents weren't old but mother had worked hard all her life and now the doctor insisted she needed a long break. My family didn't live like many rich people but I knew there was money. However, John was stunned when he heard what my parents proposed.

"He's what?"

"Taking mother on a world cruise. They'll be gone for six months. They want me to live on the farm and run it while they're away."

"Nonsense, Elizabeth. Your place is here in our home."

I fought him again on that. I think I felt it was my one chance to be halfway free again for a while. Finally, I hinted at the wealth tucked away in the farm. I was an only child, I would inherit everything, but not if my parents were so antagonised by his refusal, they changed their wills. A will could leave me an income but tie up the capital. I mentioned an amount for that possible capital which made John's eyes flicker. He'd always wanted to own his own properties, ones that he could rent. With an amount like that he could buy several and happily hold every unfortunate tenant to his leases.

In the end he agreed we'd go to the farm. I'm sure he wouldn't have done so if he'd had any idea of the disruption to his life it would involve. My parents sailed and we were there to farewell them. Mother hugged me at the last, whispering. "John's ignorant on a farm, dear. Don't let him do anything stupid." Her look met mine strangely but I ignored it. She still wasn't well.

After that we settled into the farm routine. John spending his time at our home in the city, then driving down to the farm for weekends. From the beginning it was difficult. He had no understanding of the work farming entails. I couldn't simply drop it all on the weekend while he was there. Come hell, high water or husband, the cows must be cared for every day and this was the season they calved. I was out in all weathers coming in tired and filthy even in the weekends. John was disgusted.

"Cows calved before there were farmers. Let the animals alone, I'm sure they'll manage."

Sometimes they wouldn't but it was a waste of time trying to explain. It made me scratchy though. Working a fourteen-hour day, coming back to cook for myself and then having John appear to complain in the weekends that the house wasn't spotless and he didn't *like* stew. He expected me to do all his washing and ironing as well during those two days. Why use a laundry when he had a wife.

It went on for weeks until I was utterly exhausted. I went to my old doctor for a tonic. He grinned, asked a few questions and suddenly I found I was asking him to give me a checkup and tests. He agreed. The results came back a week later. There was no reason why I should not conceive, I was fine. That weekend John arrived and begun on me at once.

The house needed scrubbing. Here was a stack of his clothes to do. He hoped he was going to get a decent dinner. He'd been working so hard all week he needed a good meal. I wondered what he imagined I'd been doing – sitting around? I'd been doing anything but. Betsy had calved only an hour before John drove in. She was a difficult cow but her calves were magnificent and her line were prize-winners from way back. My father and I could handle her and fortunately her calves never seemed to follow her in temperament. We could sell any of them for a lot of money, we had an order to buy right now for one of her bull-calves – for a sum which would make John's eyes pop.

I'd left a roast in the oven while I was with Betsy, but I hadn't had time to do roast potatoes and gravy as well. The potatoes were boiled, quickly browned and the gravy was from a packet. John mentioned these points all through dinner. I stood up once we'd eaten.

"Where are you going?"

"One of the cows just calved. It's going to be cold and windy tonight. I want them under cover in the barn."

"For heaven's sake, she's an animal. They're used to being outside. You should be cleaning up in here." He drew a finger along the bookshelf nearby, studying it. My breath caught in sudden rage so great for a moment I could barely see. I remembered my mother's parting words, the results of my tests – and a dog put down almost forty years ago.

"You know best, darling." I told him, waiting for the approving look. "But I should still get Betsy and the calf into the barn. The calf is already sold." I told him the price and watched his amazement. "Why don't you help?"

"My dear Elizabeth!" His protest was automatic.

I made my voice sound surprised. "Why not? You've always said all one needs with animals is a firm hand. My father wouldn't have any trouble." I saw him remembering that quarrel and what had been said then. He nodded, speaking graciously.

"If you really need help, my dear, I suppose this once I can provide it." I shod him in slightly too-large rubber boots, added a heavy coat and gave him a long whippy stick from the porch corner.

"I'll go and open the barn door. The gate's open, just chase the calf along and the cow will follow."

The calf was about three hours old. My father or I would have carried the small creature but John wouldn't think of it. In the gathering dusk I could see his light-colored overcoat approach the calf where it lay curled on the ground. It refused to rise and he hit it. The calf bawled. Betsy stood up, incredulous. John hit her calf again, it blatted in pain as he pushed it hard towards the barn. It staggered on unsteady legs and this time the bewildered frightened sound it made as he struck it again produced results.

Behind my husband, Betsy moved angrily forward. John turned as her horn brushed the edge of his coat. Even then he saw no danger. Just a stupid defiant animal. He hit her across the face with his stick then turned to slash the calf hard again. It bawled in pain and fear. Betsy struck coming in, horn hooking wickedly. I saw John stagger, hit out at her desperately, then go down under enraged horns and hooves. She hooked and kicked, trampling until movement beneath them ceased, then she went to her calf.

I walked away to the farmhouse and the phone. No one asked questions. I simply said I'd planned to put the beasts under cover later on. John had known how tired I was, running the farm on my own. He must have wanted to help and gone out without telling me. No, he knew nothing at all about cows.

He wouldn't have known not to get between a cow and newborn calf. Yes, Betsy had always been dangerous that way. Not to us but then she knew us and we would never have hit her or her calf like that. The marks of John's stick on the calf had been easy to see in the police flashlights.

They called it misadventure. I refused to notify my parents. Mother needed the break and there was nothing they could do. I buried my husband in his family plot, sold the hated house in the city, cashed in his partnership and insurance then banked a sum of money which would see me comfortably off for the rest of my life. I refused to have anything done to Betsy either. Local farmers agreed. If some damn fool city fellow was dumb enough to do as John had done then he deserved the results, was their verdict.

My parents came home at last. With three of us the work was easier.

Mother could rest often. I'd eventually inherit the farm, I knew, which made me think. Next door's younger son returned home soon after my parents arrived back. His marriage to a city girl didn't work out. We're about the same age and I've known him all my life. He's good stock with a daughter already. If we used my money, we'd have a bigger and better farm and a real showplace once I inherited. He's my kind, I'm his and I've seen him thinking that. That I'll also inherit our farm doesn't hurt either. I'll wait and see how it goes. I can always give him a bit of encouragement if it's needed.

My father has no idea of what really happened to John. Like the other farmers around he saw it as the sort of accident an ignorant city man could have. I think my mother guesses but then maybe she has reasons for that. Her own mother died young so my mother was left to care for her unloving and slave-driving father, helping him all hours on the farm. Her father never wanted to lose her work. She wasn't of age so he refused her permission to marry. He stopped the wedding for a year and would have stopped it another year yet though none but the three of them knew why she and my father did not marry.

Until a tractor accident killed her father. The inquest decided he'd been driving, backed the tractor up to the trailer with his leg between them ready to kick down the coupling. It was a common system in those days. Instead, his leg was trapped between them when he misjudged. That too was not uncommon. He'd bled to death before he was found.

Mother married quietly a month later. She sold up the small mixed-stock farm and put the money into father's dairy farm. Then they lived happily ever after. Nowadays I wonder, did she see what had happened and walk silently away to wait before finding him? I don't ask, any more than mother would ask about John.

There are a lot of dangers on any farm. Accidents too. I may need to mention that to my own daughter one day. Until then I'll ask no questions – and tell no lies. I imagine mother feels the same way. Some questions it's better not to know an answer. That's one of them.

THE FACILITATOR

Wizard Bingelgretson focused his spell through his facilitator and spoke the release word clearly. There was a tingling in the air as a cloud of smoke flattened out and developed a shining surface. A silver surround crawled around that and met itself. The wizard lifted the new speaking-mirror down and nodded casually at his facilitator.

"A good focus. Now, let's do it again. I'll send the second mirror to Wizard Herinton and we'll be able to communicate at will."

The rather thin cat made a plaintive sound. "Wizard, focusing your magic is tiring. We should do this in the morning."

The wizard scowled. "Are you or are you not my facilitator? Your job is to take my magic and refine it in a narrowed focus to do as I require, that's your job description. Now get on with it."

Wearily Jerris the cat focused again. The second mirror popped into being and was laid down on the workbench while Bingelgretson crooned over his workmanship.

"Yes, yes, a superb job if I do say so myself. Yes, my craftsmanship cannot be bettered. Herinton will envy this when he receives it."

"If you've finished admiring our work, may I eat and then go to bed now?"

Bingelgretson nodded absentmindedly. "Yes, I suppose so. There's food in the kitchen, and I won't need you again tonight. But be ready first thing in the morning, I plan to produce more mirrors and on Nonesday we're going to the Anver conference."

The exhausted cat bit back a tart comment and headed for the kitchen. He was seldom given sufficient food to meet his wizard's demands, and he was starving. It was every bit as tiring being a facilitator as it was being a wizard, but his person never seemed to think of that. Jerris knew he was valued, but it wasn't for himself, just for his ability, and there were times when it was as if he were a machine, something that wouldn't tire, or protest or require feeding – and certainly not appreciation.

Nonesday saw cat and wizard on the way to the Anver conference. For Jerris it was a complete bore. Some forty wizards crowded into a large room with food and drink-laden tables along both sides. Their facilitator-cats mostly sat under the tables to avoid the trampling feet, ate hugely, and listened to their partners' chatter.

"Yes, mine is so effective, why, over the past three days I've created six speaking-mirrors, as well as two nightcaps for the duke, and a reduction vest for his Lady. Jerris focuses my magic so well that none is wasted, not even the slightest overflow."

"Yes? Not bad, but mine managed five builder spells incorporated in their cornerstones, four strong-bridge spells on their keystones, and a ford-protection spell keyed to posts on either side."

Bingelgretson's cat winced. Wonderful, that was quite a lot more focus than *his* wizard had listed and he wouldn't be pleased to be outdone.

He was right. They returned home and Jerris was addressed early next morning. "Herinton is an arrogant, supercilious, braggart. Him and his cursed facilitator. Today I plan to outdo him."

Jerris made an attempt at reason. "Sir, he was lying..."

"Lying? Can you prove that? I could bring him up before the wizard's council if..."

"Well, not exactly lying, just misleading you."

"In what way?"

"You said that we had done our work over three days – as we did. He, however, claimed his feats and they *were* done, but not over the three days he implied. It took him a full seven-day and his cat was unable to work for another two days while he rested."

"Maybe, but everyone heard what he said. They'll all think that he can do better, faster work than I can. Now, be ready, first we'll create six builder spells incorporated in their cornerstones, six strong-bridge spells on their keystones, a strengthen-curtain-wall spell for Duke Monmanth's castle."

Bingelgretson rubbed his hands together. "And we'll do them in the next two days. I'll show that braggart he isn't half the wizard he thinks he is, prepare!" The cat hesitated. "What's wrong now?"

"I'm not sure I can facilitate so much in so short a time."

The wizard snorted. "That's your problem, I can always get another facilitator. Begin..." He linked his hands, pulled them apart slowly and magic grew in the gap.

That night Jerris slept the sleep of the completely exhausted. He'd spoken no more than the truth. He doubted that *any* of his kind could do that much work in two days, but Bingelgretson was determined and a facilitator in his first life must obey his wizard. He did as he was told, but by mid-afternoon his focus was slipping. He steadied himself, reached deep into his reserves of strength and hung on for the final spelled keystone. Then he sagged to the floor.

Bingelgretson nudged him with a foot. "We still have that strengthen-curtain-wall spell to do. Get up and focus." The second nudge was closer to a kick. "Apply yourself."

Magic grew between Bingelgretson's hands and the weary cat did his best, but he had nothing left. Bingelgretson shouted the invocation and the rising power back-lashed through the cat, who went limply to the floor as his abilities and consciousness faded.

He woke to find himself lying on a transfer stone. Bingelgretson eyed him sourly. "You burned out. I'm sending you where you won't gossip about me."

Before Jerris could move or speak, he was abruptly sprawled on wet ground, it was cold, dark, and his head hurt. He tried to stand, fell back, and slept. Morning gave promise of a fine day and his senses reached out as soon as he woke. Nothing. He had no idea where he was, but he couldn't stay here. He staggered to his four paws and walked forward. The region in which he'd found himself seemed to be a mixture of farmland with large areas of brush. He found water, but any attempt to approach a farm was met with barking dogs or cats in attack-mode. He plodded on, until weak with hunger he collapsed by a small spring and cursed the man who'd been his wizard.

Bad enough Bingelgretson had been violently competitive, but to be so careless of his facilitator that Jerris had been burned out and discarded against all the laws of wizardry, no wonder Jerris had been dumped elsewhere along the world-chain. Had his wizard *intended* him to die? Something in Jerris said that he had. He mourned his work, his world, and the man who should have cherished him. If he survived and found a place here for himself, he'd never again trust a human, or help one in any way.

"Oh, you poor thing, what happened to you, little cat?" Gentle hands scooped him up. "Did someone abandon you? Come home with me and I'll take care of you."

Jerris was carried to where a cottage stood. A neat vegetable garden was lined up along one side, while along the other and down the back were fruit trees and berry bushes, with a scattering of scented shrubs and patches of flowers. An herb garden lay along the front of the cottage and the scents of everything perfumed the air pleasantly. Jerris relaxed slightly, all the indications were that this human would not ill-treat him, not that he expected it. A facilitator was ... then into his mind flooded the remembrance that he was no longer a facilitator. He was an ordinary cat and could be killed at a whim.

Involuntarily he mewed, grieving the loss of what he was. The hands cradled him more closely. "Nearly home. Don't worry. There's water and food for you, and a blanket to keep you warm." The voice took on an edge. "How *could* anyone dump you out here to die? But it's okay, you can stay with me if you want to, or I'll find you a home somewhere." A hand moved away, and he heard the creak of a door opening. "Here we are, boy, home."

Jerris was placed on a soft blanket. The human bustled about and, in a few minutes, bowls containing food and clean water were placed by his head. Jerris ate, drank, and lay back, drifting off to sleep. For two weeks that was his life as he gathered strength again. People came and went. He heard them talking and gradually understood that the human was an herbalist. She had no magic but knowledge, and she also traded the fruit, berries, and vegetables that she grew.

She owned her cottage, furnished it comfortably, and was never short of food, or respectable clothing. In the world from which Jerris had been exiled she would have been middle-class, a professional herbalist with her own magic. This one had nothing he could facilitate – even if his ability hadn't been burned out. Once she realized that he'd be tossed out again. He wailed at the thought.

"Poor cat, what made you meow?" He was scooped up and cuddled. "It's all right. Nothing will hurt you here. I'll protect you." She sat him up on her lap and looked into his eyes. "But if you're staying, you'll need a name. Something of your own."

Jerris projected. If the woman had any talent at all she'd pick up the sending. Lianne felt the intensity of his stare but understood none of it.

"Hmmm," she laughed. "I know, I'll call you Bloss. That's half for Blossom, and half because cats tend to be the boss of wherever they are. Bloss? Bloss – yes, that's your name, you're my Blossom and Boss."

Jerris settled again under the stroking hands. It could have been worse, at least the human understood that cats were both beautiful and commanding. It wasn't his real name but it would do while he honored her by living in her cottage. Memory struck again. He did her no honor by being here, not a burned-out facilitator in the home of an untalented human. They were well matched – until his ability returned (if it ever did) and he could find another wizard. Meanwhile he'd remain in the cottage and maybe catch a mouse or two.

Several times in the next few months Jerris almost set out to leave, before changing his mind again. Let him learn of those who lived nearby, and what this world was like. He caught the occasional mouse, and learned. They called this area 'New Mexico' – he wondered where Old Mexico lay – and it was a wild mostly untamed land. Among other things, he discovered that this world had house imps. Lianne's cottage had one and he was surprised when he met the creature late one night in the kitchen.

"An imp? In this world? I thought there was no magic here?"

"Then you thought wrong, didn't you? Many people here believe in us and leave out a saucer of milk. Those in the township, and around came from a place named Cornwall, and some remember. We foster their belief cautiously, we bring minor luck to those who live within, but they don't see us."

"There's no magic here though?"

"Isn't there?"

Jerris gaped. "Do you say that there is?"

"I say that you make too many assumptions." The imp made a small jump and disappeared while Jerris growled after him. What was that about?

He redoubled his wanderings after the human was safely in bed. There was no scent of magic clinging to those who called on the herb woman. He studied them, increasingly irked by their attitude. Some were rude, as if they expected more than they received, Jerris thought. Why would the human accept such treatment?

The house imp snorted when he was asked. "Lianne is gentle. She can be firm about treatment, but have you ever heard her raise her voice?" Jerris hadn't. "Well, then, nor have I and this has been my house since her parents' time. They were in one of the first wagon-trains to come here near forty years ago," He changed the subject. "And what about you, are you going to stay here?"

"I'm a trained facilitator. Yes, I burned out, but often the ability returns. Once that happens, I'll find a strong wizard, someone who'll value what I bring to his art."

"And leave Lianne?"

Jerris stared. "What use would a facilitator be to her?"

"She loves you."

Jerris preened his whiskers abruptly. "Nonsense. Once I'm gone, she'll get an ordinary cat. Humans value one's abilities. What can I do here apart from bringing her a mouse now and again? Any cat could do that. No, when my talent returns, I shall find someone with power and if you think she'll mourn me, you're wrong."

The house imp eyed him, opened his mouth, shut it again and gave one of the jumps that saw him vanish in mid-air. Jerris looked after him. Funny creature, fancy thinking that the human cared for a cat, now *value*, that was a different matter. When he went, Lianne would be free to get a commonplace cat. She might even get herself a dog. This cottage was isolated, anyone could come here – he'd heard visitors talk of the Indians who could raid ... he found that the fur on his back was standing up and he stretched. What did he care about a human's isolation?

He explored, watched Lianne's visitors, and talked to the imp. Many nights before she took her candle upstairs to the tiny bedroom Lianne would write out her herbal recipes with Jerris asleep in her lap. He accepted her invitations when they were made, she was soft, warm, comfortable and her hands stroked pleasantly. Why not make use of her? After he'd been there a year, he discovered something he had not known, that the imps had minor magic. He asked about it.

"It's little enough, but it serves us in our cleaning to pay for the milk we're left."

"Could you do more?"

The imp shrugged. "We do well with what we have. Why? Are you thinking that we could give you back your ability?"

"No." It had been idle questioning, but now that the subject was raised... "Could you?"

"A working like that would take many of us. Succeed, and we'd strip ourselves of magic for a moon. We'd be more likely to fail and lose what we have to no purpose."

Jerris nodded. Or, to be blunt, the imps weren't going to take the risk for a cat that could offer them nothing, had no abilities of his own that would be of use to them, and could move on at any time.

A thought occurred and he asked another question. "The raiders, could it be that the luck you bring her keeps them from this house?"

The imp grinned and said nothing, but Jerris felt himself answered. So, it did not take great power to turn eyes from a small area, but it took more than one. Interesting.

Morning four months later brought a human male hammering on the cottage door. Medium black hair, medium black eyes, and a deep black temper.

"Open this door, woman, you cheated me."

Lianne opened the door. "Mr. Grant, in what way did I do this?"

He strode past her, shouting and snapping like a bad-tempered dog, listing her crimes as he saw them. "You gave me a salve, you gave me a potion, you said it should incline the bank manager to loan me what I required. You cheated me and I'll have my coin back."

In silence Lianne walked from the room, to return with a number of coins, which she held out. "Your payment is returned, sir. Now please go. It seems my craft can do nothing for you since you did little of what I suggested and listened to less of what I told you."

"Whore! I'll..."

"Bow politely and leave," a harsh voice said from behind Lianne's former customer. Jerris who'd been listening recognized Master Harvis, Lianne's friend from two ranches away. The customer scowled, but Harvis's shoulders were broad and his arms brawny. The customer summed him up – and left.

Harvis watched him out of sight. "What was that about?"

Lianne sighed. "He wants to buy the land old man Carron left. Carron's son has his own ranch and no wish to leave. If Mr. Grant adds that land to his place he'll have a better ranch but to add Carron's land he needs a loan. I gave him salve, a potion and advice." Harvis raised his brows in question.

"I gave him a potion to swill around in his mouth each night and morning after eating, since his breath stinks vilely, the more so in any small room."

She sighed. "Apparently he merely drank it and made himself sick all that night. I gave him a salve and instructed him to bathe every second day and apply it to his armpits and groin after he'd done so since he never bathes and his body also stinks. He used it without bathing. Naturally the bank manager was unaffected, he refused a loan. Mr. Grant came to demand his money back and I repaid him."

"And he made threats," Harvis said thoughtfully.

Lianne smiled. "An angry man says more than he means. Don't worry about me, Harvis. But if you think you should do something, loan me one of your dogs to lie by my door a few nights. If Mr, Grant returns, a dog will make him think twice."

Jerris hissed to himself. A large dog, *not* something that he wanted around the cottage. He had it anyhow but found that the dog was used to cats, a polite pleasant beast that harassed neither cat nor house imp, and fawned affectionately on Lianne. Jerris noticed its prowling outside after dark and approved for Lianne's sake – until the third night when there was a strange silence. He padded to the small window and looked out. In the moonlight he saw the dog lying still, a half-eaten piece of meat beside it.

Few cats are fools. He meowed softly for the house imp and it came. Jerris spoke quickly and the imp listened.

"There's little I can do. I cannot make Lianne fight. I cannot keep the human out if he wills to be in. I cannot fight him. My magic isn't strong enough."

Jerris nodded. "But you can do something if you will." The imp waited. Jerris spoke quickly and it nodded. "That I can and will do. And I know another possibility that may aid. Stand motionless while I work. After that, it is up to you, cat."

Jerris stood, feeling magic begin to settle over him. The imp jumped and vanished while Jerris waited by the door. It splintered open and Grant crept in, picking up the motionless cat as he went past. Lianne woke to find herself held down with an arm across her throat, a voice murmuring in her ear. She began to struggle and Grant laughed.

"I have your cat, fight me and I'll gut him and you can watch him die."

Lianne sobbed once. "No, let Bloss go and I'll do whatever you wish." Jerris could smell her fear and disgust. Her voice, however, remained clear. "Anything, just don't hurt Bloss."

Jerris felt something he had never known before grow within him. She stank of fear and horror, of disgust and hatred, but for *his* life she would allow herself to be used against her every inclination. Grant made a movement in the half-dark and he smelled her sudden pain as the man spoke.

"That's a taste in case you get too comfortable. You won't be using that wrist for a while. Now, take off your..."

The magic settled into its shaped configuration and Jerris sprang. The imp's gift had lengthened, strengthened and sharpened the cat's claws and teeth, and he hoped that would be enough. His claws sank into the man's back, his teeth deep into the thick neck. Grant screamed and bucked himself free of woman and cat. Lianne fell back gasping. In the tiny bedroom Bloss was fighting for their lives, screaming the long eerie battle-cry of a cat, to which species surrender is unknown. Lianne managed to light her candle and saw that while Bloss was inflicting considerable damage her ex-client was still the likely victor.

The man screamed again as claws raked, and snatched too quickly for Jerris to dodge. The man laughed, gripping the struggling cat by the scruff. "You and your pet, I'll teach you both." He flung the cat against the wall and Jerris slid down the wood planking, basically unhurt but stunned by the impact. Lying on the floor, he smelled what the man could not know. Lianne's abrupt fury, not for herself, but for Bloss. Her scream echoed the fighting screams the cat had uttered, and in her hand, the heavy brass candlestick curved forward with so much force that she grunted with the effort.

The candlestick base caught Grant across the nape of his neck. He dropped and did not move. Lianne fell to her knees. "Oh, Bloss, my brave one." She caught Jerris up, tears falling onto his fur. "Don't die. I don't want to lose you, please, Bloss?"

Downstairs, encouraged by a house imp, a barking dog led a man down the path. Footsteps thundered through the door. "Lianne? Are you there? What's happened?"

Jerris managed a faint purr. Harvis to the rescue – a little late, but he'd be useful.

He was. He checked Grant, found him dead, and called the sheriff. Later, he sent his younger brother to mend the door, and his younger sister to clean the blood from the bedroom walls and floor. In court he testified to Grant's overheard threats, and had a knowledgeable man swear that the dog left as Lianne's protection had been deliberately poisoned, while the nurse from a nearby township spoke of Lianne's bruises and broken wrist. The court agreed unanimously that their herbalist had acted in self-defense and Lianne went home to her cottage.

A week later, the house imp spoke to Jerris. "When do you think that you'll be leaving, I know your ability has returned."

"Yes, it may have been the magic you shared that started the return."

"Therefore, I ask again. When do you leave?"

"I am uncertain."

The house imp exaggerated his surprise. "You always said you could only be valued by a wizard. You said Lianne was a human of no magic and that she'd find an ordinary cat of as much use to her. You said she wouldn't miss you."

Jerris growled. "I know what I said."

"Then when do you leave?"

"Very well, imp, if you will have it aloud. I'm staying. Lianne loves me. She would have let that human do as he willed to save me. I smelled her pain, her disgust at his touch, but she would have suffered whatever he would do to her to keep me safe. And when the human hurt me, she killed him to save me. How can I leave? I owe her."

Unseen, the house imp smiled. "I see. It's for a debt, and is that all, cat?"

"No, she loves me, I won't grieve her by going away." His voice roughened. "And – I love her too, and I will stay with her so long as we live." His teeth showed in a cat grin. "A facilitator is not an ordinary cat. We live long. I could be here for very many years. Think about *that*, imp."

He trotted up the stairs to curl up by his human. She liked to have him there and it pleased him too. Which was the aim of any cat, to please himself. If it pleased him to stay, he would. If it pleased him to tolerate that nosy house imp, he would. And if it pleased him to love the human – that was his right too. *And no one had better argue!*

GREAT AUNT EDNA

Everyone said that my widowed Great-aunt Edna was such a *nice* woman. She lived in a nice house in a nice street in our small western town, went to church, and held nice afternoon teas twice a year from which the funds raised were donated to church charities. She also walked every morning and she really was extremely fit for her age. Edna had been the younger daughter while my mother was the older child of Edna's sister's son. So, while in the eighteen-nineties Edna was in her eighties, I was sixty years younger and Edna was my great-aunt, it didn't matter, I liked her and she liked me – she kept inviting me over for a cup of tea, scones, and a chat anyway.

I dropped in on her after Christmas that year of our Lord eighteen-ninety-seven and found her genteelly sipping a cup of tea and sighing.

"Problems?"

"Nothing you can help with, dear. It's the Fergusons next door. With Mary's health become so bad, they've decided to move back east to be with family. I'll miss them and heaven knows who I'll get as a neighbor now."

I could understand why she'd miss them. The Fergusons had lived there most of Edna's married life. He was a skilled cobbler and up until then, the township hadn't had one. Now there were three. The Fergusons were only a couple of years older but while my aunt's health had remained excellent, theirs had deteriorated over the past five years. The man who'd owned the house before them had been odd, but he'd died, and the Fergusons had moved in. They'd have received a good price for the house when it was sold, and they were thrifty. There would be sufficient for them to live comfortably once they returned east.

"Why are you worried about new neighbors?" I asked. "This is an expensive end of town. No one's likely to move in that you won't like."

Edna sipped more tea. "Josie told me that the man who purchased their home turns out to have bought it to rent out."

I snorted inelegantly. "So what?"

My great-aunt eyed me severely. "So this, dear; you know what some tenants can be like."

I did.

"If he does rent that place out, he'll charge a fortune, and surely tenants wouldn't be too bad if they're paying that sort of price," I suggested.

My great-aunt offered a cup of tea. I took it, drank and thought that she was being overly pessimistic. She'd probably find that the tenants – if tenants there were – would be a nice middle-aged couple from back east. I said that while I ate the biscuits offered and my great-aunt said nothing, merely looking at me in a way that suggested I was slightly naive. I smiled back, I wasn't naive and I was sure that everything would be fine.

* * *

It turned out that I *was* naive. I'd assumed that if people paid a fortune in rent, they'd have to be nice, quiet tenants; was I ever wrong. The only nice thing about the Smyths was their name. They were middle-aged all right, but the husband came from a wealthy family, whom it was rumored paid to see him settled well away from them. He drank like a fish, had a dog that barked for hours most days – something *they* never seemed to hear but the rest of the area certainly did – and the first time that my great-aunt went over and asked them to turn the windup gramophone down, I won't repeat what they called her. How did I know? I was staying the weekend and heard every word. Great-aunt Edna came home, and the next day I was swept off with her to talk to the town marshal.

"I wish to make a complaint about the Smyths. They are making an undue amount of noise and it shows every sign of continuing. I asked them to make a little less of a din but they refused in the strongest terms."

The marshal asked a question and my great-aunt looked horrified. "I could not possibly repeat what they said. You'll speak to them? Thank you." We went home and she waited for the next occasion.

I wondered how the Smyths would handle the marshal and was half disappointed when they turned the music down as they were told. The dog shut up. I went to bed and leapt awake again half an hour later when the noise went back through the roof. I didn't wait for Great-aunt Edna, I threw on a dressing gown, went to the back door, called the nearest urchin, gave him a note for the marshal and complained. He couldn't have gone far because he arrived back quickly and confiscated the noise-maker. I smiled, rolled over, and slept soundly, presuming that would be the end of it – and again found how wrong I could be.

A rock was thrown through Edna's window the following night, and although I called the marshal there was no indication of who'd done that – although I could make a good guess. The dog kept barking, I called the marshal who sent a deputy, he checked the animal and reported to me that the animal was well housed and fed, and they could do nothing. Wednesday night, several days after I'd returned to home and husband, another window was broken, my great-aunt told me.

I stayed the following weekend. The weather was shifting into the heat of summer and it was going to be a scorcher according to the grocery man's length of dry seaweed. Friday at ten p.m. the music started next door, getting louder and louder as the night wore on. There were shouts, yells, a crash as something fell over, and throughout most of it, the dog was going crazy, yapping until I was surprised that his throat didn't seize up.

The row died away about six a.m. I had some sleep once both the noise and some of the heat died down, and got up around lunchtime to go and talk to a few of the neighbors. Consensus was that they were surprised – the Smyths didn't look the type. I suggested to the neighbors that they take it in turns to complain once an hour on the hour until the marshal got tired of it and shut the Smyths down. They did that, and for their trouble they *all* began getting their windows broken, followed, when they continued to complain, with other more dangerous problems. The complaining stopped abruptly.

As my great-aunt pointed out, they only had to be patient for a while. House prices were starting to rise and the house would be on the market soon. It was, and to everyone's horror the Smyths bought it – an occurrence no one had hither-to considered.

"What will you do?" I asked.

My great-aunt pursed her lips. "I *could* move. Josie Toft and her husband put their house on the market as soon as they heard."

"Will you?"

"No, dear. Your Great-uncle William and I bought this house more than sixty years ago. I'll wait and see. In my experience things have a habit of working themselves out."

I hoped so, but I wasn't holding my breath.

The money changed hands, the seller took his profits to the goldfield to invest in a mine there – and the Smyths held the house-warming party to end all house-warming parties. It started on Friday evening on a hot summer's night and continued without a break until just past midnight on Sunday. By then almost all the party-goers had left, so I heard later, and it was down to just the Smyths and another couple who kept the music going, the booze flowing, and their arrogance showing.

The marshal or one of his deputies called three times during the period, each time they confiscated whatever was being used for the music, and each time it started blasting again – they must have had an entire room full of windup gramophone. The dog lost his voice around midnight, and with quiet reigning soon after that, everyone went gratefully to sleep – to be blasted awake again at four a.m. by the rumble of wheels, the shouts of a man, and a steam whistle.

As Great-aunt Edna explained when I dropped in later. "I imagine after drinking heavily all that time they slept very soundly once they stopped partying."

I agreed. I slept like the dead myself once any Smyth party had died down.

"And of course the dog had barked so long he developed laryngitis and couldn't make a sound."

"What *did* happen exactly?" I asked.

"No one knows, dear. Somehow the house caught on fire. It was Dave Marchant across the road that gave the alarm. He went to the necessary and saw flames showing at the windows. He sent for the brigade and rushed over but he said by the time he arrived, the fire was so bad he didn't dare go inside. The brigade was there only minutes later but by then the roof had fallen in. All Dave could do was get the dog away."

And that was it. A year later, a retired teacher (and his wife who was a nurse and Mr. Smyth's cousin, and who'd inherited everything) built a nice house on the empty section and moved in. They do *not* have loud parties, and they have a cat – a quiet beast and an excellent mouser. Great-aunt Edna had taken the dog, saying that he wasn't a bad animal, just completely untrained. Under her tutelage he's become sensible, a good watch-dog and a pleasant companion to her.

* * *

Twelve years later, Great-aunt Edna was ninety-six and dying. It was another hot summer, although the heat was beginning to lessen. I was nursing her at her home and caring for Pom Pom, the Smyth's dog, as well. Both were very old and I doubted the dog would outlast my great-aunt by much. Our talking tended to ramble all over and somehow that afternoon – perhaps via a discussion on the weather and harking back to that blazing summer twelve years earlier – the discussion shifted to the Smyths and I said that what had happened had been such an awful accident.

Great-aunt Edna smiled. "Ah, yes. When you're old, dear, people assume you're incompetent, incontinent, and incapable of anything physical." I wondered what she was talking about. Her next comment enlightened me far more than I'd expected – or wanted to hear. "Those who drink heavily sleep heavily, especially if someone has left a carton of mixed spirits on their doorstep right after the last visitors have gone."

I gaped, putting two and two together, as I'd never done before. "Wouldn't they have wondered who did that?"

"Not that kind, dear. They accepted it as a gift from some friend, or perhaps that some deliveryman had come to the wrong address. That was why people went home, you know. I heard their last guests talking as they departed. The drink had run out, so the final couple left."

"And no one ever found how the fire started..." I said, my tone studiously neutral.

"No, I knew that house, if you put a ladder up against the bathroom at the back and walk over the bathroom roof, you reach the chimney. Mary Ferguson's nephew did it several times in the last couple of years before they left, when she locked herself out," my great-aunt said in an equally bland tone. Adding, "They had a fire any time it was convenient or a cold night."

I blinked, realizing who she as talking about. "It was one of the hottest nights we *had* that summer."

"And they were partying." I must have looked as bewildered as I felt. Great Aunt Edna nodded once. "The Smyths didn't just drink, dear, they smoked – you know – as did some of their friends. The advantage of having a fire is that fires destroy anything thrown into them."

I understood. I don't take that sort of thing myself but I know the mechanics. Any sign of the law arriving and the opium could be easily tossed into the fire. I just didn't know how they could have borne having the fire adding to the heat of that night. But maybe if it was a matter of not being caught... Most of the Smyths' friends had been ostensibly respectable – as the Smyths themselves had been.

"By the time they went to bed, the fire was probably down to coals and they'd have put a fire guard in front of it." My great-aunt added.

"A fire guard?"

"Yes, the one Mary Ferguson left there. Very light and easily knocked over. If something fell down the chimney that could have started the fire going again, and if that also knocked over the guard, well – there was a lot of flammable items in that room." She looked at me and for a fifth of a second she wasn't nice old Great-aunt Edna. "As I said at the time, dear, things have a habit of working themselves out."

I said nothing, not to her and especially not to anyone else. I'd be inheriting and my husband and I planned to move in once Great-aunt Edna was gone – less than a year her doctor said – we'd only rented before, Tim didn't earn a lot; although as a senior clerk, it was completely respectable. There would be sufficient money besides the property, that I – we – could live very comfortably even if Tim lost his job or left it.

I watched as she took her medication, settled for sleep, and I went to my own room to read. After a while, I put my book down and stared at the wall as something occurred to me. Before the Fergusons bought that house, there'd been another man who owned it. They'd found unpleasant sketches of several upright lady citizens he'd made after he drank something poisonous and the marshal was called in. Now I knew about the Smyths I wondered about his death too. And, I thought as I lay back – had those deaths been the only ones?

In my own case, there was John Tyler, who'd wanted to marry me. He'd made a will in anticipation of that, and, while I'd married Tim, so far as I knew John's will was unchanged, and with no relations to contest that... I'd been married fifteen years now, having been only eighteen when I wed, and of late, Tim was pressuring me more and more to have children. I didn't like children. I didn't want children. And Tim could be wasteful, always wanting to spend his wage on something of little benefit. I was my great aunt's heir, and soon I'd have options. I was smiling thoughtfully as I went to sleep.

THAT GOOD FELINE

Our township had trouble once, an alien who visited but who turned out to be a blessing instead. Frangi was a good creature. He became a friend, and because of him we had sheep which brought us wealth. We kept matters quiet on that front however. Them back east tend to get excited about the strangest things. Wasn't as if our visitor was unfriendly after all.

It was quite a while before we realized Frangi had left us something else, and that *was* a problem. It took a couple of years before we began to notice and that gave them a chance to settle in and become the nuisance we finally saw we had. Rats. Not real rats of course. These critters had sneaked off the alien ship, but they were small, a gray-brown, very fast, and they were scavengers, so we called them rats. It wasn't until months after Frangi's last visit that one was even seen.

I have a son, Harry, and twin daughters, Janet and Mary, and they're good sensible hard-working children. They understand you don't get something for nothing, and it's thanks to the girls' discovery of the Yaros, the alien sheep, and their befriending of those, that our township is prosperous. This time it was my son's turn. He came clumping in after first snowfall, and glanced around for the girls. Not seeing them, he spoke, and I know from his attitude that something was wrong.

"We got trouble, ma." I focused on him and waited. "Some sort a' vermin. I noticed there's been fewer windfall apples. Thought it was likely raccoons or 'possums. Then I left a bunch a' carrot tops sitting until I could take them to the compost, but they were gone when I went back." I said nothing. Harry would tell things in his own way, and so far, I'd heard nothing to say it wasn't raccoons or 'possums.

"I figured if it was one of them, I could maybe trap a few, the furs'd be useful. I set traps and never caught anything but stuff was still going. I got to wondering, I mean, raccoons and 'possums, they do get caught sooner or later, and none did, nor

I never ever saw 'em. So, I put out some bits, peelings from potatoes, rhubarb leaves from your last pie, an' I sat up and watched. Something came to them, ma. Kinda rat-like but not a rat. I couldn't swear to it, but it seemed to have more feet. Longer, thicker coat, and the tail … well that weren't a rat."

"Why?" I asked reasonably.

"Fluffy, an' flat" Harry said. That, I thought, made sense according to his earlier comment. Rats did *not* have flat fluffy tails.

"Long or short?"

"Medium, and ma. Last few days watching, I've seen mebbe half a dozen of these critters. They all have flat fluffy tails, and all of those are either gold or silver."

I jumped to a conclusion. "Sex!" I said triumphantly, while Harry promptly looked embarrassed. I smiled at my son. "I mean gender. Likely the gold tailed ones are all male, the silver are female – or the other way around. But I bet that's it."

"I'd guess so, but ma, what are we going to do about them? I've been listening around. They started by cleaning up mostly rubbish, things we put into the compost, but they ain't just doing that now."

"Is everything they eat organic? I mean was it all once alive or do they eat other items like metal or anything?"

Harry shrugged. "I dunno, ma. It's the organ-stuff people notice gone."

"All right." I was thinking hard. I'd had an idea … well two actually. I remembered something Frangi had told my husband Bill while Bill was still alive. Frangi dropped in on us every year or so, and he'd be back soon. I grinned. We had to be the only western township with a visiting Martian, but he was a pleasant creature and he and Bill had been good friends.

"Harry." My voice was decisive. "I want you to do this without the twins knowing. Take any garbage out to the barn. Lay it out in small clumps, just a handful at a time, about a long pace apart. Then collect up other things and put them in between each clump." I thought briefly. "A few bits of really rotten wood, a rag or two, see if you can find something that's gone bad, rancid butter or fat, or oil, and some of the poisonous fungus and plants…"

It worked. The 'rats' came, saw, ate, and wandered off with, alien creatures or not, what I can only describe as smug looks. Harry put out a single trap after that, carefully baited, and we sat up to watch again. What we saw explained a few things. The animals worked in a trio. Two of the gold-tailed ones, and a silver. They sprang the trap, ate the bait, and looked, if possible, even smugger. But what I noticed in particular was that the poisonous plants and fungi they ate seemed to have no effect on them; and wasn't *that* interesting.

I'd been listening around the township meanwhile. I'd say we didn't have much time to act. But enough, if only Frangi got here in the next two months. He did. He came to my home first. We spent a very happy evening talking, catching 'him' up on events, (I say him because his people are hermaphrodite and reproduce by fission as do the 'sheep' we obtained from him,) Clearly the rats weren't of that kind as he confirmed once the twins had gone to bed and Harry and I had Frangi to ourselves.

Sheriff Ezra arrived then and we had a quiet conference. Yes, Frangi agreed, the rats might well have managed to escape when the Yaros, the alien sheep, had done so. He regretted the rats. They must be exterminated. They bred geometrically and from the sound of it, they were at explosion point. Yes, he had a method of vermin control. Yes, it could catch the Minos. I giggled at that point, Right, not rats, mice. Yes, they could eat practically anything. We put our heads together. The talk went on half the night, and our looks once we left off talking and headed to our respective beds may have out-smugged the minos.

Frangi was back the next afternoon with the Martian answer to vermin. They were called Ashos. We took one look and called them cats. Frangi said they were cyborgs: half animal, half machine. They were friendly to intelligent beings, attractive, a useful size, almost unkillable, could reproduce if certain things were done, and they were very very very fast. Frangi programmed them according to mine and Ezra's suggestion, and in hours they began bringing back minos.

Minos didn't eat solid rock or the mortar we could make. That made them sick if they even licked it. Minos numbers built up until the Ashos could find and capture no more. By that time Harry, the sheriff, Lizzy Powry the schoolteacher, and a few others we trusted, had a supply. We had a captive breeding programme. The minos tails – large, flat, beautifully furred in gold or silver – made wonderful handbags, scarves, slippers, even jackets if the purchasers paid the exorbitant price one cost.

The minos were fed on garbage, poisonous fungi and plants pulled up by the children – producing safer pasture – and other such unwanted rubbish, and they thrived. They cost us almost nothing to feed, and made no real escape attempts so long as they were fed well. It was something of a circle too, since the minos were contentedly cannibalistic if the offered item was dead and skinned.

Our township prospered further, and everyone here understood it was to their benefit to keep their mouths firmly *shut* on certain subjects. But most houses, farms, or ranches now had a rock pen out behind the barn, while inside most now had a 'cat.'

All right, so it wasn't really, but they were a very good imitation, requiring only a saucer of oil once a month, and regular affection – which they repaid generously.

We called them cats and mice once we'd settled to the system, and, as Ezra said at the celebration a year after the start of events that brought us another source of wealth. "That Frangi, he do leave this place feline good, oil right" he grinned at the howls. "An' an increase in the micechief don't do no harm neither..." I threw the first pillow.

HAPPY BIRTHDAY TO ME

It was during my sixteenth birthday, on my way back from the ice cream parlor, that I decided my brother had to go. As usual he was tagging along, making a mess of himself eating an ice cream, getting drips all down his shirt (for which I'd be blamed as usual) and attracting unwanted attention (for which I paid, also as usual.)

"Yah, yah, dummy! Hey, stupid."

A fast-moving figure ran by snatched Jimmy's ice cream, tossed it into the dirt, screamed with laughter and skidded to a halt far enough away to enjoy the fun without being within reach.

Jimmy howled, ran to pick up the ice cream and howled again when he found that on the hot pavement it had spread more than was practicable for retrieval. He continued to howl, scrabbling at the melting remains until he got the waxed paper cone free and went to stuff that into his mouth.

I grabbed it, tossing it away. "Jimmy, no. No, you can't eat that." I'd have damn well allowed him, but it was covered in bird-shit and someone would be bound to tell our parents I'd let him do that. If he were sick from eating the horrible thing I'd get the blame too. "Jimmy, I said no."

"Wanna. I wan' it, I wan' it, I wan' it!" He sat sobbing on the pavement, pounding his hands on the ground, as his voice got louder.

Wearily I hauled him to his feet. "I'll buy you another one. But this time you keep hold of it, okay?"

He was, as I knew he'd be, placated. "Oookaay, Mikey."

He ran lumbering ahead as I followed. I spent my last dollar on a replacement ice cream and we headed for home a second time, with my brother contentedly licking his ice cream. I watched for any tormentors coming after Jimmy and that was a mistake. I should have been watching on my own account.

We rounded the corner by the park and Keith Merrison was there. I watched him closely as he approached. Jimmy stuffed the last mouthful of ice cream into his mouth, licked out the paper cone, and smirked at Keith.

"Can' get it, I had it all. Hah hah!" I saw the look on Keith's face.

I snarled at Jimmy. "Run home, go on. You run home *now.*"

Keith's friends tried to cut Jimmy off but he's powerful and surprisingly fast. I'm neither and while they missed out on Jimmy, they caught me. Keith's gang may be a year younger than I am but they were four to one and all of them bigger.

I got back half an hour after Jimmy. My shirt was ripped. I had a lovely array of bruises and I hurt all over. I slipped in thorough the back door, changed my shirt, and dumped the old one in the ragbag, then went to find Jimmy. He was in my bedroom playing with the balsa-wood model plane I'd spent most of the weekend putting together and he'd broken a wing tip.

I stood there looking at the plane, feeling my bruises, hating my brother for all the time, attention, and money that was spent on him while I got the blame for anything wrong that he did. I took his beatings from the bullies. I had to look after him on summer days when I could have been in the park with friends – who didn't want him along and I wasn't allowed out without him.

He had a special tutor during school-time (when our parents couldn't find the money for me to have new boots – mine leaked and were getting too small). He went on trips to the new zoo. (He liked the monkeys. Why not? He had a lot in common with them.) Trips to plays (but we went only to the ones he liked, never anything *I* wanted to see). And he had the toys he wanted, treats to eat, rides when the fair was in town. (I got cheap things like the plane, treats that I bought from my own allowance, and if that ran out, I got no more, while Jimmy could always yell and get what he demanded. Same with the fair. If I could pay, I had the rides, Jimmy just had to howl a time or two and he was on anything he pointed to.)

It wasn't right. Okay, so he was my big brother, what said I had to put up with the injustice forever? And staring at my broken plane, wincing as I walked over to take it away from him, I decided right then that things were going to change.

I snatched the plane away. "You broke it! I spent hours making that and you broke it. You laughed at Keith, and him and his mates beat the hell out of me. I wish one day you'd go swim in the lake." And it was then that it came to me.

"Swim in the lake? Jimmy's not allowed in the lake."

"Not if anyone's around. Not if there's anyone to see you."

"Swim if no one sees me?"

"If I can't see you, how can I stop you?" That's his kind of logic and I could see it sinking in slowly. "But I never said that." He nodded and kept nodding, a big sloppy grin on his face. I was smiling too – but on the inside.

I made dinner for our parents; dad had been at work all day and mum was off volunteering at one of her church charities as was expected of anyone of our class. They came home and made the usual fuss of Jimmy while not noticing either my new bruises or that I moved very carefully.

The next day started the plan when I took Jimmy to the park.

"Hey, Mike, how they hanging?"

I grinned. "Right where they should be, Vince. Wanna play a little ball?"

"If you keep the dummy under control." I nodded. "Then, okay."

I worked at it, finding things for Jimmy to do, keeping him from spoiling the game, sending him across the park to the ice cream cafe whenever he starting whining, and it was a pretty good day all in all. I found time alone with Jimmy to twice mention that if I couldn't see him doing something, then I couldn't stop him, and each time he laughed. We got back a bit late and dad was already watching for us.

"Where you been, son?"

"Playing ball in the park with Vince and the guys. Dad? Jimmy took my plane and broke it. I'd like to replace it?"

He got this unhappy look on his face. "We don't have the money to do that, son. I wish we did."

"I had to keep Jimmy happy today," I fished out the list of what I'd spent on ice creams. "Can I at least get this back?"

"I can manage that." He fished a couple of coins out of his wallet, passed them over, took the receipt, and saw the look on my face. "It isn't like that, son. It isn't that we don't want you as much as your brother, don't want to give you as much. It's just that..." He hesitated. "Hell, I guess you're old enough to be told now. It goes back to my granddad's brother."

I listened and took everything in, and I finally understood why my brother got so much and why dad was always so careful to get receipts. Once dad finished talking, I looked at him.

"Jimmy's my brother an'..." I managed to look embarrassed. "I love him. It's okay now I know."

Dad clapped me on the shoulder," Good lad, I knew you'd understand."

He'd have been surprised at what I understood.

I let things slide for a year. But during that year, every few times I took Jimmy out with me I mentioned casually how nice it was to swim in the lake when it was very hot. That you could jump off the end of the dock. And that if I couldn't see him doing something, then I couldn't stop him doing something. It got so that he'd repeat what I said, clap his hands and look to me for approval – I'd give it. "But you don't say that to anyone else. Understand?"

"Not tell anyone. I won't, Mikey."

He wouldn't, I knew that. He might be a moron – literally – but he could keep a secret if he thought it was to his benefit and I made sure it was. I'd say that stuff about not seeing, he'd tell me what I wanted to hear, and I'd buy him an ice cream. That went on for twelve months until the day after I'd turned fifteen and Jimmy was two months over eighteen.

He'd had a lovely big party for his birthday: a clown, balloons, a couple dozen of his pals – just for the party and the day, they had no use for him otherwise – and all the food they could eat. My birthday was ordinary food on our table and a magic show – one Jimmy had been making a fuss about wanting to see and that bored me rigid. The magician was crummy.

It was a hot summer that year of 1898. Dad had had a heck of a lot of overtime that he'd accepted because I only had another year to go at school before I'd have to leave and he wanted to buy me a few things before I started working. Mum was volunteering at the church charity a couple of nights a week and I was looking after Jimmy. I hated the idea of leaving school. I'm not lazy and I'm smart. I wanted to go on to university and do something in an office, have a long comfortable life, maybe make a name for myself in something. But to get anywhere these days you have to have education and I wasn't going to get any more of that, unless...

By the end of summer, everyone was scratchy from the heat, people argued a lot, snapped at each other, grumbled, and I knew I'd never have a better time. Besides I'd taken the opportunity to do a bit of sneaking into drawers in my father's study, and I'd realized something – something that could be very useful.

"Jimmy, wanna go to the park? We could see if the van has strawberry ice creams."

"Strawberry. I love strawberry." I knew that, it was his favorite flavor and the van had been out of them last time. "Go park for ice cream, Get strawberry."

"That's it, big guy." He ran ahead eagerly, while old Mrs. Gennero from next door stopped me.

"Taking your brother to the park, are you?"

"Yeah, he feels the heat. I said I'd buy him an ice cream."

She patted my arm. "You're a good brother. It isn't every boy who'd look after one like your Jimmy the way you do."

"He's my brother."

She took it as more than the statement of fact that it was and teared up. "I think it's wonderful. You're a sweet, kind, caring boy and I'd say so to anyone."

I dug a toe into the asphalt. "Nothing's going to happen to him while I'm around. I gotta go, Mrs. Gennero." We could hear Jimmy calling, chanting about a strawberry ice cream and she patted my arm again. I took off, leaving her smiling approvingly after me. I hid a smirk, a useful witness.

It was almost dusk, so there weren't many people around and the parlor would be shutting the doors in half an hour. I bought Jimmy an ice cream, a large strawberry one, and he started licking it. I moved sideways to him and managed a clear look around the park. Yup, there was Keith and three of his pals.

I waited until half the ice cream was gone and Jimmy slowed down on it. "Isn't it hot, Jimmy?"

"When it's hot it's nice to swim in the lake, I could jump off the dock."

I nodded, waiting until he'd taken a few more licks. "It's so hot, but you can't do that while I'm with you but if I can't see you doing something, then I can't stop you doing something."

He giggled.

I started us walking towards the lake, Keith saw us and I saw him say something to his pals. He trotted along the path, and as he passed Jimmy from behind, he reached out, grabbed the ice cream and tossed it away. I'd been waiting. That verbal back and forth wasn't all I'd taught Jimmy.

I kept my voice too low for anyone but Jimmy to hear. "If I can't see you doing something, then I can't stop you doing something." Then, "Pretty pretty wave, Jimmy."

Jimmy turned to face Keith and stuck his fingers in the air. It went as I'd been expecting it to after that. I had time to hiss, "I can't stop you doing something," as a final reminder before Keith and his three friends landed on me. Jimmy took off for the lake. I thrashed about in their hands yelling his name, once he looked back and smiled before he took off again even faster. I waited until, from underneath Keith's beefy arm I saw Jimmy run along the dock, and then I reared back, yelled Keith's name in apparent protest, and slammed my head against a tree root. I made it a good hard whack and I saw stars. I went limp and stayed that way.

Keith got off me and I felt his toe in my ribs. "You ain't hurt, get up." I stayed limp.

"Hey, get up."

I heard an adult voice intervene. "What's going on here? I saw you jump this boy." Keith spluttered something. "You boys go home right now. I'll be having a word with your fathers. Four of you attacking a boy that's smaller than any of you."

"He's older."

"I don't care how old he is. He's smaller and four to one isn't right. Get going."

They did.

I stayed down. I heard the guy, whoever he was, calling for help. That came after not too long, and I stayed limp still. Truth was that my head honestly did hurt. I felt sick, and I'd bet I had a nice new crop of bruises where Keith had kicked me. I was loaded on the horse-drawn ambulance just as a deputy marshal arrived. I lay there listening to the stranger say how he'd seen a pack of boys attack me. The kid with me had run off, and I was being kicked and punched into unconsciousness when the man intervened.

The deputy was a local man; he knew the area, my family, Keith's mob – and Jimmy. "You say the boy with this one ran away. Which way did he go?"

The man must have pointed, because the last thing I heard before the ambulance horse started off were footsteps running towards the lake. Happy Birthday to Me. I let myself fade out.

They were too late.

No one blamed me. Mrs. Gennero talked at the inquest and was indignant on my behalf. "He was always so kind to Jimmy. Why, that last day he was taking him to the park to buy him a strawberry ice cream especially. They hadn't had that flavor there the week before. You'd never meet a better or a more caring brother than Michael Rogers!"

There was a lot of discussion as to whether they could charge Keith and his friends with something, but they concluded that it'd be difficult, if not impossible, to find a charge that the jury would buy. Mum and dad told me over and over how it wasn't my fault. I was in the hospital overnight with a concussion, and in bed for six more days. I went back to school after a week and everyone was real nice to me.

A month later, dad sat down with me after he got home from work. "I'm sorry, Michael, but we have to move. After the end of this month, we can't afford the rent with Jimmy gone and his money with him. I could lose my job too. I can't afford to travel that far every day. At the least we'll have to move to a much cheaper place nearer my work."

I knew one thing from the start; mum and dad aren't that bright. They've never been able to figure the angles, not the way I can. I'd guessed that completing my plans would take time, but I'd had time, and I have a lot of patience if I know it's going to pay off. And as I said, I'd also managed to get a look at their copy of the will.

"No, dad, we don't have to move, or lose the money for Jimmy. I'm your son too."

Dad looked baffled. As I said, he isn't that bright. "The money's Jimmy's."

"No, dad. The will says that the money was left to provide

lifelong care for your son, for him to travel, be entertained, live separately if that was necessary, to study or have tutors if that was possible and suitable, and to care for him in all ways so that he would have a happy and fulfilled life. It didn't say James Rogers; it said the son of Christina and Marvin Rogers. And I'm your son."

"But... you're adopted."

"Yes, but I was your nephew when you did that, so I'm a blood relation, you adopted me legally. that makes me your legal son. What's more, you adopted me more than a month before the old man died, and he was sensible right up to the end, you said so. He could have changed his will, added in Jimmy's name to make things plainer, but he didn't. Ask the lawyer if I'm not right."

It took a while, but the court agreed with me. Lawyers an' judges aren't interested in the spirit. They stick to the letter of the law and by that, the money was there so I could go to university, travel over the vacations, and be entertained. I kept my head down until I'd completed school, then finished my first year at the university. After that, I had a lawyer I'd hired on the quiet check the situation. Could I get a place of my own? Just hypothetically. I could. There was only one problem. Mum and dad wouldn't like that. They might start wondering exactly how Jimmy drowned, remembering some of what Keith had claimed, and if they mentioned those doubts to anyone else...

The fire was a shame. I was away overnight with friends, but I lost everything, all the mementos I'd had of my brother, and my mum and dad too. People were nice again but I told everyone I felt I couldn't stay around where I'd lost so much. I moved across the country to a different university, and bought a very nice house in its own grounds – I hadn't realized just how *much* money was in that trust – and hired a housekeeper.

For entertainment I have a nice little blonde who comes in a couple of nights a week, I have good clothing, a really good horse – and a tutor so I'll get my degree with high marks. It all worked out for the best and I'm expecting to have a long and very comfortable life from now on. Thanks to Jimmy, whose carefully trained and willing cooperation was far and away, one of the best birthday presents I *ever* had.

LONE STAR JACKSON - OUTLAW

A s the professor used to quote, 'there's more things on heaven and earth than you ever dreamed of, Horatius." An' as I used to remind him whenever he said it, "Geeze, Prof, my name isn't Horatius, it's Horace and you know nobody calls me that anyways."

They didn't. I never liked that name and anyone that wanted to stay on my good side called me "Boot". Why? Because if there's one thing I learned being a town marshal, it's that you have to look after your feet, an' I always wore the best handmade leather boots Sam Garcia the cobbler could craft for me. At the time this business began, I'd been back east seeing my ma who was poorly. I'd left young Joe Keegan looking out fer the town an' after six months gone, I was looking forward to being home again.

I caught the train all the way west and we were less'n twenty miles short of my township when the train come sliding to a stop just before the final rise, and I heard a commotion coming closer toward the carriage I was riding in. There were yells, some woman screeching, a couple of men shouted, there was a shot, an' another. Next minute the carriage door crashed open and there he was in the doorway.

At first, I didn't know but what he was an ordinary train robber and I moved fast. If he saw I was a marshal he could start shooting and there was folks other than me could get hurt. I slipped my badge down back of the seat, an' dropped my wallet with it. I still had a small leather purse I could give up that hadn't nothing in it but a coupla dollars in nickels and dimes and an old copper ring I was given once by an Indian I helped.

The robber come down towards me and without showing it I was taking a good look at him. An' that was when I realized that he wasn't nothing human. His face was silver, with eyes and a nose and mouth, but all them was silver too, and there was no hair showing below his Stetson. He was wearing

109

regular clothing though, an' his two-gun-rig was a good one. But what really gave it away was the tiny trickle of steam coming from a sorta vent where his Adam's apple should'a been.

I stayed quiet, let myself look a mite scared, and waited until he reached me, but all the time I was watching an' listening, and remembering everything I could. He got to me and when I looked up, I saw that the places where his eyes would be were black, like bits of glass and nothing showed behind them. He spoke up real polite. I'll give him that.

"Your money and valuables, please, sir."

"Who are you?"

"Lone Star Jackson, sir. Now, your money and valuables please."

"Or else?"

His tone never changed but it felt as if he leaned towards me threateningly. "Or else I shall be forced to kill you, sir."

I suspicioned he'd already killed at least one person in the previous carriage because I could hear a woman still howling and crying, and I'd heard those two shots. I handed over my purse, an' he looked at me."

"No other valuables, sir? No watch? No keepsakes?"

I looked as harmless as I could, not knowing how well he knew people. "I ain't nothing but a poor dirt-farmer, Mr. Lone Star. Can't afford no watch, an' you taken the only keepsake I got. It's in my purse, I got that copper ring from my pa before he died and it's the only thing I got to remember him by."

He nodded, and I swear his voice got softer. "I won't take it then," he said. An' damned if he didn't open that purse and hand me back my ring.

I put my hand out and he dropped the ring into it. He wore leather gloves but his hand under them had the size and shape of a real hand. I nodded at him and spoke up. "I thank you kindly for that, Mr. Lone Star."

He nodded stiffly. "I am a train robber, sir. Not a thief." An' to contradict that, he went on down the carriage demanding people's money and valuables, and when a woman at the far end of the carriage refused to give him her earrings, he took them right out of her ears. Me, I thought he'd given me my ring back because it made him look good and he'd seen it was worthless. Her earrings were diamonds, and I notice she didn't get those back, no matter how loudly she begged.

The long and the short of it was that he cleaned out everyone, and left the train, running away across country towards a clump of scrub (there were several shots fired after him and from the clangs I heard, some hit home, but none had any effect I could see) an' a few minutes later I saw him coming out of the trees mounted on a horse and riding not so badly, in fact it was that which gave me the notion I knew where he could have come from. The train started up again an' in less than an hour we pulled into town an' I was first off the train looking for the professor. I found him in the saloon, pulled him over to an empty corner table and started telling him all about my trip. When I got to the part about the train robber he sat up.

"Describe the robot?"

"I know it was steam-driven. It had a vent in the throat with steam coming out in tiny puffs, they were faster when it moved or spoke, slowed down when it was waiting."

"What about the head?"

"No hair I could see, although it was wearing a hat. The face would have looked normal 'cept it was all silver. Oh, and it told me its name was Lone Star Jackson."

The professor nodded. "That's well observed. "Now, can you remember the exact words he said, to you, or to anyone else?"

I remembered most an' I told him. Then I leaned forward. "You made it, didn't you?"

I'd wondered about that from the minute I saw the thing, I knew the professor tinkered about, but he was an honest little man and I couldn't believe that he'd have made a robot that'd go about robbing people.

He looked shamed. "I didn't make it to do that, Boot. I made it to be an actor."

And right then and there I understood. He'd been tricked, and by golly I'd find the men who did it, get back everything that robot stole, and jail the men who'd cheated the poor professor and brought shame on him like that.

"Tell me all about it," I said, an' he did.

"Two men came to me the week after you left for the east. They said they were the managers for a theatre company, that it was hard to get actors, and they figured if they had a robot to act in their main play it'd cost a lot less, and they'd have one actor that didn't get drunk or quit. They said if all went well, they would come back and buy another one or two, but it wasn't the money, Boot, although they did overpay. It was doing something new, people would see my robot and they'd know I'd made it. They even said that they'd add my name to the playbills once the tour started."

In a pig's eye, I thought. Or maybe they would at that, sharing the blame if they got caught or even trying to shift the whole of it to the innocent professor.

"An' you taught him to speak?"

The professor got all excited. "It was an excitation of the Babbage concept," is what I thought he said. "A mutation of the principle of random cause and strategic consequence. But once I had it geared, I could teach the robot and use the, 'if that then this, if this then that' logic tree. There were a few bugs I hadn't worked out, but the men didn't care once they saw it working. They were delighted, kept shaking my hand, and saying I was a genius, and that my robots would be in demand by every theatre manager in the west."

"And the whole train robber speech, you taught it that?"

His excitement faded fast. "Of course, they said that was the first play they planned to put on in Abilene. It was called 'Outlaw, Lone Star Jackson,' and they gave me a script. I taught my robot all the words, and what to do in the part. He did so *well* too. He's geared to shoot too, but he was supposed to be provided with special bullets that just made the sound.

He certainly had learned to shoot. The two shots he'd fired at the man who refused him could have been covered by a silver dollar. So, what were the 'bugs' the professor was talking about? I asked. He told me, and it gave me an idea.

"This is what we'll do..." I had a word with a few people both on the railroad and elsewhere, and they spread the word quietly.

It came back to me in two days, with growing talk of a big consignment in the next train coming west. It would be carrying a mine payroll, and the train owners were taking advantage of the guards on that to add valuables of their own to the shipment. In view of that, it was said they were putting on a separate train, just the engine, coal wagon, the guarded mail-car and caboose. That way the train could move faster, and they'd send the regular train on well ahead.

It worked. The regular train went through with no holdups, and the smaller train with the supposed valuables come up the rise a few miles short of town and hit grease on the rails. It hung there on the brow of the hill, wheels screaming and sliding, and the robot swung itself into the caboose as neat as you please.

I was there dressed as an engineer and it turned to me. "Sir, please have the train stopped and no one will be harmed. I'm a train robber not a killer." I gave the agreed signals and the train's screaming wheels slowed then stopped. "Thank you, sir," said the robot. "Please tell me where the valuable shipment is kept."

Meek as a nun I led him to the car, and slid open the door, noticing that it didn't seem to worry him that there were no guards to be seen. "Please, Mr. Lone Star, don't take all the gold."

His head turned to me. "I must. It is why I am here. Open the lids of these chests."

I opened them and he peered at the contents. "That is most satisfactory. Tell your friends not to get in my way and no one will be harmed."

I halted him as he went to pick up the first chest. "Mr. Lone Star, in case you trip, let me put the padlocks back so the gold won't be spilled and put you to the trouble of gathering it again."

"Thank you, sir. You may do that."

I snapped padlocks shut on all five chests and he picked up the first chest and carried it over the rise and down the other side. He was back within minutes, picking up two chests and carrying them off. This time the steam from his neck vent blew out in a long hissing sound as he hefted the weight. It was continuing to blow when he returned for the last two chests, he hefted those in his arms and the steam became a long thin shriek. I waited until he vanished over the rise.

"Professor?"

"Any minute now."

And with that there was a sound like a buffalo stampede hitting an iron plain. I heard a cut-off screech, a bang and after a minute the professor was running toward the top of the rise.

I got there as fast as he did an' it was a sight. There was an old half-ruined cabin a' ways down the other side, with filled saddlebags that likely had the loot from the last holdup, and there was two riding horses an' two pack horses, sitting back on their tether-ropes, eyes rolling half out of their heads in fright – they'd been lucky though, they hadn't barely a scratch.

Couldn't say that for the two fake theatre managers. They'd been hit by a couple of chests full of gold-painted washers the robot had been holding when its steam-boiler exploded, and they was about as dead as I ever seen any man.

The robot was still moving, and the professor was kneeling at his side. The thing looked up at him and managed a weak question.

"Am I in the hands of the law?"

"Yes, and now you pay the price of crime," the professor replied in such a way I knew it had been part of the script.

I felt sort of sorry for the robot. It hadn't done any more than it had been built to do. It was people who'd used it wrongly. There was a pause, before the professor spoke again.

"The play is ended."

The robot shivered. "Was I a success?"

The professor patted its shoulder. "Of course you were, hear how the audience is cheering. You were a triumph. In a minute you must take a bow."

The thing hadn't a face that could shape a real smile but I think it would have smiled then if it could. A final puff of steam escaped and it stiffened, shuddered, and the head fell off. It was done, and that was it.

"Professor," I asked, "you're not going to make any more of them things, are you?"

The little man looked down at his dead creation. "No, Boots, I won't. I did try to warn them that it the robot was overloaded it could cause a problem with its boiler but they didn't seem to understand. They just laughed and laughed when I said it."

I blinked. "What exactly did you say?"

"Why, that if they weren't careful, things could go with a bang."

SUCH A CUTE PUPPY

"**M**iz Richards, Miz Richards?"

Elizabeth Richards, widow of Jeremiah Richards, cattle rancher in a small way, opened her door and looked at her cowhand. "What is it?"

"Rustlers."

She suppressed a word that that would have horrified her employee. "How many cattle have we lost this time?"

"Five good steers from the bunch in the far canyon."

Liz nodded, keeping her expression neutral. "Very well, move that herd to Spring Canyon, and have Joe spend the next couple of nights in the line camp there."

She knew Joe wouldn't like that. The Indians had had peculiar tales about the canyon but needs must when the devil drives the wagon. She shut the door and retired to sit on the edge of her bed, motionless as she remembered.

She'd been a seventeen-year-old bride when Jeremiah brought her here, she'd fallen in love with the tall shy young man the moment they'd been introduced at a soiree back east – and he with her. He'd brought her to this land and she'd fallen in love with it too, with her ability to ride for miles without stopping, with the shades of red and yellow, green and gray-green, and the wide clear skies. They hadn't had much money but they'd used her dowry to buy land, built their cabin, then worked hard and prospered, until in the eleventh year of their marriage Jeremiah had been thrown from his horse – three years back. He'd died where he fell, and she missed him so much at times that she thought her heart would break.

Just that first year after his death though, then Marty Spence had moved in, purchased three of the small neighboring ranches, staked claims on more land, expanded, and expanded again, until he owned land on three sides of hers, and with almost four times the acreage. He'd settled in, and within months she began to lose stock. Never more than a

115

handful at a time, but a steady attrition that, if it continued, could ruin her.

The gong sounded for breakfast and she joined the hands. "Miz Richards, Miz Richards," came their quiet acknowledgment as she was seated. She took her plate, waited until everyone else was eating and spoke.

"You've all been here since the start of this ranch. You know what's happening, and you know that we'll be in trouble in a few years. The town marshal says that it's out of his jurisdiction. I could sell up. I'd get sufficient from Spence to live in moderate comfort back east again. But if I do that, you're all out of a job, and I love this place, I don't want to leave. Has anyone any suggestion on how we could save Circle Two?"

The five cowhands looked at each other, their plates, and back at their employer. Johnny Lee spoke for them all.

"We talked about it. We can't think of a thing. Spence has a dozen hands, about half of them better than any of us with a gun. An' if we start a fight then he's got the excuse to roll right over us. There's talk of the town electing a sheriff to do the outside-of-town work, but even if he's fair, Spence can keep rustling until we go broke and without proof, there's nothing you can do."

Liz Richards sighed. "I see, thank you. Finish your meal, and Johnny, I'd like you to go into town and lay a complaint about those five cows. I want it on record that there's rustlers around."

The men finished eating, drained the last of the strong black coffee in silence, and tramped out, while the cook gathered their plates to wash. Liz saddled her horse and went out to ride over her beloved land while she thought. She was still young, well, at thirty-two she was youngish. If only she and Jeremiah had had children. They gave you an anchor, something to fight for. And children grew up fast out here; their first could have been thirteen by now, a right hand to her, and someone to inherit the Circle Two.

Deep in thought she rode on, further and further into the mountains where the foothills bordered her land. When she came to herself, it was to find that her mount had followed the thread of Indian trail to the plateau just above the end of

Spring Canyon. The ranch-hands cut hay here in the fall, and there was a small stone cabin there – one that Jeremiah had built and where more than once they'd gone to be alone together in the early years. She couldn't face the long ride home. Her men wouldn't be worried. Now and again she came here, and they'd guess where she'd gone.

Liz gathered sticks from the lean-to beside the cabin and built a fire. It was midnight before she banked the blaze and walked to the door to look up at the stars – an odd flare of luminosity caught her attention as it showed in the corner of an eye. Liz turned. Nothing showed in the blackness. She stayed looking at the sky, reluctant to leave the beauty of the night. The stars glowed, the fine sliver of new moon barely lit the earth below, but it glowed softly, lovely beyond pearls.

She turned to go inside and heard a tiny whimpering cry. She halted, waiting, and it came again. Somewhere out there a small creature was alone and afraid and her heart melted. She was the same, alone, and afraid that she would lose her land as she'd lost Jeremiah. The whimper came again and she followed it, cabin lantern in one hand until she was standing, looking down at the creature that cried its loss.

It was small, furry, an odd-looking little thing, a puppy obviously, but not of any breed she'd seen before. Not a wolf or coyote, she'd seen those. But it was a puppy, lost and afraid and its misery called to her.

"You're such a cute puppy aren't you, and all alone? It's all right. I've got you. I'll take care of you." She scooped it into her arms and cradled it against her, and after a final soft sad whine it snuggled into her warmth and relaxed.

Liz smiled down at it. "First things first. You may be hungry. Now what can we find for you?"

She found the tin of powdered milk and made up a drink. Offered that, the small creature drank, reluctantly at first, until she warmed it and stirred in a pinch of sugar. Then it drank eagerly, a small bowlful and another before it fell unexpectedly asleep in her lap. Liz made up a can of the milk and set it aside. As soon as they both woke in the morning, she could put that to warm and save the time she'd otherwise spend making it up. She crawled into the blankets on one of the cabin bunks and the puppy came with her, nestled at her side, making tiny sounds in his sleep, and snuggling closer as it chilled in the early hours.

He came home with her mid-morning, stomach rounded with warm milk, small blocky shape amusing the ranch hands as he chased and pounced on a ball Liz made out of a leather form stuffed with straw. She'd finally recalled the dim memory of a sketch her father had once showed her, and she'd guessed at a number of possibilities, but none of that mattered. Now named Max after Liz's father, the puppy slept in her bedroom, on the bed with her until he was too big, and then on a fur rug beside the bed where her hand could fall on him if one of them needed comfort.

She loved him and while he grew at tremendous speed, he was devoted to Liz, always gentle, and the hands who liked him, seeing him every day, never quite realized how large he'd become. He was still thought of as Miz Richard's cute puppy – even by Liz – until the day that one of Spence's men met her while she was riding a long way from the ranch house and alone save for Max who was scouting far ahead of her.

"Pretty lady like you shouldn't be out here alone. You could meet a man."

"I appear to have done so," Liz said dryly.

"Yeah, you have, an' a man like me knows why a pretty lady's out here." His hands grabbed, her mount jumped away, and Liz found that she was half hanging against her attacker's horse, while he smirked down at her. "Yeah, I reckon I can give you what you're looking for."

He maintained a bone-crushing grip on her arm as he dismounted, dropping the reins, and reaching for the neck of her shirt, tearing it open. Liz yelled, a sound of fright and fury. Her hand came up in a vicious punch under his ribs. He yelled and slapped back open-handed, the blow sending her to the ground before he was on her, rolling her face down, ripping at her clothing. Liz was fighting, snarling at him as she fought with all her strength. He punched, and the breath was knocked out of her. She was losing when ... abruptly he shrieked hoarsely and fell away from her.

She became dimly conscious of a terrible sound like rolling thunder in her ears, a crunching, tearing, somehow *liquid* noise. For long seconds all she could do was gasp for breath, her eyes shut as her diaphragm heaved for air. Then she found sufficient to fill her lungs again and her eyes opened. Beside her on the grass Max ate the prey he had killed, the creature that had dared to attack his adored pack dam. And as he ate his reminiscent snarl rumbled in the still air. No one should hurt Liz, she was his, *his*!

Liz sat beside him considering. Women are pragmatists. The man was dead and that couldn't be changed. Max had killed him to save her, but if she said so then Spence would insist Max be shot. If she and even the law refused that, then Spence would see that one of his men shot Max on the sly. She'd need to clean up the remains once Max was done, take them somewhere they wouldn't be found, circle the horse around and let it go to return from a different direction. If no one knew...

No one did. The remains were found months later, the death put down to a fall and the state of the remains to scavengers. But by that time another man had gone missing. Liz heard about that when she was next in town.

The livery stable hostler was grinning. "They say that he didn't like working for Spence. Everyone knows the man's cheap. Reckon Manny got tired of being short-changed an' rode off. Funny he'd leave his bedroll though. But then, maybe he'd been offered a better job and figured not to need the hassle Spence would have given him if he'd given notice."

"What about his horse?"

"T'warn't his. Spence is mad about that an' he's put up a small reward."

Liz did her shopping, and chatted to a number of town's-folk while thinking. Of late, Max often spent part of the night roaming the ranch. It could be that Manny Bick had been on her land with an eye to picking up a cow or two for Spence. Max understood that the cows on their land belonged to her. If he'd found Manny taking them, Max might not have been pleased. She listened, prompted comments and further gossip, and put two and two together. Once she returned, she took a horse and rode out with Max.

She was right about the second place that she checked. There wasn't much left of Manny, and the horse looked as if it had tangled with a bear. It was alive though, and could walk.

She gathered up Manny's remains, packed them in a sack and led the horse very slowly on a long roundabout trail into the mountains to where a small box canyon with little grass bordered on the far side of Spence's ranch. There she left horse and remains. They were found weeks later, and this time Manny's death was put down to the bear that appeared to have attacked his mount.

In the remaining months of the year as snow blanketed the land, five more of Spence's hands vanished. Each time Max had been gone for much of a night, and Liz was amused to note that the rustling of her stock had ceased. If two and two didn't make four, she'd be a monkey's aunt. Liz continued to ride on the better days of that winter. She saw things and learned more, and Max as usual was always with her, friend, guard and defender. The remains of the missing hands were found once the snow melted in spring, but by then the scraps were too far gone for anyone to make any assumptions as to how they'd died except that they hadn't been shot. And no one but Liz and her hands knew about Max.

Marty Spence rode up to her ranch house on the first day of summer. He'd been seen coming and Max had been ordered into hiding. Liz looked at her enemy and heard his offer for her home.

"No. Thank you, sir."

"Now, Miz Richards, don't be hasty. You've had trouble with rustlers an –" Liz cut in politely.

"No, we've had no trouble for months now. Maybe the gang or whoever they were have moved on."

"An' maybe they could move right back again. You ever think of that? No, I'm making you a fair offer and a wise woman would take it. Things can go real bad for a woman out here." Liz raised her eyebrows. "I'm just warning you," Spence said hastily. "Wouldn't want anything bad to happen to a good woman. But sometimes it does, and that's just how things are."

Liz saw his gaze turn towards where a haze lifted as cattle were moved to await a buyer. A stampede would ruin their condition, time would be lost in which they'd have to be rounded up again, and probably the buyer wouldn't or couldn't wait. She put an unpleasant whining edge on her voice.

"I have no intention of losing my home. As soon as I sell these cattle, I'll have all the money I need." She turned away, tossing a final comment over one shoulder. "Two more nights and I'll be rich."

She cocked her head sideways, sufficiently to see his face without making that obvious. Yes, he'd taken the bait. Tonight or the next he'd be here with his remaining men. Not that he had so many now. Of the original dozen, Max had dealt with seven, Spence had hired a man in spring, but that left him with only six hands plus Spence himself, while she had five and Max, and Liz was a very good rifle shot too.

She went inside after giving slightly odd orders to her men, went to her bed and slept away the day while Max drowsed on the mat beside her. Once it was dark she woke, fed Max and ate a light meal, before saddling a dark bay pony – a good color for riding at night. It was a sensible beast that was used to Max, and not at all prone to panic while being fast on its feet at need. She rode to the herd, which she'd had bedded down in Spring Canyon. Tonight was the new moon again, and she waited in the dark. Max sprawled comfortably at her side, the dark bay pony standing hip-shot.

At midnight by Liz's small pocket watch, Max sat up. The odd luminosity flared, Max howled softly and deep cries answered. In the starlight Liz could see shadows drifting silently over the land, and a second set that resolved into men on horseback. They closed in on the sleeping herd and Liz waited. A torch flamed to life, shots brought the herd to its hooves, bellowing as men whooped, and Liz mounted, reaching down to touch Max's head.

"Now boy, get them."

He flung back his head and bayed, low howls responding back to him from a wide half-circle and then there came human screams, shrieks of fear and horror, then of agony. The cattle shifted anxiously, but the sounds were in front of them and that was the canyon mouth, their only path. Soon enough the sounds died away and the cattle quieted. Liz dismounted. Something loomed out of the night smelling of blood and fur, and she tensed. A wicked snarl warned it away as Max joined her, crunching noises continued for an hour or two before dying away, as Max and Liz waited for dawn.

That came and Liz was busy. That afternoon she rode in to see the town marshal. "I have to report an attempt at rustling my cattle, the herd I have waiting for the buyer."

The man sat up. "Who?"

Liz lowered her gaze, looking distressed. "My men worked hard for days gathering and cutting out the best cows so I said that I'd take night guard and they could have a night's sleep. I had the cows in a box-canyon so all I had to do was camp by the mouth of that with a light fence pulled across. In the early hours half a dozen men came riding in shooting and yelling. I don't know what they were thinking of, the herd stampeded right over them."(Well it had, once she'd hauled the remains into the canyon mouth and started the herd running.) "I don't even know who they were, I couldn't see them in the dark, and once the herd had passed, well." She shuddered delicately as the town marshal made soothing noises.

"It's terrible. Even if they were rustlers, I wouldn't have wished a death like that on them. Can you come out and look at things?"

He could, he assured her, and did. Only half surprised to find that sufficient remains could be identified to suggest where to look – at an empty ranch and bunkhouse next door, where once Marty Spence and his men had been. That was almost the end of the story. Liz sold the cattle, used the money and other savings to buy half of Spence's land and stock, and when, a year later the area got a sheriff, she married him and found herself still young enough to have a son and daughter.

And Max? Max went home on a new moon when a gate opened to a faraway time when dire wolves roamed and now and again a tiny cub was lost to the luminosity that was a temporal rift.

Max returned to lead the dire wolf pack he had chosen. The pack that had come at his call to help his adored human, a woman who was also wise enough to know when to let him go free. But for all of her life, Liz remembered her cute puppy, and a long string of large dogs on the Circle Two ranch were named Max in his memory. After all, when you have a dire situation, what could be better than something else 'dire' to counter it?

A STEAM-POWERED CAMERA

Janfrey, inventor of the steam-driven bicycle and convener of the current meeting of London Adventurers, pointed and a man stood up from within the body of the meeting. It wasn't a large group, only twenty real enthusiasts with five committee on the platform. They had met for this occasion in one of the buildings that dated back to the start of the Victorian Age and which was a riot of crimson velvet, gold curtain-cords, polished wood furniture and a series of depressing portraits of hard-faced bewhiskered men, and with a large potted aspidistra in one corner.

The man who spoke was a little more modern. He was clean-shaven, and while short and slightly stout, he gave the impression of a man who was also physically fit. However his brow was furrowed, and his tweed cycling suit was disordered as if he had been too preoccupied to straighten even his tie. His face was serious and his tones grave as he addressed his fellows.

"I am Michael Dibdin and I have a dilemma," he said slowly. "I'm a writer and a ghost-hunter. I'm fortunate enough to have written a book about an adventurer who flies an airship all over the world fighting crime and righting wrongs and that caught the English public's fickle little minds. My publisher persuaded me to write a second book and a third. This provided sufficient money for me to write during half of each year and the rest of the year I am a ghost-hunter.

"I investigate old places, setting up my cameras and debunking rumored ghosts when they fail to appear. I sell articles to the Psychical Society and a certain mystery writer has spoken well of them. Naturally I use Mr. Janfrey's steam-driven bicycle to which I have added a covered, lockable trailer. I find these items most convenient in country lanes, and ascending steep hills requires no effort. I should say that it isn't that I don't believe in ghosts. But so long as I never see one, I felt free to pour cold water on the idea of their existence. I was sure I wouldn't be seeing one in my latest haunt either. So far as I knew there *were* no legends of ghastly or horrific deaths there. My quandary, gentlemen, is one for which I can show you proof later, but for now I shall merely describe it..."

Michael Dibdin paused, remembering how it had begun. "My articles about ghost-ridden buildings – supplemented with photos – impress editors and I command ready sales. Mr. Janfrey had listened to my requirements and produced the prototype of a new form of camera for my work. It has a wide-angle lens mounted on a small steam-driven turntable that allows the camera to take a photo across long strips of film so that almost an entire room may be seen in one frame. On it the film, once developed, can also be shown. During my latest tour I planned to call in on a couple known to me who live in Sussex. This I did and it was almost dark when the conversation turned to the church.

"I should say that the village, housing my married acquaintances, Gerald and Molly Symondson, is a picture postcard hamlet; a public house, twenty cottages, and a Big House, originally the Squire's home but now the property of my retired and well-to-do hosts. Three small shops serve the village with the church opposite them. This building, which I planned to investigate, is the usual sort of church for a village like this; a section of Anglo-Saxon wall, a Norman altar, with the church later rebuilt and embellished with Victorian ornamentation."

Michael Didbin continued his tale.

* * *

"So, it has no ghost?" I asked.

My friend Gerald had laughed when I asked that.

"Not one, old fellow. I know with something that old, there should be a ghost but the village is a backwater. The plague passed it by. As did Cromwell and his church wreckers."

"What about Good King Hal?"

"Oh, the church was originally catholic of course. So was the family who built this house. We bargained for the records to be thrown in when we purchased this place and as the original family had died out and their collateral line had no interest, we were permitted to retain the lot." He grinned. Gerald dearly loved a bargain and he was still smiling as the butler entered. (I admired the steam-driven robot, allowed it to help me to a whisky and soda and sent it on its way while Gerald resumed.)

"It took two wars this century to wipe out the family. The grandfather fought at Trafalgar, while both his grandsons fought in the Boer war. Death duties and little money remaining in the family, left the place in a mess. They took the roof off one wing to avoid paying exorbitant taxes, and the other wing burned down in a fire. After the old lady died, we bought the property, cleared the remains of both wings, planted gardens there and redecorated the center section."

Molly giggled. "You might find your ghost there, Michael. Tonight is the anniversary of her death. Go over and see if you can see anything."

I glanced out of the window at the last gleams of daylight. It would be a fine mild night for the time of year. I wanted to take photos of the inside of the church anyhow. Another whisky wouldn't go amiss before that. I said so and Gerald summoned the butler who arrived in a veritable cloud of steam to dispense rather warm whisky. I settled back. It was almost midnight when we finally stopped talking, Molly had long since retired, and I looked at my watch again.

"Good grief! Well, if I want to take photos it had better be now."

In fact, I had little option. As Gerald had warned me, during the morning the church would be filled with a wedding party followed by a christening. The building might be free the next night but I'd planned to leave after breakfast I wandered out to my bicycle, opened the covered trailer and removed the photographic gear I carry everywhere.

I moved around outside taking shots of the old stone church against the moonlit sky. I'd done little the previous day since there is little effort involved in using a modern bicycle, and I had energy remaining. A few shots of the interior and I could set up my ghost traps for an hour or so. There'd be nothing, which would allow me to add a few sarcastic paragraphs, along with photos, to my current article – already bespoken by an editor who paid an advance.

I entered the tower quietly. My indignation was considerable when I found my intentions preempted by a mere youth with very old-fashioned photographic equipment, and an air about him that indicated he was used to getting his own way. I approached him politely but firmly.

"Young man, do you have permission to be in here?"

His reply parodied mine. "Old man, have *you* permission to be here?"

"Yes," I snapped, "I have, and unless you can say the same, I must ask you to leave the premises." I was aware I sounded stiff, but the boy's insolent attitude called for it. He snorted derisively.

"I was here first and I'm staying. If you don't like it *you* can leave."

I had no intention of bandying words with this pup. But if I went to make inquiries, by the time I returned the boy could be long gone and I'd lose my own chance of taking photos. I decided to ignore him and set up my camera, ectoplasm detectors, thermometers and steam-powered wide-angled lens and film pack camera in silence.

Not so the boy. He made would-be witty remarks about my gear, my person – rather old to be out so late? And my technique of setting traps – futile really! After all, he added, he'd waited to see the old lady for a long time and had never seen anything. An old man with no idea of what he was doing had far less hope.

For the first time in years, I lost my temper. I told him that he was an insolent little swine and that in the morning I would make inquiries about him. If he were trespassing, I'd see that charges were laid against him … For a brief period, I seemed to have lost time, then he was looming over me, his face twisted like that of a fiend as he hissed explicit threats I was too shaken to answer. I am no coward but he overawed me and I retreated. There was an aura of such menace about him I dared neither remain nor retaliate.

I packed my items and headed for my bicycle trailer. Once there I stowed the equipment, then retired. By morning I'd regained my equilibrium. No old lady had appeared but I'd had little faith in her. I had good pictures of both outside and within the church, the second portion on the long, single, photographic-strip. I'd pass a pleasant hour or two with my hosts and depart after late breakfast. Mute but not of malice. Why should I spoil their day? In reply to questions over bacon and eggs I shrugged and merely said that I'd seen no ghosts.

Later, while Molly was in the village shopping, Gerald produced scrapbooks, several of which dated back many years, containing early photographs, some delicate sketches drawn by Mary, and old clippings. I flicked through them casually. The later ones were culled from local newspapers whose subscription area covered that of the village. I smiled over such items as the local flower show. An escaped bull had broken down a number of fences to the wrath of local farmers.

A headline caught my eye and I read the information below. It described a series of tragedies that occurred almost thirty years earlier when one by one, four village girls had been brutalized and left to die in the small wood near the church. The crimes were eventually brought home to the only son of a local family. The boy had been promising but, in the weeks, before his death, his friends had noticed changes. He'd become rude, quick to argue and then almost savage, even dangerous, in his manner.

I read on. The boy was said to have developed an unhealthy interest in ghosts, persuaded a wealthy friend to buy him the latest equipment and gone hunting the phantoms. Gerald leaned over my shoulder to see what I was reading. He grunted softly. "A pity, all that. A real pity." A cold feeling crept down my spine. I turned the page quickly. Gerald pointed. "That's his picture."

I knew before he spoke. The face of the young man with me in the church last night looked up. I kept my face blank with difficulty. "What happened to him?"

"He kidnapped another girl and her father caught him before he'd done more than tear her clothes off. The father emptied both barrels of a shot-gun into the boy's belly and left him to die before telling anyone. The doctor said that the lad would have taken an hour or more to perish and that he would have died in great agony. Oh, and there was an autopsy. He had a brain tumor."

After taking my leave I rode slowly through the countryside with one sad thought roiling about in my mind.

Further clippings had reported his parents as saying the boy feared death was the end of everything and was trying to find proof it was not.

* * *

Dibdin straightened as he addressed the meeting. "That is a basic account of my trip, gentlemen. But worse has followed. I took a number of single photos, in none of which does the boy appear. But with my new, steam-driven, wide-focus lens and camera, I find that I have a photograph of the lad standing within the church.

"Fellow Adventurers, it is horrific, they show him as he must have appeared at the moment of his death. Blood covers all his clothing, his body cavity is torn open and one can see the mutilated organs within, his face is twisted in an expression of such rage and despair that even I gave back when I first laid eyes on that strip of film.

"The worst if it is, that as the film passes through the spindles and the camera lens pans along the room, he appears to advance. His face, his attitude, is demonic. I am an Adventurer, but I confess it, I am afraid. I believe that it is the camera that has allowed this and I do not know what may happen if he reaches me – or any other who is present when the film is shown – and yet, that film is proof that ghosts *do* exist. Therefore, I ask all of you, what should I do, is there someone to whom the item could be safely given?"

Janfrey nodded to him as he sat down. "My dear Michael, I think I can find those eager to assist in this matter. Leave the film with me and I shall make arrangements."

Michael Didbin was weak and agreed, although even then he feared the outcome.

* * *

Newspaper item. April 3rd 1897:

> The terrible discovery was made last night of rooms in the London suburb of Finchley in which four men lay

horribly murdered. They appeared to
have been watching an amateur film
using a prototype steam-powered
wide-lens camera. The men were
listed as Jonathon St John Janfrey
the well-known inventor, Father
Eccleston from St Monica's, and two
members of the Psychical Society of
Finchley. They appeared to have been
disemboweled by a series of blasts
from a shotgun. However, no shotgun
was heard or found, no pellets were
evident in the bodies, and the door
had been locked from the inside. Sir
Arthur Conan Doyle has taken an
interest in this case.

    In another outrage, a young girl
was found unconscious in a street
nearby. She had been brutally
treated and might have died but for
her discovery by a passer-by. After
treatment she recovered sufficiently
to give a clear description of the
young man responsible and police are
seeking a man of this appearance.
Sketch; page 10.

Michael Dibdin of the London Adventurers, stiffened in
his armchair as he turned to page 10 and looked at the well-
drawn sketch. Oh God! It was as he'd feared, the film had
released its subject... His hands begin to shake, he tried to rise
from the chair but was unable to move. He had to get away, he
could be out of the country in two hours. He'd always heard
that ghosts couldn't travel over large bodies of water.

    Behind him the door to his rooms creaked gently, his eyes
started in his head, as, afraid to look he crouched in frozen
terror, newspaper crackling in his convulsing fingers. Light
footsteps advanced. From behind his chair the voice of a
young man spoke to him in tones that were horribly,
terrifyingly familiar to the Gentleman Adventurer.

DOING THE RIGHT THIING

We're such an unfortunate family. My great uncle did eventually marry when he was older and more settled. She was a pleasant woman who came of quite a good family. She died soon after her son was born and my great uncle who'd long since come to the conclusion that civilization was a snare and a delusion moved far back into the mountains to an isolated cirque valley to live with the boy.

He raised him alone, never letting him come into town or meet anyone else. They needed no more than themselves, being a cirque, the valley was self-contained, and they had only to place a short fence at the mouth. The land my great uncle owned was a pretty large area, almost twenty thousand acres and James, the boy became an excellent rancher, always concerned for his stock and taking care that they were never ill-treated. But when he turned twenty-one my great uncle had a problem. He wanted James to inherit the ranch, and, to do that, he needed to take him into town to sign papers acknowledging they were father and son, and James was his heir.

Great Uncle Matthew worried for weeks over this. A town could be a corrupting influence and he'd spent twenty-one years making sure the James was innocent about the wickedness of the world. But it had to be done so he sneaked them into the town before first light, spent the day in the lawyer's office – having told the man that if they could stay there, unseen, he'd double his fee – and meanwhile they carefully read and signed all the necessary papers.

Just before dark, Great Uncle Matthew went out to get the wagon, brought it round to the back door of the lawyer's office, got James into it and started for home. They were just driving past the new schoolhouse a little out of town when the door opened, and a young woman came walking out of the building and down the road right by the wagon.

James stared at her, and she slowed and stared back. I have

to admit, that having seen a sketch of James as a young man he was astonishing handsome so it wasn't all that surprising. James turned to his father.

"What odd clothing that young man is wearing."

"That was a woman, son. You've read about them in the bible, and now you've seen one, we can go home."

But it was too late. James was captured. "Father, if that's a woman, I want one to take home with us."

"No, no, son, women are a snare and a delusion, you don't what to have anything to do with them."

"But Father, I do. Please, get her for me. Persuade her to return with us."

My great uncle sighed. It'd all end badly, he was convinced, but if James had set his heart on this young woman, it could have been worse. She was modestly dressed, obviously educated, and he believed that she wouldn't have any relatives to pester them, or she wouldn't have been working. So, he dismounted from the wagon and called the girl who halted to listen.

It took some talking but James was very good looking, Matthew explained how much land they had, and offered to build a whole extra set of rooms for them after the honeymoon and in the end she agreed. James wanted her to come with them right there and then, they found a minister, and by ten o'clock James and Miss Mason were married and all three were on their way back to the ranch in the mountains.

Great Uncle Matthew put a pack on a spare horse once they arrived, saddled his mount and stepped into the saddle." A man should be alone with his wife for a while, son. I'll take a swing around the boundary to check everything is all right. I'll be gone for two weeks. You take good care of your wife, always do right thing, and be kind to her."

"I will, Father."

Great Uncle was gone for those two weeks and by the time he headed for home he was looking forward to his daughter-in-law's cooking and a seat by the fire with some good conversation. So as family history has it; his horse walked into the corral and James came out to meet his father but there was no sign of the girl.

"Hello Father. It's good to see you back."

"It's good to be back, son, now, where's that pretty wife of yours?"

James looked sad, "I guess we won't talk about her, Father."

Great Uncle was horrified. Surely the girl can't have gotten sick of marriage this soon? "Why," he asked. "Where is she?"

James gave a long sad sigh. "It was like this, Father. Two days ago, she went down to the corral to saddle up for a ride. Her horse got excited. He was swinging around while she held the reins and she lost her balance. She slipped and fell, and her leg was broken."

"What, the poor child. So where is she now?"

James pointed towards the back of the ranch house where in the distance there they could see a line of stones. "Why, father, you told me to always do the right thing, so I did as we'd do for any good horse, she was in such pain I had to shoot her."

A FRIEND OF GRANNY JARNI

"**I** didn't do it!"

"What?"

"Anything. Honest, Granny, you know the police, they hassle a guy just for the hell of it. I haven't done anything for them to be after me."

Granny Jarni looked at her grandson. She saw the lean length of him, wiry rather than bulky – although he was strong enough, thick black hair, brown eyes like hers, and a cocky grin covering sudden uncertainty.

"Yes. You did. You know it and I know it." He met her gaze defiantly and she shrugged. "You can't lie to me, boy, so don't try. You're a fool. You beat up that boy, and him and his girl are gone."

* * *

Johnny Anaru was startled. "How'd you know about that?"

"Maybe the spirits told me. But the police were here looking for you yesterday evening, even if they didn't seem to be quite sure what it was that they wanted to ask you about."

"What did you tell them?" His tone was half-pleading, half-threatening, and her head came up sharply.

"I told them nothing. You're my grandson, but don't think to frighten *me*. You and your hellhounds. You know what they call your friends in the city? 'Johnny Anaru and his dogs.' Fine thing for an old woman to hear!"

Her tones softened. "Why, Johnny? You had a good education; you could have done something with your life. You still could."

He shrugged. "What? Working nine to five at some office job for a dollar a day, listening to the boss telling me what to do all the time. A week a year holiday, having to wear a suit, and getting a few dollars rise in pay if I kiss up enough. I do a lot better working for myself."

He figured his grandmother didn't know what he was doing to make most of his money. But in 1897 often there weren't jobs for a man who was part Indian anyhow. Not that he looked it as much as Granny did – who was half-blood – Johnny was only an eighth, but even that was sufficient to trigger prejudice if someone knew and had that inclination.

"Yes, I know you do, but there's downsides and a boss comes with any job. Bringing alcohol in from that place of his down at the wharves for Sam Anton. You think he isn't your boss? At least in an office the boss won't have you beaten up or killed if you make a mistake."

Damn! She did know; how'd she *do* that? Johnny scrambled for a reply, met his grandmother's unhappy brown-eyed gaze and suddenly felt bad for her. When his Mum was ill for a couple of years before she died, Granny Jarni had quietly stepped in and taken Johnny home. She'd stayed up at nights when he was sick, stretched her money to see he had everything he needed, and listened patiently to his woes when things were difficult at school. But damn it, he had his own life to live.

"Sam's okay. He pays good money and it isn't as if I'm selling the stuff around the streets. People who want it will get it somewhere, might as well be from Sam."

"Sam Anton?" Her voice was vastly contemptuous. "You think if there's trouble, he'll stick by you? He won't be able to dump you fast enough. If the police even look as if they have anything on him, he'll toss you to them like a bone to a dog and clear out."

"Sam wouldn't." *No*, Johnny thought, but wisely didn't say. Sam was making a fortune here. He wouldn't be leaving the seaport city any time soon and he wouldn't toss Johnny to the cops anyhow, he knew too much of Sam's business. "I don't have any problems with old Sam."

"And the police?"

"They don't know anything. They just think they do."

"They knew enough to come knocking at my door," Granny said tartly.

"Yeah, well, I'll talk to them." He nodded casually, then saw the real distress again in her eyes. "I will, Gran, honest. I'll go today. Look, it's okay, they don't have anything on me and they never will. I just go up to the wharves, collect a parcel and bring it back for Sam. It's sealed all to hell and gone. I don't open it, so the cops can't prove I know what's inside. Sam always tells me it's business information to keep him up with what the opposition's doing.

"Sam's a smart man. They don't have anything on him either. He's never done time. Hell, they've never been able to lay a hand on him. Don't worry. I dunno what the cops think they're doing anyhow, coming here and upsetting old ladies. I guess I'll have to have a word with them about that."

He managed a swagger as he left. He'd talk to Sam and ask for his advice on this. It was true, the cops didn't have anything on any of Sam's people – but it was also clear they had to be suspicious about something. They wouldn't have been asking Granny Jarni about him if they weren't. It could be the trouble he'd had with that kid, and then again it might not be. Sam wouldn't like it that the cops were asking for Johnny either way.

* * *

Sam Anton didn't. He was minding his own business and the cops should mind theirs. He didn't want any clear links between Johnny, who collected the stuff at the wharves, and Sam who allowed it to trickle quietly through a collection of middlemen and their subordinates onto the streets of the city where it was quietly added to the booze at certain establishments. The cops knew what was going down, they just couldn't prove it. Some were doing nicely out of not seeing anyhow, and Sam would like things to stay that way. No evidence, no charges, and no trouble.

"I'll tell you what, Johnny boy. I'll have a word with my lawyer."

"And I go to him?"

"No, no." That was the last thing Sam wanted. The cops knew what firm he used. "No, he'll make arrangements for a lawyer from a firm that's nothing to do with me. He'll get back with a name and I'll let you know. My chap will tell your lawyer that the money's okay. Once we know who you're to see, you just go there and tell him how the cops are harassing a poor old lady. Make them say why they did that. They can't have anything on you and it'll embarrass them trying to explain why they were out banging on your granny's door. Your lawyer will make a fuss, their superiors will tell them to lay off, and everything will be sweet. Okay?"

"Yeah, thanks Sam. I knew you'd fix things."

"'Course I will. My people know they can always rely on me."

Sam called on his lawyer, talked, returned to his office, and sat at his desk thinking about business, Johnny, the cops, and if maybe he shouldn't get out. He'd started to make very good money ten years ago, and seriously big money over the last five years. There was another guy who'd buy him out if Sam agreed. If the cops were really onto the whole setup, it might be a good idea to skip the country.

His father had come from the old country, but there were still ties back there. With the money he'd made, if he could get it out safely, he could buy a small estate in Somerset where his dad had come from and be landed gentry. Sam's eyes narrowed. In fact, it was something he really should consider. He could start a trickle of his money going to a second cousin who lived where Sam would like to buy. Give the man limited rights to deal with it.

As for Johnny and his granny, they could rot. He grinned, a predatory smirk. People thought she knew things and went to her for advice, some even thought she could *do* stuff and one way or another she made a living from the gullible. Well, so did he. The difference was that what he sold, worked.

There was no proof, but Sam knew the cops. They'd keep digging until they found some. They never quit – and Johnny and his granny were weak links. The boy would happily beat up anyone. Sam suspected he'd killed at least once. But he loved that old woman and if the cops found the right lever to use against her, Johnny would talk. Maybe if they were both gone? But the boy was useful just now, reliable too, and Sam didn't want to lose him. No, he'd see what the lawyers could manage. And then he might think harder about taking his money and going back to his dad's country.

He grinned at the thought of his cover trade, which had the police at a standstill so far. He ran an agency that supplied aspiring models for advertisements; billboards, newspapers, patent medicines. All sorts of people came and went from his business. If the police started trying to watch all of them, they'd run out of followers a lot faster than he'd run out of suspects for them to follow. The cover made good money. If he went back, he could set it up in London, put in a manager, and keep having an estate in Somerset quiet. Neither end would need to know about the other.

The police would have trouble proving he'd ever been anything but a simple businessman anyhow. His grin widened until he resembled a hungry shark. Come to think of it, that's all he was. A simple businessman meeting demand with supply. Someone tapped at the door and he called them in to hear how things went on this problem. He'd put a man on it as soon as Johnny was gone.

"Jeffers and Harte? Okay, I'll tell the boy. No, no connection, just a kid I know. But the cops are bothering him and his granny for no reason and the kid's upset. He came to me and I told him I'd see what I could do. Yeah, I'll pass the name on. You told them I'd cover the costs? Okay. Thanks."

He sent a note and Johnny came in later that day to be told what had been done for him. "Go and see Jeffers and Harte. They're up on The Avenue. Tell them about your grandmother. They'll talk to the cops and sort it for you. No, s'okay. Oh, and Johnny, I'll need you to make a run to the wharves again for me in about a week. Yeah, usual deal and the same money. Okay? Yeah? Good."

* * *

Johnny Anaru walked out with a blank look but his eyes showed concentration. Sam had fixed things – this time. But Granny Jarni could be right. There'd been something in Sam's voice, a faint tone of something Johnny couldn't quite identify. Word was that Sam had several of the police brass in his pocket, but that they were demanding more. Then too, that other lot were starting to push. Granny heard things, sometimes things that hadn't come to her grandson's ears yet. After this last trouble, she'd sat him down and talked quietly, and Johnny had listened. Sam *could* be getting ready to clear out as Granny suggested – and, where would that leave Johnny?

The police listened politely to the lawyer, and the detective in charge of the case advanced reasons.

"Mr. Anaru was seen in proximity to some sort of attack or mugging in the central business district. We wanted to speak to him to clear up the matter, but he was – ah – rather elusive. His grandmother's address is on record as being his place of residence so we merely went there to ask if he was in or if she'd seen him."

"I see." The lawyer looked at them. "Of course you have a statement from the person who was attacked?"

No, they didn't. The person seemed to have disappeared. No, while someone involved with the victim had – ah – suggested that Mr. Anaru had been responsible, they too had disappeared without making a statement. The police were concerned however. There'd been blood – quite a lot of it – left on the pavement, and they had wanted to find Mr. Anaru to see what he could tell them about any of this. No. No intention of charging him with anything, or of harassing him – or his grandmother.

Johnny broke in angrily there. "My gran's an old lady. You come banging on her door after dark, asking for me, and scaring the life out of her. What do you expect, she's gonna be happy about it?"

Ah, yes. Well, a policeman had called earlier and the lady was out. It hadn't been very dark and certainly it wasn't late when their man called back, it had only been about seven o'clock. Nor had Mr. Anaru's grandmother appeared frightened.

The lawyer was stern. "Nevertheless, it must not occur again. Mr. Anaru is always willing to help the police, but I suggest that next time you speak to him directly. His grandmother is not to be approached. Now, as to this alleged attack. Do I understand that you have no complainant, no witnesses, no statements, and no reason to discuss it further with my client? I do? Then good day to you, gentlemen."

He swept Johnny out and once on the street he turned to him, speaking quietly. "They'll leave your grandmother alone in future. It won't do them any good to have some reporter pick up a story about their scaring respectable old ladies. There were hints of their being heavy-handed with one a few months ago over some council problem." He eyed Johnny sternly.

"But you should be careful. I knew one of the men in there – the one sitting at the back and saying nothing. He's from the police's Alcohol Investigation Unit, and if he's sitting in on your interview there, it wasn't about any assault. I'll say no more, but I'm sure you understand me."

"Yeah, thanks. I mean that, really, thanks."

"No need to be too grateful," the lawyer said dryly. "I'll be sending Mr. Anton a bill."

Johnny paused to shake hands before slipping off through the crowd, paying close attention to that back-of-the-neck feeling that might tell him if the police had someone tailing him. He hadn't said what he was thanking the lawyer for, and he noticed the lawyer hadn't asked. It had nothing to do with putting the police on the back foot over Granny Jarni. It was the information provided about the man at the back of the interview room – and who he was.

Just as well the lawyer had insisted on a plain interview room. He'd said that they were interviewing Johnny, not charging him with anything. Or were they? They weren't, so it had been the small plain room. That had brought the man into the room where the lawyer could see and recognize him. As the guy had said, there was likely to be only one reason for the man's presence. Sam had another courier job for Johnny soon, he'd said; maybe the cops had heard hints of something coming in. Maybe there was a leak in Sam's organization?

Johnny figured that the cops on the wharves could be watching for him. Sam paid very good money and Johnny wasn't at all stupid about money. He'd been saving half of every payment Sam made and not just in an account. It had been going into places where he got good interest. A friend of Granny's had given him the advice. Once Johnny had the next payment, he was planning on looking around for a small property – the ideal thing would be a one- or two-man business with a house attached. But if the police could prove anything – well, you couldn't spend much cash in prison. On the other hand, Johnny reckoned he would take a chance, one more time anyhow. Maybe after that he'd make other arrangements.

There was something else too. Sam had contacts. If some

special outfit was after Sam, he'd know about it. But he hadn't said a word to Johnny. The guy Sam always said was one of the few men he trusted. So maybe Sam trusted Johnny. The question was becoming, just how far could he trust Sam?

He wandered around the shops thinking as he watched for any sign of a follower. He was due to bring dinner to Gran's place tonight as he did most Thursdays. He'd pick up something nice for Gran too. She liked stuff that smelled of roses. He stopped at the perfume shop and found a small bottle of "Attar of Roses". He bought it, wincing at the price, but only the best for his granny. He brought her grilled spare ribs, baked potatoes with corn cobs, an apple pie and arrived with them and the perfume that evening.

* * *

Granny Jarni opened the door and studied her grandson. A look of innocence, food, an expensive gift, and a rather smug grin. She summed those up even as she was letting him in, giving him a hug, a kiss on the cheek, and setting out the food while exclaiming over the expensive perfume before making them cups of strong, sweet tea and sitting down to eat.

So – he thought he'd managed to put the cops off his track, did he? He'd have gone to Sam Anton, who would have found him a good lawyer and they'd visited the cops on the spot. No proof of anything. The cops would have admitted that, and her fool grandson thought that that was the end of it. Granny knew better – and if she didn't, she had friends who enlightened her. The police were gunning for Anton, they were determined to get something on him and put him out of business. And Sam was no fool, he'd know eyes were on him.

Granny ate, chatted casually, and watched Johnny. He wasn't a bad boy; he'd just lost the right path. One day he'd come good but she didn't think it was going to be any day soon and things could go very wrong for him before that happened. She was far more worried about him and his dealings with Sam Anton than she was telling Johnny – who wouldn't have believed her.

But Granny Jarni knew things about Anton. The man looked like a prosperous businessman, gave to charities, ran an honest agency for models, had a nice home, a couple of expensive vehicles – and the habits of a great white shark. Johnny seemed to think that because the man was always polite to him, paid him big money, told Johnny how much he was valued, and even found him a lawyer when the police harassed him, that Sam was okay.

* * *

Sam was far from okay and she smothered a sigh. Children nowadays, they didn't listen to a grandmother; she was old, what did she know? She could have pointed out that living a long time often meant that you had accumulated friends who told you things. You had knowledge if not wisdom. And being of her blood, she got information where others didn't. Besides that, some couldn't pay for her assistance in cash, so shared information instead. But her grandson wasn't likely to listen. He'd always thought her abilities a sham too. She'd just have to see what she could do for him behind the scenes.

Sam Anton was in his office talking to a contact a week later. "Yeah? You sure? Okay. Yeah. You'll get your money. Go and have a quick lunch in a couple of hours. Joe at the Copper Kettle will say you dropped an envelope and give it back to you with your change. If it's ever queried, say you had a private bet with a friend. Tell them you're not saying who until he tells you it's okay to give his name. Let me know if the cops do ask an' I'll see someone's ready to swear to it. Right."

Sam put down the phone and found he was sweating. Hell, he'd been right. The cops were after him. They didn't really have anything on him as yet, but they had a special bunch just starting to dig. His contact worked in the clerical section of the main police station in the city. He wouldn't take any risks, not even for the money Sam paid him, but he hadn't had to. So far, he'd quickly learned the basics of what was being done and been almost as quick at telling Sam – as he should be. Sam paid enough.

Sam pondered. He'd better think about sorting out a buyer. He could stay in the city if he dropped his shadier method of making money. But if he sold the business as a going concern and kept his head well down for a while … The cops would realize it was someone else doing the job and go after them. They might even think it had been someone else all along if he picked the right buyer. Connie Mikalis would be a good man to sell to, the man was ruthless and the cops would go a long way to bring him down. Besides, Connie was the man who'd starting cutting into Sam's territory. It'd be an amusing to do things that way.

And – Sam's brow wrinkled as he thought. Really, he wanted to leave, go back to the old country and be a squire. A different type of power, and maybe more fun. Certainly safer. But better he left no loose ends whichever way he chose. The only one who really had anything much on him was young Anaru. The kid had an excellent memory and he could tell the cops a lot about his trips to and from the wharves to pick up parcels – and who'd given them to him up there and where the handovers had taken place. The kid could even make a deal if – hang on, yes, in another ten days the boy was heading there to collect a parcel on the last trip Sam had planned for a few weeks.

Sam opened his ledgers and studied the bottom line. Yeah. He was rich enough – especially if getting any richer came with a jail cell. He'd gone into this as a business, a way to make big money. That was all he wanted and he had pretty much achieved it. Now and again a special job made him a single very large sum. He could shuffle the money that came from this last trip, sell the distribution business – and the information, the additive that made it so successful – to Mikalis and go legit. But Johnny knew too much. The street dealers didn't know Sam at all, the middlemen who supplied him couldn't prove anything and wouldn't dare talk, and so far as the cops could prove, Sam Anton was whiter than white. And if he ended up in Somerset as a respectable squire, they'd shrug and forget him. Yeah, that'd be safer. He'd start to liquidate his assets and be ready when the time came.

He smirked at the thought. But Johnny Anaru could talk. If the cops offered the boy a big enough bargain, he sure would. That damn grandmother of his would see to it that he took any bargain the cops held out. Maybe if she had an accident? Nah. If she did, the boy would guess who'd done it no matter how convincing it was and Sam knew the kid would talk for certain then. No, he needed to get Johnny first – but then the old lady would be screaming bloody blue murder. He had to get them together, that'd do it. No one left to make a fuss, no one left to complain and make the police listen. Yeah. Both of them.

* * *

Granny Jarni was walking on a far beach at dusk just as Sam Anton was sitting down at home eating dinner and listening to his wife. It was dark enough so that Granny couldn't be seen from more than a few meters away, and just barely light enough so that she could watch her footing on the sand. Beside her, the great black bulk of a very old friend kept pace as he listened to her worries.

Granny was talking. "I've had word, there's a special police group in town. They want Sam Anton and they'll probably get him unless he sells up quickly."

"Then Sam will know that and he will sell. Why are you worried?"

"Because of Johnny. He's been working for that man for almost five years now. Sam hired him because Johnny has an excellent memory. Give him long complicated directions and he never needs to write them down. He just remembers them. He's done all sorts of things for Sam and he could tell the police a lot if he talked. Sam knows that."

"And you think Johnny would talk? Why?"

No," Granny Jarni shook her head slowly. "I think Sam Anton will try kill us both before he can."

There was a commotion in the water as if her companion thrashed in anger. "Why would he do that?"

"My grandson knows too much and his boss knows if the police take Johnny, I would make him make a deal. Sam can't afford that. But if he hurts me, Johnny will make a deal with the cops for my safety or to ruin Sam if I'm killed. If he hurts my grandson, he knows I will make such a fuss the police will come looking. And no matter how careful Sam may be, there could be something for them to find. His best way is if neither of us are around to talk to anyone."

"You are my friend. I would protect you."

Granny smiled. "I know you'd do your best. But in the city,

you'd be like a fish out of water." They both chuckled at the pun.

"Still..."

"I promise I'll tell you if you can help."

After that, there was only the soft hiss of the waves and a crunch of sand as two friends walked in comfortable silence together, each considering problems, possibilities and solutions.

* * *

Ten days later Johnny was unobtrusively heading for the wharves. It was a bright sunny day. He was going to do a little errand for which he'd be very well paid, and everything was just great. Fine day, pleasant trip, good cash money at the end of it and nothing to worry about. He spent the night anonymously on the outskirts of the large area devoted to ships, sailors, and their needs, and around seven a.m. he tapped gently at a door and was hauled inside.

"Hey, Charlie, less of the grabbing. What's the excitement?"

"Cops!"

"What? *Here*?"

"No, but this guy's been hanging around all week. He doesn't seem to be sure of the address but you can never tell with the police."

"Which?"

"Special alcohol task force. That's why Sam's selling. Here, didn't Sam tell you?"

Johnny put two and two together with remarkable speed, came up with seven and a half and spoke casually. "Course he did, Charlie boy. I expect Constantine Mikalis will want a different courier system though – that's who's buying, isn't it? And I didn't know the alcohol squad was on to you, that's all. Is there any sign of the bloke around now?"

"Yeah, it's Connie Mikalis who's buying, and no, I haven't seen the guy around today."

"Okay. I'll get out of here once you've done a couple of things for me."

"What things?"

Johnny explained and Charlie grinned. "Not bad. Okay, I

can get that done, I've got contacts. It'll take a couple of hours, mind?"

"Just get it done. Sam's expecting me back tonight and he doesn't like to be kept waiting."

Left alone in the shabby room, Johnny put his wits to work. Charlie tended to learn things he wasn't supposed to know. A trait of which Sam was unaware, but Johnny had been at school with Charlie. So Charlie had discovered Sam was selling to Mikalis? A good idea on Sam's part. If the squad were after Sam, as soon as they heard who'd bought him out, they'd probably drop chasing Sam and take off after Mikalis – although they could come back to Sam at any time – if he stayed around. But Sam hadn't mentioned any of this to Johnny, which meant he wasn't supposed to know. Why not?

Johnny Anaru was no fool, and he felt a cold chill slide down his spine. He wasn't supposed to know because he could talk, but there was one way of making sure he didn't. He shivered suddenly. And there was someone else who would have to be kept quiet too. Maybe if Johnny had a card or two to play, he could slide both himself and his granny safely out of this? He had to get word to her.

* * *

Granny's door knocker rapped that evening and she jumped to open it. A boy at the door offered her a sealed envelope. She recognized the handwriting, accepted it, paid, and retired to read in her parlour with the fire cracking quietly.

Gran,

There may not be much time. The guy I met up here – you remember Charlie that I was at school with? He says Sam's already sold out to Mikalis apart from this last run. Sam never said a word to me even when he saw me yesterday morning before I took off, and I can think of a good reason why. I should have listened to you. I should be home tomorrow night around six o'clock. I've got an idea how to deal with Sam. We'll talk when I'm back but I thought you should know about this now.

Be careful,
Johnny.

Granny Jarni read the note twice, consigned it to the fire and nodded slowly to herself. "And I reckon I've an idea better than any idea you'll have."

She put precautions in place and waited until the next day when Johnny rode up to her back door via the narrow alley. He led the horse into her large shed, loosened the girths, ran the stirrups up, took his mount's bit out and gave it hay to eat before scuttling in quietly via the back door, and settling into the chair Granny indicated.

He would have talked but she looked at him, and he said nothing while she told him some of what she knew. She explained her idea, while he listened. After which, there was silence for a minute before Johnny answered her slowly.

"Yeah, yeah. That sounds good to me, apart from the end of it. How are you going to keep Sam from killing us?"

"I know a few things. He'll not say or do anything against us."

"You sure about that?"

"Trust me, grandson."

"You'll have everything waiting?"

"Yes. Just do as I've told you. It'll be all right, Johnny, I promise."

"But what if Sam won't play along?"

"You think he'd break his word to you?" Her voice carried a slight edge of sarcasm and Johnny was nettled.

"I guess I know Sam. Yeah, he'd give me up, but only if it's to his advantage."

"So, we'll see that it isn't." She sighed. Her grandson was bright but he was rarely subtle. She'd have to be subtle for both of them until this was over. She knew what would have to be done and she didn't like it much, but worse things had happened in the city in her lifetime and Sam Anton had been responsible for a few of them. She didn't plan to be a ghost wandering the streets and cursing his name.

She made a few calls on various people before taking her pony down to the beach to call an old friend. "You said if I needed help, I should ask."

There was a low chuckle like rippling surf. "Explain your plans, tell me how I can aid you, and I will."

Granny Jarni nodded. "My grandson has got himself in

deeper than he intended." She explained what she knew of the police, Sam Anton, her grandson, and the parcel he was bringing back. She described the plan she had made, and waited.

"It sounds unpleasant and dangerous for you. How do you expect to resolve it all?"

Granny's voice was tart. "It's called cutting the Gordian knot. That's where you take the simplest path, straight forward and right through the middle of any obstacles. In other words, let obstacles pay the price for being what they are." There was no actual answer, but her friend was old and wise, and she saw his head nod in understanding and agreement.

* * *

On the main road from the wharves, the mount carrying Johnny Anaru was racing for the city. It was probable that the police had an eye on him and didn't want him stopped before Sam's office. But he was careful to be as unnoticeable as possible. Granny's plan called for him to arrive safely and on time. Johnny grinned as he rode. Charlie had got him everything he'd needed, now if granny had done her bit, everything could work out for them. It was about an hour short of dusk when he slowed his weary horse and saw his grandmother waiting down on the beach.

"Right on time. Good boy."

He tied his mount by her pony and walked after her to the water's edge where a dinghy leaned to one side, water washing lightly against the faded paint. His grandmother looked at him.

"Do you have it?"

"Yeah." He tapped the breast of his leather duster. "I didn't have anyone following that I know of. Still, we should move fast."

Granny nodded, laying a hand on the boat. "Get this into the water for me, Johnny, I can row but it's too heavy for me to move."

He heaved the small boat into the waves, scooped up his grandmother, and carried her out a few steps as he towed the boat with him. He placed her into the little vessel, climbed in, and balanced his weight. Wordlessly, she took up the oars and rowed out in a straight line from the beach. It was no great distance to the small island that nestled in the bay. Once there,

Johnny stepped out, hauled the dinghy onto the sand and, turning his back on the distant beach, produced the sealed tin from the front of his jacket.

"What do I do now?"

"Follow me and do as I tell you."

The tide was receding. In another hour it would turn and start up the sand again. Granny Jarni made a calculation based on time and tide and moved along the beach to where a small spit of rock ran into the sea. In the sand partway along that she pointed.

"Dig a hole just here." He obeyed and she tucked the tin into it. Johnny nodded when she looked at him. The rock spit made a clear landmark that he'd remember. His grandmother nodded back and he filled in the hole before returning to the dinghy.

She spoke once as she was rowing back. "You know what you have to do now?"

"Yeah. I'm just not sure why." She shrugged and he said no more.

* * *

They left the dinghy drawn far up on the sand and parted, Johnny riding his horse to Sam's business, while Granny Jarni went home to wait at her small house further from the bustle. It took several hours before Johnny returned to tell her of events.

"Police closed in on me near Sam's office. Said they knew I had a parcel and I was to show it to them immediately. I said it was Sam's, I was taking it to him and it was expected. They asked what it was and I said it was business information, things about those in his line." Johnny's grin was wide. "One of them ripped it open, and guess what? It was. I said they were gonna get me in trouble. They opened the parcel, they gotta come and tell my boss that it was them opened it. Okay?"He grinned again and Granny's smile matched it. So far things were going as she'd planned.

Sam had gotten into the alcohol business, then he'd made the accidental discovery that if you added very small amounts of a certain drug to the alcohol it produced better effects. You stayed as it were, more sober, but the experience was more enjoyable, more intense. Your health deteriorated, but if you kept taking the doctored drink you wouldn't notice. Others did and had however. Some were the police who didn't like alcohol anyway, and liked Sam's version still less. The more so as now and again if the payment was large, things could be expedited for a client who wanted someone gone.

It had taken time for them to narrow the sales – and deaths – to Sam, and just about then, Connie had found something that was almost as good for all but the deaths, and had starting cutting in on Sam. Granny had heard a lot however, including Sam's sale to Connie, how much, where, and when. And she'd added some of that to her plans. She listened as Johnny talked.

"Sam asked what was going on when we got there. Police said they'd heard I was bringing some sort of drug in. Sam, he didn't believe it, I was a decent kid who just acted as a messenger for him now and again. The police said they were sorry. They went, and I told Sam Charlie'd had someone watching him and he was bothered. I thought if it was true, better safe than sorry. So I got Charlie to do me up another parcel. I got a message to you, you met me before I got all the way back, and I gave the real parcel to you. You hid it where they'd never find it."

Sam had grunted at Johnny then nodded. "Looks as if you were smart. So they grabbed you and all you had was business papers, ones that looked as if they'd been copied by someone I'd paid to find out about others in my other line of work?"

There was a grin in Johnny's voice. "Yeah. Reckon they won't be so keen next time. Oh, an' one thing Mr. Anton, I heard that you might be gonna sell the business to Connie Mikalis. That true? I mean I've done good work for you but he won't use me. My income's gonna go down some if it's true?"

Sam Anton ignored the question. "So where's this safe place?"

"Dunno, gran knows. I'll have to go back and meet her. She'll take me to where she's stashed it and I can bring it to you."

Here comes the kicker, Granny Jarni thought as she listened. She could almost hear Sam's mind ticking over from the time and distance of Johnny's explanation.

"Nah. I'll come with you. We get the parcel, I pay you, and we split up."

"If you say so?"

"I do. Hang on a minute, I'll pick you up a nice bonus from my safe. Can't let my best man down, can I?" There was a pause. "Here. Don't spend it all in one place."

"No, I sure won't. Thanks, Mr. Anton. That's twice what we said."

"Yeah, but like you told me, Mikalis won't use you an' your income's gonna drop. This gives you a bit of time to look around."

And besides, Granny thought, as she listened to her grandson. You can always take it off the boy's body once you have the parcel you want. Letting him have it now just keeps him happy and trusting. Johnny finished his tale and she slipped out the back, taking the pony, Johnny would explain she'd gone ahead when he rejoined Sam.

She was sitting peacefully on a rock near the sea when the two men came walking. Good boy, he convinced Sam to come by the old carriage they'd hired from Mr. Gunston. It made sense. The police, if they were watching for Sam, wouldn't expect him to be traveling on a carriage that dated back forty years and looked it. With a bit of luck, Sam and Johnny had given the police the slip completely. Sam confirmed that.

"Yeah, no sign of them." He laughed harshly. "Guess they never found out that I own a couple of other businesses in the building, both on different floors. One has a window at ground level. Now, where's my parcel?"

Granny pointed to the island, dimly visible in the half-moonlight. "There."

Sam gaped at her. "What, out on the island? Why?"

Granny smiled. "Why not? Do you think the police would think of looking there? And they'd have to dig up the whole place to find it even if they did. I can go right to it. Of course I'll need Johnny to do the digging."

"Why don't you stay here and wait for us then? He can row us over too."

Granny shook her head. "No, he never learned to row that well and the tide's running. You could end up out at sea, and if the boat capsized in this rough water with the rips here, you could drown unless you're a very good swimmer."

She knew from a friend that Sam wasn't. He grunted irritably. "How long before the tide's running towards the shore again?"

"About an hour. Once it turns it's no trouble coming back. Even a boat that isn't rowed will drift straight back to the beach with the current."

That should persuade him to leave his move until she and her friend were ready for it. It seemed to have done so. Sam made no further objections as Johnny hauled the dinghy to the water and loaded them all in. She moved the spade so they could sit comfortably and took up the oars. She rowed smoothly, making it look easier work than it was, as if the tide were ebbing and taking the boat with it to the island.

* * *

Sam was running possible events in his mind as the old woman rowed. He would let her get them all over to the island. He'd let Johnny do the work of digging up the parcel. Then he'd kill her grandson and let the tide take the body out to sea. The old woman could be threatened into rowing Sam Anton back. If she refused, he'd kill her too; he had only to wait a short time and the dinghy would drift back to the beach on the incoming tide without any problems – or so Sam believed.

The dinghy keel crunched into the sand and Johnny stepped out to haul it a little higher. "This way, Mr. Anton." He shouldered the spade in the half-moonlight and his grandmother followed, with Sam behind them. Once they reached the rock spit, Johnny starting digging. His grandmother moved casually through the sand until she was standing on the beach, Sam Anton turning to watch her while she faced the beach.

* * *

She glanced up at the sky. Just after dark, about half-past nine. If all worked out, she and Johnny would be back at her home in a short time, and there would be the item. She'd seen to it that Sam had been delayed for her to find that and reach her home, then the beach before him. He'd condensed his wealth into a single suitcase – a trunk held his clothing – laid on that the ticket for the boat he planned to catch to London the next day, and he'd gone to his office believing no one, not even a burglar would find them.

Granny smiled as her grandson dug. So much came to her ears, one of the things being from one of Sam's mistresses, that there was a secret room in his home. Nothing special, it had been a dressing room off the main bedroom. He'd had it boarded up with panelling that matched, and a door under a tapestry on the other side. Sam hadn't known the girl knew either. He'd paid her off, she'd gone, told granny, and died soon after. Granny could move fast when she wished, and she had. The suitcase and ticket reposed in her own home now. She had plans.

Behind Sam against the night something moved and she gave a small, unnoticed nod to the great shadowy figure.

The sealed tin appeared and Johnny picked it up with one hand while he started scraping the sand back into the hole with the shovel edge. The tide was coming in now although Sam, with his back turned, hadn't yet noticed – nor what moved with it.

"We don't want to leave any signs." Johnny said as he finished. He appeared to catch his foot in a clump of seaweed as he moved away from the smoothed sandy surface; he stumbled awkwardly and dropped the tin. Sam swore.

"You clumsy idiot, that's worth more than you'll ever be." He grabbed the parcel. "Not that it matters now. I've got it and I don't need you anymore." The moonlight flickered on the metal of the sleeve gun.

Behind him, in the low surf, something smelling of salt water and age reared up, black bulk massive, against the sky. It came down over Sam Anton. There was a startled muffled cry and he was gone. A few seconds' pause and a gun and a sealed tin were spat up on the sand. Johnny went weak at the knees. He could only stare and shiver at what faced them, eyes glimmering opalescent in the half-darkness. Granny Jarni opened the tin and threw flour to the wind before hurling the gun out into the sea.

"That's that. Now we go home and forget tonight."

Johnny managed to speak, although his voice shook slightly. "What did you do with the real stuff?"

"Emptied it into the drains before I came here."

A deep rumbling noise became words. "You called him a great white shark."

"Yes," Granny said briskly. "He was."

The sound rumbled into a chuckle. "Indeed. But now his spirit knows, even the largest shark bows to the Atunkai in his own part of the sea."

The shape splashed and the blackness of it, the scent of age and power, was gone. They went home in silence; Johnny breaking that only as they parted, his grandmother off to sell the ticket, while considering where best to invest the case's contents, Johnny to spend the night trying to convince himself he'd seen nothing – really. Although maybe he'd take up another line of work. One where you didn't run into – things like that he'd never believed in – and had now learned how wrong he'd been, that his granny was no fraud, and more than he'd ever realized.

"You said you had an old friend helping us." His tone was slightly accusatory as he hugged her good night.

His grandmother snorted. "I've known him since I was a child and we've liked each other since we met. Who is he then, if after sixty years he isn't an old friend?"

There was no reasonable answer to that, and her grandson attempted none.

BATH SALTS AND BEDLAM

Our sheriff was here today asking if I'd seen some wandering male person, I could have *sworn* he said was named Bob Jonquil. I didn't take it the wrong way. I'd seen the sheriff coming from my neighbors' farm and watched as he went on to my main ranch then my other neighbor after I assured him I hadn't seen any man at all on my property this week whether he was named Bob Jonquil or Merriweather Anstruther Daffodil. My neighbors would have been saying they hadn't seen this Jonquil person either. That's because I knew where he was, not that I'd actually seen him, but I knew all the same...

It all started with my new bath salts. I have a damaged leg, from a riding accident when I was a child, (probably why no man married me, although of course, they would have, had they known how much my grandfather had in a bank back east and that in time it would all come to me) and there's nothing that keeps me pain-free like a good long soak in very hot water before I go to bed.

My cabin's bathroom has one of those long deep cast-iron, claw-footed baths that's absolute bliss to lie back in when it's filled with hot water, and I do, regularly, once Annie my maid, housekeeper, and general factotum has heated the water and carried it to the bath. And for a good soak you can't beat bath salts. About a year back a man had come by in a covered wagon selling all sorts of strange items from the tailgate. One of the things he had was bath salts.

The man had brought out a few bottles as I walked up and I looked them over. They were an odd shade of blue-green, the lady with him said they were mostly made from Epsom salts and 'herbal additives', whatever those were, but the stuff smelled pleasant, and I bought a couple of bottles. Once I'd paid, the chap spoke to me quietly.

"I can see you're a lady who knows good merchandise when you see it." I did, but that didn't mean I didn't see *him* for what he was. A quack if ever I'd known one. I waited to see what he wanted to sell me now.

"Them bath salts, lady, they're the good stuff alright. S' just the color puts some folks off. But I can do you a good deal. Gotta a case of it, another thirty-four bottles like the ones you bought. Sell them to ya for an all-in price?"

I considered. "How much?"

He named it and I kept my face from showing surprise. That *was* a good price and spread over all of the bottles it ended up around a fifth of what I'd pay for that amount of anything of even reasonable quality on any trip I'd make to one of the larger cities. It could be the whole consignment, three dozen bottles counting the two already bought, and it made sense if he could sell them all for a single price.

"Just one thing, lady." I nodded that I was listening. "You don't want yer dog drinking the stuff. It don't go well with them."

I saw no need to go into long-winded explanations as to why I didn't have a dog. I merely said I'd be very careful and paid for the case. Once he drove off, I carried it to my barn and left it there shut into a stall.

After that, I went back to my cabin. It was time I fed my creatures, something I did to raucous approval from the geese. I bought two geese fifteen years ago, six months after there were two family tragedies in succession. The first was not unexpected. Grandpa had a heart attack and died in his sleep, and I inherited.

What was not expected was that on a train trip to the city there was an accident, the trail derailed, and my parents were killed. I sold their small farm, and with the money for that and my inheritance from grandfather I purchased a larger ranch, installed a foreman, a cook, and five hands, and they ran my property most efficiently. On the other side of the property there'd been a large cabin, and I took that for my own along with the ten acres around it which I had fenced off. I doubled the size of the cabin, added comforts, and hired Annie who, because she was deaf had found it almost impossible to gain employment.

She lived in, having a day and a half off every ten and usually going home for that night to her family. I paid her standard wages and with her own very spacious room at the cabin, she was extremely happy. The more so as I had no dog, she was afraid of those. But I'd already purchased the geese. Every so often they raise another gosling, it joins the gaggle, and over the years, the numbers have seesawed as goslings arrive and now and again something gets one of the adults. It's been steady on nine adults for a couple of years now and that suits me.

I lost one some time back when an intruder kicked one of the older geese to death. I think the gaggle mourned her. She'd been the matriarch, and I have to say I wasn't that happy about it either. I got the original pair as watch-geese, and they do – watch, that is. Anyone they don't know sets foot on the property and they scream like something on the rack. After dark, and even if they know the intruder they still scream.

And while usually it's all noise, if they have goslings or eggs or are feeling territorial, it can turn very nasty. I'd only had the place a year when a saddle-tramp targeted my sheds; they left, not so much running as low flying – unlike their pursuers – with the geese hot on their heels. (My geese are Sebastopols, they're big strong birds, but they can't fly, which is convenient since I don't have to worry about clipping their wings, but they certainly can run if they need to.)

I opened the gate and greeted them. "Okay, okay, I'll feed everybody." I did, and while they and the hens were busy, I managed to haul the case of bath salts out of the wagon and get it inside, using the small trolley I normally employed for sacks of feed and which Mark, Annie's brother had made for us. I stacked the bottles on a shelf in the bathroom linen cupboard, and took the light crate outside. It'd get used; probably as kindling. Then I looked at the time and nodded. Annie could put dinner on and I'd have a bath while it cooked.

With dinner started and the the bath gently steaming I added a generous amount of bath salts, climbed in and relaxed. The salts smelled great, and I could feel the heat soaking through my damaged leg. The cat wandered in, leaned over and took a mouthful of bath water.

"Oi, Fluffy, get out of that." But then, the bloke hadn't said I shouldn't let the cat drink the stuff, just about dogs, so probably it was okay. I climbed out, reluctantly after a while, dried off, dropped a long robe over my head and went to eat dinner.

Things were quiet for weeks after that until the bathroom waste pipe broke – the one that drained the bath water into my septic tank. I'd let the goats in to eat the grass down around the house and one of them – there's always one – had jumped on the pipe and broken it. So now the bath water ran into the small hollow by the drain instead of down into the tank.

I didn't worry much, in fact it was probably good, I wouldn't need to get the tank emptied for a lot longer and believe me, when you live out outside the township getting that done is an expensive nuisance, so I left it be. I noticed the geese drinking now and again after I let the bath empty, and sometimes the cat took a drink too, but that was okay, the water soaked away in hours and everything was fine.

About six months after that, I heard the geese yelling one night. They quieted down pretty quickly though and I went back to sleep. In the morning, I checked the sheds, and one of the doors was ajar. I figured some idiot had been sneaking around to see if there was anything he could steal and the geese had seen him off.

Nothing unusual about that. Our little township is between two larger towns and it's surprising how often some tramp or boy from a poor family thinks it'd be advantageous to come sneaking through my sheds and see if there's anything both valuable and portable to be had.

That was why I got geese in the first place. They cost less to feed than a couple of big dogs, and they're more effective than a dog too, I can't count how many times I've seen some big burly wagon-driver delivering something to me, back away when the gaggle advanced. It's their beaks, snapping at just the right level to intimidate that does it. I don't have any trouble. They know me and Annie, and we know them, and before now, I've helped an injured one so they trust me and I suppose you get fond of someone who feeds you too.

They were in full cry again a few weeks later, same as last time. They went quiet again after a minute or two and I went back to sleep. It happened again a month after that and I was getting annoyed. Next time I'd get up, and if I saw whoever it was, I'd have something to say to them. Annie slept through these events of course, and I never got around to mentioning them to her.

It was the week after that I noticed an item in the two-page local broadsheet I picked up while shopping. nothing much, just a brief paragraph saying three men from the larger town six hour's stage-coach journey to the north had gone missing. All were known criminals so I'd bet no one was asking many questions. I grinned, on a spree most likely and they'd be back once they ran out of money – probably surprised anyone had even noticed their absence.

Well, more petty criminals went missing. I kept getting woken up by the geese and all that kept my leg from going mad about my walking about on it too much, was that hot bath and those bath salts. And then I had a burglar when I was still awake. It was almost one in the morning and I'd been caught up in a book I was reading. I'd put it down, made myself cocoa and I heard the gaggle start to scream just as I placed my empty mug on the kitchen table by the door.

I scooped up the old cavalry saber I keep handy and I was outside before the first yell died away. "Okay, who's there?"

There was a sort of squeal, a thrashing, and something was floundering on the ground. The geese closed in and the thrashing stopped. I flicked my torch in that direction and held the light there a moment. Then I went back inside and shut the door. I have a good imagination but I know when something is that and when it isn't. That hadn't been. I waited until daylight, went out to feed the geese, and noticed they didn't seem to be hungry. Thinking back, I suspected they hadn't been hungry after each night there'd been a commotion. And that's when I knew for sure I hadn't imagined what I'd seen.

I waited until the next day, and this time when I fed them I did it by hand. They came up one by one, took the wheat gently from my palm as they always had but this time, I reached out and carefully moved their heads so that I got a look inside each beak. Then I blinked. That certainly explained the missing burglars and the gaggle's lack of interest in breakfast on certain mornings. I thought about things over the next week and decided to say nothing. My friends don't sneak around my cabin in the early hours, and if for some reason they needed to, they'd hail the house loudly as they pulled up.

I couldn't see that my area was any poorer for the loss of a sprinkling of thieves either. So, there it was. I'd leave well enough alone, and I did. Over the weeks following I heard the geese tune up a time or two and stayed in the house, wondering as I listened to their yells, what had caused their change? And as I soaked in the bath one evening, the water dyed that odd shade of blue-green, I looked down – and two and two suddenly made nine. The bath salts!

The seller had said to keep my dog away from them. Maybe what he'd *really* meant, was 'all animals'? I asked about very quietly to see if I could find the man who'd driven that wagon, but no one knew anything about him. Just another traveling quack selling dubious items. But I wondered – where had the bath salts come from and what exactly were the claimed 'herbal additives'? What did they do to a bird or animal that drank enough of them and was any change permanent? Could whatever drank the stuff control the change or was it random?

Sixteen days later, I had an insight into that when I saw the cat hypnotize a mouse into coming out of hiding and walking right into the cat's jaws. It looked as if the change was geared to what the animal wanted. The geese hadn't liked their matriarch kicked to death in front of them, so maybe they'd wanted a way to make sure it didn't happen again? And the cat wanted an easy way to catch prey.

What else could have drunk the wastewater? It would only have been my cat inside, and outside the geese were usually around the hollow the moment they heard the water running out. It had taken months of regular drinking to make the changes. I used two bottles so far and for about one and a half they'd had all they wanted.

The other question was, once all the bath salts were gone, and there were no more to drink, would the cat and my geese revert to ordinary? Somehow, I thought so. Or I could put the bottles to one side and see now. I did so, and by watching Fluffy carefully I saw that the effects wore off in about a week or so. That was all right, if it took a month to begin, and a week to stop, I could safely have my bath salts every three weeks. And I'd bought all the peddler had had.

And then I remembered. I'd given three bottles of the bath salts to my friend with whom I'd stayed the night soon after the peddler had been. She led a miserable life with a husband who used her money, beat her, and ill-treated her big gentle coonhound as well. Andrea adored that dog and it adored her. And I wondered, if Smudge had been drinking the bath water, (and that's something house dogs often do) just what change would Andrea's dog wish for – how long would it take before my friend and her husband found out – and should I do anything?

I decided not to. Who'd believe the cause if anything did happen. Andy would be better off without him, and – I remembered my last visit – he'd come home early, just before I was about to leave and I'd heard his comment when she said I was there.

"Crippled cow, no use to any man. Oh, well, so long as she's going."

No. I'd do nothing – nothing but hope Smudge *had* been drinking Andy's bath water, and that the outcome would be 'suitable.' After all, what the geese had done had suited me – and all the decent folk hereabouts even if they didn't know it. I smiled.

THE WHEEL

Within the human condition, the great wheel of time has turned thus.

The lowly are now the exalted, the exalted are now merely dust.

I was asleep when the bugle rang out. I bolted upright, threw on overalls – they can be donned quickly, you can move freely in them, and they cover a multitude of sins – kicked on shoes, and ran for the school gates. Once there, I looked at Henderson.

"Virus Carriers?"

"Aye, Miss. Guess another crowd of them got to heading this way and arrived."

I looked at the massive gates halfway down the hill where the creatures we called carriers beat silently at the thick iron bars, until even those gates could buckle if this wasn't stopped. "Can you drop the portcullis behind them?"

I can, Miss. But that'll only catch the first hundred."

"That's a start. Do it, and alert the fire teams."

I listened as he gave instructions, the messenger raced away and ten minutes later I went to meet the teams as they turned out. "Carriers," I told them. "We'll see how many we can clean out before we call in the – ah – experts."

There were soft giggles as my girls lined up, tanks on their backs, flamethrower nozzles at the ready. The portcullis dropped, trapping carriers, the first fire-team moved down the road and lit up. I watched unmoved as the first installment of carriers died, and the second, the third, the fourth, but with the fifth…

Henderson arrived at my side. "Miss? We got no more fuel left."

I checked through the night-vision goggles and clamped my lips shut on unseemly words. We'd more than halved their numbers, but if that many broke through, there were still sufficient to slaughter or change every one of us they got their teeth into. All right, time for those who knew how to deal with carriers. I raised my voice in a long ringing call – and they came. Lining up on top of the wall along the edge of our plateau. Then they opened their mouths and sang.

Their singing was a low sound that rose and fell, not melodious to human ears as it increased, louder and louder in pitch, climbing to an edge until it rang in my ear-bones. Below us, the carriers began to shuffle back, that movement became a panic – as much as carriers *could* panic – and they pushed and shoved in their eagerness to escape the sound that was destroying them.

I smiled as the first of them plunged from the road. The plateau is high, and the narrow road that winds up to the school is cut into the side of the cliff's stone. To step off it in the final third of the path up to the school is to plummet some three hundred feet down, and that was exactly what those carriers were doing. The fall wouldn't kill them, but it would break so many bones they'd remain where they landed until I found time to take a killing patrol out. More carriers fell.

Henderson was chuckling happily. "That's another one of them b..." he cut off the word. "Sorry, Miss. But it's good to see them die."

I laid my hand on his shoulder briefly. "Yes," I agreed. "It is."

I left him and his assistants to clean up our road and escorted the fire-teams back to the school buildings where they could leave their equipment and return to bed. Behind me trotted the singers, now and again raising a questioning voice. I smiled; they knew they'd be paid for this night's work. We'd killed somewhere between three and four hundred carriers, which was excellent. And there had been at least another hundred carriers the singers had driven off the path to their permanent disablement before the remaining mass of them had fled. It'd been a fine night all around.

I paid the singer's price and retired to my own bed. It would be dawn in another hour and I normally got up then. I wouldn't sleep, so I'd spend the time writing my diary and checking supplies. With fuel for the flame-throwers used up we'd have to make a trip off the plateau in the next day or two. I needed a list.

I wrote one, and then sat back against my pillows enjoying the silence. A singer arrived, landed on the end of the bed, curled up and fell asleep while my hand stroked lovingly down his back. I thought of previous events and snarled silently. I'd never known who developed the virus, not even sufficient to know if it had been someone of the North or the South. Both were possible. Those of us in the South had been losing, but we'd cost the North dear, and more and more of those in power there had raised their voices on the topic. For myself, I thought it likely to have been the North, not by official agreement, but at the hands and knowledge of some rabid enthusiast.

Towards that belief was the fact that the first of the virus carriers had appeared on the Northern side of the Mason-Dixon line. I believed there'd been some sort of medical facility there and that a carrier had escaped it. It had taken time – too long a time – for it to dawn on those nearby what was happening, and by then it was too late to do anything effective. Carriers multiplied, over-ran whole areas, and entire cites became wastelands. You could shoot them, but they were tenacious of life. It was then a Major Lindly came up with the flame-throwers, which *were* effective, and then, the singers appeared.

Without them, we might still have survived, but not easily, and we'd not have done so well. And we, that is, those of the staff and school, *had* done well. I'd been the assistant headmistress of Talyn School when the virus broke out. The school took in those children who were without one parent, or orphaned but with an estate. Some were the children of diplomats from a number of countries, and whose parents wanted them where they could visit while continuing to receive an excellent education and finally there were those whose parents were simply extremely rich. The only requirements were money for fees, the ability to speak reasonable English, and the common sense to obey our rules. We could deal with anything else.

I'd always been an effective teacher, and an animal lover. When ten years ago in my late twenties I'd won a national sweepstakes – collecting the sort of money I could only dream of – Talyn's headmistress had come to me and made an offer.

She wanted to expand the school and its security as well. If I put in the money required, I could have a thirty-five percent share in the school, a place to keep my animals, and I'd be assistant headmistress.

I went to look over Talyn and a week later I'd agreed. After that, I went over the contract with my lawyer, signed, and paid up.

One of the new security methods put in place with my money over the years following had been to acquire a couple of flying machines. I gained a license over the two years following that purchase, and only months before the carriers first appeared, I had bought one of the very newest types for my own enjoyment – to find it would become our lifeline.

My money had also heightened and strengthened the wall that surrounded the school's hundred acres, and added small watchtowers in six places, including one at the top of the road where new arrivals would pass massive gates into the grounds. It was those precautions – and a few others – that had saved us when the carriers came.

Morning bell rang and, in the distance, I could hear the chatter of girls as they washed, dressed, and prepared for breakfast. I met the headmistress, Elise Anvert, as I emerged from my room. "My dear, was that a carrier attack last night?"

I nodded. "Don't worry, we killed several hundred and the singers drove the others off. I'll take a team down to finish the ones that fell."

"When?"

"During sports time."

Her faded hazel eyes twinkled at me. "I suppose that's appropriate. But be careful, Janice, we can't afford to lose any of you."

I smiled back. "Oh, I'll take a singer. Only one won't hold off carriers for long, but long enough for us to get back to the flyer and take off." I knew that was so. It wouldn't be the first time it had happened.

"Good, and burn the bodies if possible."

I certainly would. We'd discovered this in the second year after we were overrun, that animals which ate carrier bodies sometimes became carriers too. In isolated places where carriers hadn't reached them yet, there might still be animals we could be sure weren't infected. But I didn't know of any. We had a farm here, a small herd of cows, a piggery, a flock of colored sheep, and free-range geese and hens. I'd brought the geese after one of my initial trips. They were noisy, aggressive, and left slimy smelly deposits where ever they went, but they'd long since paid for themselves; in eggs, in roast goose, and in warning us when carriers in ones and twos had made it to the plateau and tried to get through the gates. They were of a breed that couldn't fly, so we didn't have to worry about them abandoning us either.

"My dear. When are you making a shopping trip?"

"The day after tomorrow, I think," I said absently, thinking of my list. "We need more fuel for the flame-throwers, I want to raid a doctor's home for possible medicines, or first aid things, and any equipment we can use, a general store if I can find one that hasn't been looted, and I'll look for clothing and footwear or leather and fabrics and sewing supplies." I looked at her. "Why? Did you want to come with us?"

"If it isn't too much trouble?"

Impulsively I hugged her. "No, it isn't. Anyhow, I want Marion to fly the other flyer, so there should be plenty of room."

"Is she ready?"

"I've been training her – and Pam James and the Inali twins – for months. We have to take a chance sometime. If we can find another flyer or two of the same type, we may be able to expand as you suggested last year."

Elise pursed her lips, looking down at the planking. "It would help. We need more grazing." Her head came up and she met my gaze. "It's been five years since the virus. I know last night there were hundreds of carriers, but I believe numbers all over have decreased. It may be that in another five years they'll be gone."

"Along with ninety-nine percent of the population," I agreed heavily.

"Yes, so we must continue to be careful. My dear, you know, I'm so glad I asked you to join me. You've been a tower of strength, you and your singers, and I don't believe we'd have survived without you all."

I halted in the doorway and took her hands. "It was the best day's work I ever did, accepting," I said softly. "Right down to that statue."

Elise laughed. "Well, it wasn't doing anything in the museum, they had no visitors anymore; and I've always liked it."

I grinned. So did I. When the carrier plague struck, we'd been in the final stages of improving the spaces between school classroom blocks. We'd put in lawns and raked gravel paths, and the last feature had been intended to be a fountain with a sprite on a plinth. We had the fountain working, but we'd never received the sprite – the town from which it was to have come had been over-run a week before delivery. So, towards the end of year One I'd listened to Elise and gone in my flyer to a museum where they had an exhibit of genuine Egyptian statues. I'd brought one back and we'd installed that on the plinth. It had been greatly admired by everyone ever since.

A bugle blasted an urgent summons, I heard a saucepan hit the floor and stepped hastily away from the doorway as a rush of girls passed me going to their posts. Elise walked into the dining room and sat down. "You go ahead, my dear. I'll have breakfast and not get in anyone's way." She grabbed up several apples and a chunk of cheese, passing them to me. "Here, eat as you move."

I bit into an apple as I trotted for the gates again, muttering. That was the trouble with carriers. So far as we understood it, they didn't have genuine intelligence, but they had a sort of sly cunning that told them where we were, and that we were prey. Some aspect of the infection drove them to seek out uninfected humans, and at Talyn there was a concentration of us that had drawn them here month after month after year … the bugle sounded again and I ran faster, three of my singers coming from somewhere around the buildings to bound behind me.

Henderson was already at the gate. "They're trying again, miss, the first lot have hit the half-way gates. What do we do?"

I knew what he was asking. Flame-throwers were wonderful at dealing with carriers, but we were out of fuel after that last attack, and things could get desperate if there were enough attackers. However, I wasn't out of methods yet. "Hand out bows. Tell the girls to form ranks of three." Once we had the arrows shared out, I spoke. "Jessie, Meg, Amabel, you're runners. Make sure the archers always have sufficient arrows of the type they use. You archers in reserve, be ready to step up when anyone in the ranks tires. Now, follow me."

I led them down to where the carriers thrust against the gates. "On my signal. Hold, and – first rank shoot. Second rank shoot, third rank..." We were initially using long bows. Each arrow drove thorough a carrier and into a second. Linked, they often fell from the road as they fought each other to get free. As each rank of the girls fired, they stepped back to reload and the next hail of shafts struck home. By the time the longbow arrows were used up we'd also exhausted twice the ranks of archers, and I called for the crossbow-women to fall in.

"Fire at will." They were using the modern system of slot-in spring-load quivers that allowed them to fire ten bolts before needing to reload, and with five archers in a line, the amount of fire that could be poured out was tremendous. Carriers went down in heaps. Headshots will take them out very satisfactorily and after five years, my girls were experts. But there were so many carriers, we shot and shot, girls fell out, too tired to activate the crossbows or to hold the weight of them. They were replaced, and still the carriers came.

Henderson was plucking at my sleeve. "There'll be no more arrows left in a couple of rounds, Miss."

I looked to where a final group of carriers plodded up the road. Maybe eighty or ninety of them, but beyond that I could see no more. If we could deal with these coming then we'd have time to retrieve arrows, let the girls rest, and I could make a foray outside for the things we had to have.

"Henderson. Stand by the upper gate. When I call, open the mid-gates and be ready to close the upper gate again if required."

He eyed me, a solid elderly man who'd been a soldier before he became Talyn's caretaker, keeper of school legends, and secrets, and right hand to Elise and I. "You gonna use that thing you and the twins been working on?"

"I see no other choice."

"Taking them with you?"

"Certainly not," I said briefly.

He turned away, hurrying back up the road as we began to retreat, firing our last bolts, the mid-gates clanging shut behind us, latches clicking home. I shepherded the archers through the upper gate and saw that safely shut. There was an engine's roar as Henderson drove up the tractor. We'd fitted it with a bulldozer blade, one that was as wide as the road and which could be tilted from side to side. I'd need someone to ride shotgun, I opened my mouth to ask, and Henderson stepped onto the side ledge, leaning back against the curved rest.

"My job, I reckon."

He looked at me and I could only agree. He had two sawn-off guns, crossed bandoliers filled with shells, and a belt full of them as well. I put the tractor into motion and as I did so, Alex the singer leaped to join me. I slowed the tractor and received a supercilious glare. What? I thought he shouldn't come too; didn't I know that *no* one told a singer where he could or couldn't go? Actually, I did. I shut up and drove on down the road to the mid-gates, Henderson called back to Pam as we reached them and they swung open. I charged, whooping in a mix of terror and rage.

It was a melee from then on. I used the blade to sweep carriers off the road and over the cliff edge but some managed to cling onto the machine and begin climbing towards me. Henderson shot and shot, blasting them from their holds as I flung the tractor back and forth, carriers died, but there always seemed to be more. The sounds had brought others within hearing and they'd joined the attack. Unexpected silence fell, and I gasped, knowing it meant our death. No more shells. Sooner or later, unless I retreated, the carriers would reach us both, and if I reversed as slowly as I'd have to on that narrow road, they were faster than the big tractor. My retreat would only bring them to the gates – which would have to be opened to let us in and that I couldn't allow. We would die here, better to die here than open Talyn to death for everyone.

Then my Alex moved forward, opened his mouth, and sang; a song that was soaring razor-edged warning and threat as well. To kill us they must pass him, and that he would not allow. We were his, his, *his*! His song rose to a pitch that sent the carriers staggering back, some falling from the edge, others lurching into reverse down the road as the notes in his song addled what passed for their brains, slashing knife-edged into their cells and causing ultimate disruption. And I followed, sweeping my blade back and forth so that by the time we were on the lowest reaches of the path we were alone, Henderson, the now silent singer, and I.

We backed up the road to loud cheers, the upper gate opened and what looked like everyone at the school surrounded us, hugging, praising, and weeping in relief. Alex was swept into pair after pair of arms while his eyes almost crossed, so smug did he look.

Dinner that night was a feast. In the morning, I decided it would be better to deal with the shopping list first and two flyers lifted away mid-morning.

We went as far as half a tank of fuel would take us, found a depot with two more of that type of machine and, having landed just outside a town of some five hundred buildings that was well into the desert fringe and had the fuel bowsers. We returned with four flyers filled with our plunder. During the flight I had noticed too, that the carriers seen below us were few and far between. They seemed to exist only in small numbers and I wondered if what Elise and I had discussed was happening.

"They're unnatural," Elise had said when the plague began. "They can't reproduce except by infection. Where a group of animals is infected, I've seen they don't have newborn young ones with them, carriers don't have babies either. Once all those infected have died, there'll may well be no more."

"The question," I'd pointed out, "is, how long will it take for them all to die? They seem to have an unnatural vitality. They live on anything at all that they eat and they endure horrific injuries."

"Quite so, my dear. But eventually there must be a last one of them."

It couldn't come too soon for me, I thought as I parked my flyer and the other three dropped into line. With us was a tiny group of eight soldiers I'd found a few miles short of the town, trying to reach us – heading desperately for the almost mythical place of refuge their leader had heard about a year ago. Sergeant Hoyt was staring around as he exited the 'copter.

"Hell of a place." My singer approached and patted a khaki-clad knee. "And who's this? Isn't he a big cat? What breed is he?" He scooped up and cradled Alex who purred approval.

I stretched out a hand to rub under my cat's chin and the purr redoubled. "He's a singer, when I came to Talyn I bred cats as a hobby. The year before the plague, one of the females escaped. She returned in kitten and we believe the father may have been a wildcat or an unusual breed of some variety. The kittens were huge, they could also 'sing' in an odd way. Some sort of mutation with a pitch that drives off the carriers. The cats hate the creatures too. Alex was the one that came with Henderson and me in that last attack I was telling you about. If it hadn't been for him, we'd have died and carriers of the virus might have overrun the school.

"So, he's the one? A proper warrior, eh fella?"

We walked around the edge of the buildings towards the fountain and Sergeant Hoyt grinned at the statue on its five-foot plinth. "Real cat-lovers here huh?"

I smiled as I nodded. The statue was of Bast in her cat aspect, in the common seated posture and even then, a good three feet in height, carved from black stone. I saw with interest that someone had placed a pectoral around her neck, made from a number of gold chains and several necklaces I recognized. A tribute to the singers which had so often saved us – and to my beloved Alexander who done so in front of everyone?

I didn't comment, not then or later when I found some of the girls were murmuring requests or thanks to Her as they passed. Nor did I say anything when we expanded into another isolated area two years later and the new group asked for singers to go with them. Not ordinary cats that might be found elsewhere, no, they had to be the Singers of Talyn.

And late at night, in my bed after they and their chosen singers had gone, I thought of the future. The carriers were definitely fewer these days. They could be dying out as Elise believed. But it might be a generation – even two – before the last of them were gone. While they lingered, singers would be prized and for so many more years as people remembered. The wheel had turned. Cats had been sacred, then creatures of the devil to be burned, then beloved pets, and now, for a while again at least, they were the revered singers of songs that protected humanity.

And while so many people had died, I thought, I'd bet most mice and rats had escaped the carriers. We'd need cats to deal with them even after the last carrier died. I reached down and cuddled Alex as he thumped me affectionately with his head. Maybe, if I carefully indoctrinated those who listened, I could see to it that the next turn of the wheel never came. The cats of Talyn, Singers and Protectors, it had a pleasant ring to it.

A MAN WITHOUT MERIT

Felicity usually lived up to her name – but once in a while … And in this case, that's how it was on the Heston Ranch the evening of the accident. Felicity was a good girl but John Press was a bad man. What he liked though, were good girls. He'd left a string of them, no longer as naive or gullible – or by the way it was seen then, as good – weeping into their lemonade. While their parents plotted hurriedly to find a nice boy who hadn't heard of their daughter's downfall.

That was in an area well removed from Bodie, and so it was that the small township was where he chose to try his luck next. What he'd ignored was that with the advent of mail coaches, one of the new routes went through Bodie, and so it was that Felicity received a tear-stained letter from her cousin. It detailed exactly how Rosie had been caught in John's web, deceived, defiled, and utterly devastated.

> *…And so my parents say I have no choice. I'm to wed a local rancher, but Flis, he's old, he's ugly, and it's said his previous wife killed herself because of how he treated her. I too would rather be dead - before such befalls me. So this is farewell, but beware of John Press. He is utterly convincing in his protestations, but do not believe him should he cross your path. At least should he do so, watch what he does, and learn. Not as I did, too late, but in time to save yourself.*
>
> *Rosie.*

Felicity only hoped that her cousin hadn't done anything irrevocable, to find that there'd been another letter in the weekly mail, from her aunt to her parents, announcing the accidental death of their daughter. Felicity wept with them, saying nothing of her own letter, but she knew, she remembered, and when a month later a well-dressed man arrived in town to stay a few weeks, she knew precisely who –

172

and what – he was the moment she heard his name. This was the man responsible for the death of her best friend and kin.

Press meanwhile was looking over the current crop of young ladies. He settled on Abigail Swenson, only child of parents who had married late. (With luck he'd inherit quite quickly,) The Swenson parents discovered that Press had a private income, that his parents lived in New York, and that his grandfather had been a general.

Not that any of the tale was true. Press's parents had been dirt-poor ranchers who died penniless of influenza and were buried in the boot hill of a miserable hamlet. As for his private income, he'd worked for a man in New York, absconded with a large sum, used that to buy good clothes and guns – he could shoot well – which had led to more money via a number of successful – and illicit – schemes ranging from blackmail to bank robbery.

Felicity watched him, allowing it to be seen – but by him alone – that she might be seduced if he moved carefully and without his intentions being recognized by any but himself. Press had no way of knowing that Felicity watched him, listened to the gossip about him, and was far more aware of his comings and goings that Press would ever have believed.

"He's so good-looking," Abigail sighed in the sewing circle. "He came to dinner, I cooked, and he kissed my hand. He said my cooking was as delightful as I was." And a week later. "He dances so well. Mama played the piano after dinner. He complimented me on my lightness of foot."

It took three months of careful skulking, looks of encouragement, and then she had a piece of good fortune. A small rumour ran down the back alleys of Bodie that the next coach would bring money to buy gold from the mine nearby. And – really useful – the coach should be entering town after midnight. It would be a full moon, and if they didn't hurry, it would be safe enough. Press had heard the same rumour. At the church dance that evening he spoke to Felicity, and buoyant from the news and rather a lot of good wine he made a comment that left her thinking.

After which everything was going Press's way or so he was convinced. He held up the mail coach, collected a very large sum in gold eagles. Secreted that beneath a pile of rocks just outside town, circled and rode in from a different direction. No one was about. He stabled his horse, slipped back into his rented room, and slept the sleep of a man entirely without conscience.

Felicity slept similarly, so far as she was concerned, she was Nemesis, and that lady needed to regret nothing. Two nights later after a soft word in passing, Press appeared atop a ladder at Felicity's bedroom window. She drifted to him, beribboned lawn nightie fluttering, eyes demurely cast down – and a loop of curtain cord in one hand and partly concealed behind her back.

The window wasn't large. To climb in he must bend double. Felicity flicked out one hand, then the other. Her eyes met his – half dazed as he now was, and her voice was very soft. "Rosie was my cousin. She died because she loved and trusted you."

She reached out, took his shoulders in her hands, and thrust with all her strength. He fell backwards, was brought up by the curtain cord looped about his throat and hung there, the blow she'd struck first leaving him too dazed to save himself as he choked to death. She waited briefly, then screamed, and screamed again. Piercing sounds that were answered by her parents' footsteps and voices calling to her – while she looked down cold-eyed at the man who had caused the death of her best friend, and who had now met his own.

The gold now reposed behind a board in the Heston barn. If it was ever needed, it would be there to hand. The marshal found the empty canvas bank-bag under Press's small-clothes, and had prizes been given, it would have been Bodie's gossip prize-winner of the year. John Press had been a stage-coach robber. Abigail Swenson's suitor had tried to climb in through Felicity Heston's window at midnight. Uninvited – or so she said. But was he? Of course, said others, why else would she have pushed him out again?

In the end it was decided. There should be a trial, Felicity Heston *had* caused the man's death after all. Abigail Swenson testified. No, she was not engaged to Mr. Press, it was quite true he'd been courting her, but she'd decided against him. She had intended to tell him so on his next visit, and with her father's approval. The jury considered this and in an interim announcement stated in their opinion Miss Swenson was an intelligent girl.

The marshal testified. He'd found out a number of things about John Press. He detailed them, adding that Press's possessions would go as some compensation to the men who'd lost the purchase money for the mined gold, he was congratulated on his contacts and decision.

Felicity testified after that. Mr. Press had been pursuing her. She had disliked him, given him no encouragement, he had taken that amiss, and in some wicked attempt he had appeared at her bedroom window and sought entrance. He had proclaimed his unalterable determination to make her his, and in fear for her virtue and her life, she had pushed him and he had fallen.

No, the curtain cord often hung looped at the window. He must have accidentally inserted his head as he tried to enter a window which was almost too small for a grown man. She had screamed desperately for help as he fell. She had feared he would be injured when he struck the ground, or that if he were uninjured, he could attempt entry again and attack her. And that, she explained, weeping crystal tears to the jury, (who unanimously acquitted her,) was the whole tale of 'how John Press was hung.'

THE BOOKLOVER

Mrs. Ross was a widow. Her husband had died during the Civil War and left her well provided for. She had no relatives remaining, no desire to remarry, and her father's bequest of his library. So, she came west to find a place where she could live, unbothered by those who thought she should marry again, and where she could purchase a home to house her father's book collection – which she loved as much if not more than he had.

She found a house. It was insufficient in size for the library but she also found an ex-soldier who was a good carpenter and he built her a room that would house the thousands of books, complete with in-built shelving, a moveable ladder, and a small bathroom off the room, so anyone spending hours with the books need not leave the room by more than a few paces. Over the years of the war her books had become her life. The people in them were her friends and as the years passed, she cared less and less for real people and more and more for those in the volumes she cherished.

Gradually one or two of us learned her story. The daughter of a scholar, and a scholar herself, she had never been pretty. A small plain girl she had matured into a small plain woman, so her father was mildly surprised when out of the blue a suitor appeared. Thomas Ross was a man of good family and an inheritance, although this was not apparent at the beginning of the courtship.

He won Miss Anderwood's heart with little effort, never before had she been important to anyone besides her absent-minded father. And it must be said that she enjoyed the attention she received from Thomas and also the envy in the eyes of the other girls she knew when they noted Thomas' good looks and air of breeding.

Her father was a man who'd always been comfortably off, the son of a merchant. He had been well educated, and had made a good match with a girl from an impoverished family of minor nobility. She had married Mr. Anderwood with some regret but had managed to do her duty to the tune of two sons and a daughter. However, both sons had been lost in the war, along with the husband, so, when her father died five years after the war ended, Mrs. Ross had inherited all that might have gone to them along with her husband's wealth.

The library had had its genesis in a shelf of books her great-grandfather had acquired along with his family home. Her grandfather had found them worth keeping, and begun, on his own inheritance of his father's property, by adding to them with novels of the day published in the most expensive editions. Her father had added to that considerably, slowly filling the shelves with good editions of the classics and first editions of books he was particularly fond of. As Emily grew, she had been permitted to read from the shelves and by the time she was twelve, she was an avid reader.

Two years later her period of mourning upon her mother's death was leavened by further reading – and by buying entire boxes of new volumes – as she discovered that buried mentally in a book she could forget her unhappiness. As she read more and more, she also became interested in books for themselves and began in a small way, with her father's encouragement to involve herself in the rarities of the book world. Sometimes she managed to purchase one or two for the library, and her father, happy to see her spirits improving, added to that by setting up a library fund and allowing her to buy books from that.

Emily was given a Siamese cat on her fortieth birthday and after that, she was never without one, the present incumbent being replaced upon his death by another exactly like him. All were seal points directly brought – illegally so far as the originating country was concerned – from Siam, and all were devoted to her as she was to them. Upon her husband and her brother's deaths Emily clung closer to her father and her books. By now she was becoming known as a collector and catalogs began to make their way to her mailbox from booksellers and sale houses, as well as private dispersal sales.

The original library had outgrown the single small room by now and after discussion, she and her father enlarged that. Then her father, after a period of poor health, and their discussion on what she might do when this occurred, died, and within weeks the house was sold, all she possessed was packed up and stored, and Emily set forth to find a new home for herself, her books and her cat.

She did so in the small township in a western state where I lived, and while I would never have called us friends, I could honestly say that we became good acquaintances, and I liked her. The house she had purchased was a substantial one outside of town, which had belonged to a retired high-ranking soldier. However, he and his wife had no children, and on his death, his wife had sold the house to Emily and gone east to family.

After that, she was happy to live there alone, save for the latest Siamese, a housekeeper who came in daily, and her library which by now was heading towards the twenty thousand mark. The only thing she left the house for was yet another sale, another purchase of books. Gradually the township almost forgot that anyone lived at Embury – as the house was known after the previous owner – and the local children used to dare each other to walk up the drive and peer through the huge heavily curtained windows in search of something to see.

But few things never change, and over the years, Emily's health also began to fail and for the first time she became frightened. What would happen to her beloved books and her cat? She emerged from Embury and for the first time in ten years she traveled to town, not for a book purchase, but to see her lawyers.

The doyen of the firm produced sherry and biscuits and listened to her worry. He smiled; there was no problem. Emily had a considerable amount of money and nothing could be easier than to utilize this to ensure the safety of her books and cat. He gave advice, Emily heard, and a will was carefully drawn up and signed later that afternoon.

Emily returned home and to the stunned amazement of the local newspaper proprietor visited the paper and announced she wished to place an advertisement. She produced a piece of paper with this and paying him, left a somewhat flabbergasted man to sort out the typeface and position of one of the most interesting advertisements he had ever received.

Staff are wanted for positions at Embury. Required are a gardener, a cook, and housekeeper. All positions are daily, and generous remuneration is offered. Applicants must be cat lovers and an interest in books is preferable. Apply to J. Wiggins, c/ — Wiggins, Wiggins & Spratt, enclosing references and written application.

To say that there were indeed applications is laboring the obvious, even in our small township and with the surrounding area but lightly populated. Mr. Wiggins was kept busy sorting through letters and even busier for longer interviewing those applicants who passed his screening. Eventually he found three persons he believed perfect for the positions, and they were dispatched to Emily for a final interview.

The gardener was not particularly important to her, and the interview was cursory. He knew his work, had excellent references, and was a polite middle-aged man who would not presume. She hired him and turned to the next hopefuls. These were more important. They would be in the house with her and must be suitable. But Mr. Wiggins had chosen wisely. The cook was a comfortable woman who had left previous employment only upon the death of her employer.

The other servant accepted, described in the advertisement as a housekeeper, was myself. My husband had died two months earlier. We'd had little savings, and I was in need of money. I had chosen not to apply for the work directly, that could be seen as an imposition on our knowing each other. But as Emily knew I loved books and could do the work, I was chosen from among the four possibilities for that position.

Almost a Victorian, Emily might have been horrified the first time she confronted her true emotions towards me. Instead, there was a flush of love that flowed so sweetly between us she was unable to summon any feelings of guilt. She might have considered herself too old but my honest and patent devotion was balm for any such idea.

And so, the years slipped away. The library became more and more a haven for us while the rest of the house ran like a well-oiled machine. Long since we had fallen into a warmth of cherishing that flowed over to every aspect of our lives together. We were friends, sisters, two old women who lived for each other alone and the books that were almost our children. But time stops for no one, not even the most devoted of friends.

My Emily's health was now precarious. She became terrified as to what would become of me when she was gone. Mr. Wiggins was summoned and again he provided comfort, advice and finally a draft. Nothing could be more easily settled, the will was signed, witnessed and he departed. I saw his gentle smile as he went and guessed at his thoughts.

Perhaps he should have disapproved, but our love was so clear, he could not find it within his heart to condemn us. There were no close relatives left. That Emily had left all in trust would create no legal crisis for a semi-retired lawyer who wanted no more than peace by his fireside these days.

The house, garden and most of all, the library, all were left in trust, together with Emily's wealth. I was to become the mistress of their estate. Never to leave, unable to be sent away from the home and books I too loved. The money would go to paying for all to be kept in order, to portion out for taxes. The surplus each year was to be held available to purchase further books. Even the current Siamese was not forgotten. He was listed as a staff member, a stipend arranged, and I could choose successors when he departed the house and life. Embury, the library, and resident Siamese would continue. Emily regretted she must one day, leave her home, her love, her books and her cat. But she had done her best to see that even without her they would survive.

After that, she grew frailer. Our love burned as truly, but now the fire was a softer glow. A nurturing, caring love, that warmed old bones. Emily's bed became her resting place for much of the day. In the evenings I read to her, and while we ate, we discussed possible purchases from the many mailed catalogs received. As Emily weakened, she began to dread leaving her books. What if I died too, what if the new manager would not love the many tiered volumes as we did?

It became my love's obsession that her books were calling. Sometimes she fell asleep to dream drifting dreams, in which her books shared strange knowledge with her. I understood, accepting, since I too had come to love the books passionately. I could understand how terrified Emily was that someone might come, someone who did not care for them as we did. I made a decision then. Saying nothing, I had a comfortable bed moved downstairs into a corner by the great fireplace. It was accepted with all the love with which it had been done.

Soon my Emily no longer moved from the library at all. It was just after this that her dreams began to change. As though they had been awaiting the right time, her books invaded her dreams again and again. Emily was still unable to be sure of their message, but she knew it was vital to her and she strained to understand. Hoping that one day she would know what they were trying to convey so urgently. She would talk of this and I listened – hoping.

Then one night the information came to her. The words – so blurred until now – shifted slowly into something she could understand. Emily woke me to talk and talk she did. Clear detailed instructions were given and I swore to carry them out. I was unsure of some of it; could it be so? But I loved Emily with all my heart, if this was my beloved's last wish all should be done as she wanted.

Five nights later, Emily slipped away in her sleep. For an hour after I woke to find her gone, I lay holding my love and weeping my loss. Finally, I forced myself to calmness, to send for doctor, lawyer, and the undertaker of the new modest parlor in the township. The ceremony and subsequent cremation were swift and attended only by myself and Mr. Wiggins. That was the first part of Emily's instructions, After the rites concluded, Emily's ashes were carried into the library and I set out to complete the remainder of Emily's request. I wept as I did so, praying her belief was correct. That her books had indeed told her a secret.

Nights passed without result. After three months had gone and Emily's hope was still unrealized, I moved back to our upstairs bedroom. When Emily had been dead a year, I spent the anniversary compulsively cleaning the library and remembering our love. How incredible it had seemed to me and how I missed her and all we had been. Once the great room was spotless, I remained, unable to leave. The bed had remained in the corner and grieving and weary I lowered myself onto it, drifting into sleep.

And in my dreams, someone was calling. I recognized the voice, starting up with a leap as I called back and before me, Emily stood. She smiled, all our long love in her eyes, drifting to the shelf and selecting a book, she handed it to me. Then like mist, she flowed into the books and was gone. Alone, I froze, clutching a book in silence. Yet it was only an outward silence. Within me, sang a hymn to the Goddess, a song of love and joy!

I had never really believed. But out of love and hope I'd had taken the ashes. On the inside cover of each book, I'd carefully rubbed a speck her ashes from the urn. That was the message of the books. That if belief is strong enough, it can create a reality. Emily's belief had stood the test. In the library I cradled the volume, still seeing the mist that was Emily, as it vanished into the books.

I felt my face crumple into a quiet radiance of joy and final belief. If I also chose the right person when my own times came and they obeyed my instructions too, one day Emily and I would be together always, and not only that, we'd be from that time and forever a part of our beloved books.

* * *

They say that outside a small western town there is a house no one can see save at certain times and only then if you are the right person – a true booklover.

KIN TO THE PUMA

I was driving quietly down the road, Rabbit (because of how fast he could spring away) between the shafts, my silver Tiger cuddled comfortably into my side, and above me a blue sky. It may seem odd to take my cat visiting, but Tiger is a smart sensible animal and doesn't panic, besides, he enjoys meeting new people, and usually they enjoy meeting him. My husband had suggested I not go out today, some gossip about a small renegade group of Comanche being in the area. I hadn't said I wouldn't, I thought as Rabbit jogged along. I'd just nodded. It was probably all nonsense anyhow.

We rounded the bend, came out of the shadow of the clump of trees there, and I found to my consternation that perhaps I should have listened to my husband – I only hoped I'd have the chance to hear him again. There were nine of them facing me. Eight were young, no more than thirteen or so, skinny... I looked closer, and that wasn't a natural leanness, it was hunger. Then I saw the man behind them.

He would be around my own age, in his late forties, but unlike the young men, his clothing was clean and while he too was thin, there was muscle there. I hastily looked elsewhere. He was naked from the waist up and not something a respectable woman should be looking at. We regarded each other, a comfortable middle-aged ranch woman, and nine Comanche – all armed, I noticed. One of the boys moved and I saw him half-raise his tomahawk.

Tiger meowed sharply and all attention shifted abruptly to him. The older man looked surprised. Tiger meowed again, and the man approached my cat. I didn't want to start anything I'd lose, but he wasn't going to hurt my cat. "Glosbe," I said, stroking my cat. It was about the only Comanche word I knew, one I'd heard some years ago from a passing trapper. It meant puma and as I said it, I indicated a small size with thumb and forefinger. The man halted by the buggy, repeated the word and gesture, then reached out a tentative hand. My cat

183

considered this new human, found him acceptable, squawked politely, licked the forefinger offered and rubbed the side of his face against the hand. One of the boys giggled. I smiled involuntarily. The man smiled too, and suddenly we were no longer strangers who should be enemies.

I moved slowly. It doesn't do to startle people. I hauled out the stuffed hamper from under the buggy seat, opened the lid on each side and presented it. The Crawfords weren't expecting me today, and they wouldn't miss the contents of this hamper anyhow. Nine pairs of eyes focused and I realized they had probably never seen a hamper before. Tiger had however, he promptly stuck his head inside, stepped back with a handkerchief-wrapped pack of sandwiches, and I took it from him smiling. I had no idea if my unexpected guests spoke any English, but they'd understand gestures, surely?

I unwrapped the food so they could see what was offered, and handed it to the nearest boy the tallest – and the thinnest. I could count all his ribs. He may not have recognized a ham sandwich, but he knew food when he saw and smelled it. He said something to his companions, tore a corner off and gave it to Tiger who was only too happy to share. He ate the ham, moved onto the battered bread more slowly, but in minutes he was done and looking hopefully for more.

The boy grinned, the older man took the food, shared it out among them and they all simply sat down on the ground to eat. I stepped out of the buggy, bringing the hamper with me, hooked Rabbit's reins over a corner of the seat, and let him wander. He never went far. Then, ignoring the dust, I sat cross-legged on the ground, and item by item distributed the hamper's contents – apple pies, blackberry tartlets, bottles of lemonade, more sandwiches – roast beef this time, a homemade cake and several types of biscuits.

Tiger went happily from person to person, being talked to in Comanche and petted, while he purred and head-butted his acknowledgement of the attentions. How truly was it said, "God created the cat so that man may caress the tiger." It didn't take a lot of time before there were only crumbs and a drop or two in the bottom of the bottles – the sweet lemonade had been a real favorite.

Tiger made a final round of his friends while the older

man's gaze met mine. He inclined his head to where Rabbit had wandered, and I rose, walked to my horse, led him back to the hamper, and the man placed that carefully into the buggy. I climbed in, he lifted his hand, said something of which the only word I could distinguish was 'Glosbe,' and stepped back. The boys smiled at me. I smiled back. Tiger who was now on the buggy-seat beside me, gave a feline chirp, and I took up the reins.

Something made me pause then. Perhaps he was half-naked because he lacked a shirt? Impulsively I caught up the woollen lap robe and handed it to him. "Please," I said. "I want you to have this. You need to be warm to look after the boys." His fingers closed about it, and slowly he inclined his head in a formal gesture. I inclined mine, and clicked to Rabbit. He walked forward, and when I looked back a few minutes later, the land was empty. Well, I'd always heard the Comanche were good at vanishing.

I was home again before Luke got back and I said nothing of my day. He wouldn't have approved, and, come to that, nor would anyone else I knew, but somewhere in a corner of my heart I cherished the memory of a couple of hours when my silver tabby Tiger had brought together two peoples who were not so different that they didn't both like cats.

* * *

I heard more of the story months later. How the army had attacked a group of Comanche women and older children, how the surviving children had been taken away and placed with a church mission to be taught better. Three months later, the boys had escaped, possibly with help from someone outside. The girls had remained anther month before they too escaped.

I remembered the hunger in child eyes, the cheap shabby ill-kept clothing, the thinness of young bodies, and how they had smiled at my Tiger, petted him, and I acknowledged that had the man with them wished, I would have been dead. All I owned could have been taken as payment for dead mothers, aunts, and elder sisters, who had done nothing to deserve death from ambush.

I hoped that wherever they were now, whatever place they had found in which to hide, that they were safe, that they were relearning happiness. And, here I grinned to myself, that wherever it was, I hoped too that they might have a cat to share that place with them. While Luke was out, I wrote the events in my diary next day, and still smiling at the memories, I returned it to the hiding place under a drawer in my bedside table.

* * *

Three years later – no, I hadn't altered any of my bad habits despite that scare – I was driving back from a visit to friends, Tiger by my side as usual, Rabbit between the shafts, when a man slunk out of the brush by the road. I glanced up. Through a gap I could see there was a dead horse there, blood drying in a long swath over one shoulder. Just inside the brush by the road there lay a saddle and bridle, along with a pair of stuffed saddlebags. I didn't have to look twice to make the assumption whoever or whatever he was, he was up to no good, and a man of poor character. He grabbed Rabbit's reins, hauled him to a stop, and leered up at me.

"All right, lady, get down, I'm taking the horse and the pretties you're wearing. Pity I don't have more time or that wouldn't be all. Shame you don't have a gun too."

Tiger moved forward to stand between us, looked up and hissed, then he wailed. I'd heard the sound before and I knew it for what it was. A declaration of war. I snatched at him even as a hand struck out. My cat ducked neatly, and a set of claws ripped the length of a grimy arm. His victim howled, said several things I shall most definitely not repeat, and produced a knife. He stabbed at Tiger, and without even thinking I interposed my arm, screaming in pain as the knife tip gashed my wrist.

Tiger howled again. Ears flat, mouth open, he moved forward, and someone rose out of the brush behind the distracted man who'd waylaid us. A rock came down with the sound of an axe into a watermelon. My enemy went flat in a way that said he wouldn't be getting up again and I was face to face with someone I remembered. He'd been the tallest and the thinnest of the boys, the one who'd petted Tiger first. He stooped over the body checked its status and his look was pure satisfaction. Tiger sat back and chirruped at our saviour and the boy smiled, reaching out to stroke him.

"Glosbe," he said making the gesture for small, and I laughed pointing where the ripped skin and blood showed on a limp arm.

"Warrior glosbe."

A nod. I fumbled out my handkerchief and bound my wrist. The injury could have been worse, but that I was wearing a wide silver bracelet which had mostly protected me. I took that off slowly, let the boy see I was studying the dead man, then I inclined my head in the formal motion I had seen made before. I held out the bracelet. "Thank you. From a glosbe warrior to a Comanche warrior." I saw he got at least the sense of that from his nod and his hand running down Tiger's back again before he slipped the bracelet over his wrist, pausing briefly to admire it.

I pointed to the saddle bags, saddle and bridle. He handed them up, then with a final stroke for Tiger and a nod to me, he faded into the brush and was gone. He left the rock lying by the body and I smiled unpleasantly to myself. No evidence to tell against my story. The body bore Tiger's marks, anyone can use a rock, and, I opened the nearest saddle-bag and found what I'd guessed to be there. Banknotes, coins, and women's jewellery. My attacker was a bank robber. No one would ask too many questions.

Now, I glanced about. No sign of anyone yet although I'd wager that somewhere there was a posse hunting furiously. I dropped from the buggy, hauled the body into the brush, and checked it and the dead horse over. That had been shot – a rifle I thought and not initially a lethal bullet. The man's body had no gun, just an empty holster. Dropped probably and no time to stop to grab it again. His pockets were empty, but I found the knife scabbard, took that, put the knife back in it and tucked it under the buggy seat.

By now, my wrist was aching quite painfully, and I climbed back up, set Rabbit in motion and headed for town. Half an hour later I met the posse riding towards me, halting them with an upraised hand.

"Marshal, there's no hurry."

Jack Howard's known me most of his life. "Miz James, now why'd you say that? Could be you know something?"

I nodded. "Could be. What I do know is that there's a dead man and a dead horse a few miles back that way," I pointed. "And I've a pair of full saddle-bags here I took off the man, that you might be wanting."

I hauled them out and he lifted them easily.

"Miz Emily?"

I smiled. "Yes."

"Thank you. Banker says if we'd lost it all the bank would have had to close an' a lot of good people would have been left with nothing. What happened?"

I gave it to him briefly. I'd been for a drive with Tiger. A man came out of the brush, made me stop, ordered me down, said he was taking Rabbit. He gone to hit Tiger who'd clawed him. While he was holding his arm and distracted, I'd picked up a rock, hit him, then found the saddle-bags, guessed what he'd done and started for town.

It all ended very well. The bank-robber was dumped in an unmarked grave. The marshal said the man's gear was mine – spoils of war – the bank gave me a reward, and Tiger was made much of any time we came to town. And me? I wrote it in my diary a day later, making a note that I owed that boy. I'd shared food with them when they were starving, but he'd saved mine and Tiger's lives. Not to mention that Luke and I had money in the bank too and now we had it back.

That was the year my brother's daughter came to stay a month. A wild thirteen-year-old who rode constantly, and got lost regularly. But we loved her, and she loved us and Tiger. We had no children, my brother had three, the other being two boys, both several years older than their sister, and I knew who would inherit from him. Diane came back to stay every two years after that, then our mother left her sufficient of an inheritance that Diane didn't need to marry if she didn't want to. Instead, she became a women's nurse and between profession and inheritance, she was happy, staying with us every second year, and guessing perhaps, in time the land she loved would come to her.

* * *

And then, seven years later, winter came and we discovered that it was going to be one of the worst – if not *the* worst – ever seen around here. Rabbit was retired. Tiger was near fourteen and I thought I'd need another cat come summer, something I found a real grief to think about and my Luke turned sixty.

The weather remained odd. One day it snowed steadily, the next it was a fine day and if there was maybe another one fine day after that, the snow partially melted on those second days, to begin again with the next colder day or night, and Luke studied me over breakfast one morning.

"Remember last time we had a winter like this?"

I did, we'd married two years before. We had a single elderly hand, and we'd done a deal with him and his five-years-older older brother who was the blacksmith in the tiny township twenty miles away. They'd come to us two days after we married and they laid out a proposition.

"Neither of us getting any younger. Day's gonna come when we can't work an' what happens then with no family to care for us. I got savings, so's Steve but they won't be enough. I thought about what else we could do and I come up with an idea."

We listened, agreed, and set to work. Luke and I, Steve and his brother, plus a couple of friends who owed Steve a favor all filed on a standard six hundred and forty acres section, part of which total blocked off access to more land into the hills behind. Land was plentiful, cheap, and no one was going to bother with the other part we didn't own but that would be all but impossible to use without us allowing passage. Steve stayed with us a year in the ranch house Luke's Pa had built before him on their section and Luke's ma took the fever and died.

During that time, we built a cabin for the brothers. There was a small cirque backing into the hills behind us. We built it there, turned the sod and planted – all of this near forty years ago now. But when we were done, Steve and Mike had a comfortable sheltered three-room cabin, a vegetable garden, fruit trees, two fenced paddocks, one containing their horses, the other with two milk goats and a billy. We'd signed a deed too. The land and everything on it was theirs, so long as they lived, and in that bad year it saved us.

The winter then had been worse than we'd ever known, worse still that Luke had just spent every cent we had on buying a small herd of cheap cattle, weaklings from a herd going further south. There were two old cows, both well in calf – accidentally so far as the trail boss was concerned and he was annoyed about it. Half a dozen yearling heifers, all runts, nine younger calves who just couldn't keep up any longer, and a baby bull whose mother had died from snakebite. We managed to mother him on to an older cow and he was doing fine – something he wouldn't have done if he'd stayed with the trail herd. Nineteen cattle, not much of a herd, but they were a start we thought, until that winter struck.

The snow came – and stayed. We'd cut hay over much of the summer from small lonely valleys, stacked it in the half barn, half cave that was a very fair size, and it would be sufficient – probably. But the winter got colder and colder, and colder still. And partway through it, Luke turned to me.

"I don't think the cattle are going to make it, love." I nodded, but that day I rode over to talk to Steve and Mike. My dad always said with age comes experience, and I hoped with all my heart they might have advice that could save us. They listened, I invited them to dinner, and that night they pointed out something neither of us had seen.

"Our valley's sheltered beyond anything else around here. It's those winds that kill cattle, more so t' young'uns or the older cows," Mike said thoughtfully. "If we run them into our place, right down the back where the cliff's higher and there's that coupl'a acres of scrub, wind'd pass over them."

We listened, and while bigger places lost half their stock, we didn't lose a beast. Mike died twelve years later, Steve three years after that, and the cirque was ours again. We kept everything the way it'd been though. I'd come to realize that vegetables and fruit trees grew better there, that in the cliff's shelter the land below stayed warmer. I dug in a couple of blackberry bushes and they did well. Then, after a discussion with me playing pessimist, we used their cabin to store half the hay each year, grew potatoes where Mike and Steve had, and stored them in the cabin as well.

Other things changed too. The government had started offering land for a cent an acre, and we'd bought the land we didn't own but used, Luke had gone riding then, found another valley, a good-sized one we hadn't known about, but it was on our border and we bought that as well, camouflaging the entrance and gating it off.

This summer we'd cut back on the cattle. We'd lived long enough to know it was going to be a hard winter; if not just *how* hard, and we'd cleaned out almost all but the breeding herd. There were five hundred head, plus the horses, and the milch goats. The six nannies and the billy could live in the barn, the horses in Brothers Valley.

Luke smiled at me. "We can run the herd into Far Valley. It's four hundred acres, there's deep caves and if we pick the right days, we can move most of the hay there too."

We did. And in a week, we could see the cattle were going to make it, while again, some of our neighbors wouldn't be so lucky. In the big old hay barn, I had five yearling steers, due to rejoin their friends once there was a clearer day. The other half of winter arrived first in a blinding storm. Luke had gone into town and would have to stay the night. I was alone but I'd been alone before. I rode to Brothers Valley and as I neared there, a horse came plodding out the valley mouth and nickered at me.

I looked at it, making a guess, took the beast on a lead. reached the cabin, ran both mounts into the lean-to, heaved the cabin door open and they were there. The older man, the nine boys, all ten years older now. And with them were young women and small children, several dogs, and at the valley back I knew there would be other horses. The warriors looked up at me with dulled desperate eyes, the women's expressions changing to bitter resignation. They knew what I was, and they expected nothing.

And I remembered. I remembered how we'd sat and eaten together as friends, Tiger making them laugh as I hadn't known they could. I remembered how, wrist slashed, Tiger about to be killed before me, one had risen up and saved us both. Tiger had liked and trusted them. I owed a debt. I leaped for the back wall, dug my fingers under a particular board, and dragged it sideways. I freed two more, and there was the entrance, just sufficient for someone to crawl through into a narrow room, running the entire back of the cabin.

In it was cut kindling and logs, stacked so they wasted no room. Enough dry wood to fuel stove and fire for maybe fifty hours. And in each corner were sacks, flour, grain, three sacks of molasses impregnated oats, plus other supplies. The brothers had planned the cache in case we ever had a winter as bad as that other, and they were caught here. It had become a tradition, and when they were gone, Luke and I retained tradition and supplies – just in case.

I lit stove and fire. Made pancakes, coffee, and sweet tea for the children. I shared the hot food and drink around, and saw bodies thawing. Minds starting to work again, and once they could move, howbeit it slowly, I left for home. My mount was a solid animal, not fast but powerful, and used to snow. Even so, I pushed him, and once I was home, I loaded a packhorse. I turned then and started back. Little use to those in the valley if all their mounts died. I arrived, dumped more hard feed for the horses, pointed to what I'd removed from the cache, and started for home again.

Once back I studied the weather and the time. Not enough for another journey, and I was exhausted, they have food and fire for tonight and tomorrow. I ate, slept, Tiger cuddled close, and at first light, having already eaten I was on my way again. I had no way of knowing that in the township Luke was frantic, the road had filled with drifts and he was in town now until matters improved.

I had no time to think of that. I chased the steers out of the barn, and herded them to the valley, cursing cattle, weather, and events that come upon a body unexpectedly. Once I was there, I found my friends in far better condition. I also found that in the interim, the young man I recognized had learned some English. I led him to the door, pointed to the steers where they huddled by the lean-to, and spoke slowly.

"Meat for you. Cut wood from trees where the horses are."

His black eyes stared into mine. "No gun."

Without a thought I handed him my rifle, saw his astonishment and made explanation. "Small glosbe is my friend. Your friend too."

He straightened, his hand coming out to take the weapon that would see his people had meat to survive. "We are puma, you have glosbe too, kin."

I nodded, a sudden warmth enveloping me. "We are kin. It is good. I am Emily O'Donald."

"I Wolf-Brother."

And so, I learned the name of one I'd known for ten years, whom I owed a life. "Wolf-Brother, I will return tomorrow."

I did. The drifts over the road to town lessened, Luke came home, but the day before he did so Wolf-Brother and his people were gone on recovered mounts. And again, the years went by. Tiger died that summer and I grieved. Diane, my niece, came to live on our ranch, knowing in time it would be hers, and twenty years after the last encounter a boy came calling, carrying a basket. He was about thirteen, and I knew who he must be as soon as I saw his face.

"Wolf-Brother is your father?" He nodded. "Your father, I, friends."

He spoke. "My father say so. Say we do not forget. He find small pumas, say bring them to you. We are kin. Is good?"

I had already caught sight of what the woven basket held. Where they'd come from, I had no idea. Even now the area wasn't heavily settled, but here were three small kittens, tabbies, one black, two silver. I thrust aside a thought that said a family could have died and I accepted the basket as it was held out.

"Thank you. Wait." I took the basket inside, sat it on the deerskin rug, and dived for my pantry. There I flung biscuits, a cake, and three tins of treacle into a flour bag, and returned. "Gifts for your father. We are friends, kin." There was an instant when the impassive face broke into a flashing grin, I grinned back, half in reaction, half because it was such a shining look that transformed his face.

"You, us, glosbe-kin," the boy confirmed, turning to where a pony waited. He vaulted onto its back and was gone, sack balanced on the pony's withers while I looked after him. Then I returned to the wailing kittens.

* * *

Diary entry – 3ʳᵈ **of April 2030.** *Tomorrow, I marry the man I love. This entry is in my own diary, but a copy goes into the diary of Emily McDonald who was my several times great-aunt. Her niece Diane inherited the McDonald's ranch and our family has lived there ever since. The ranch next door has been owned by the Puma family for several generation fewer, but our family has known them from long before that. Tom – the American version of his name, Tosahwi – and I have been best friends since we were first walking, and I think we always knew one day it would be more.*

His ancestor saved the life of Emily, as she saved his earlier, and there's been a link between our lines for always. The families joke they're the family of the big puma, and we're the family of the little puma. To mark it, Tom's brother took me aside yesterday and told me they'll have a special wedding present for us. I saw it, and I had to laugh. He's a big silver tabby, wearing a red plaited-leather collar and with a silver name tag on it that says Tiger. (It's special, that was the name of Emily's cat who first made friends with the puma clan, and let both sides see they had something in common. He was a big silver tabby cat too, and it's nice we'll have a 'Tiger' of our own in the old house.)

I remember when I first heard the story, and later when I was old enough and allowed to read her ancient diary, people discount cats sometimes, but neither of our families ever would. Tiger the first brought friendship, showed two peoples they were the same at heart. And, typical cat, ensured there would always be homes for his descendants – and didn't it puzzle all those earnest ethnologists for years, that a small Comanche clan had *cats*, ordinary much-loved moggies, and every single one of them, a silver tabby.

LIFE IN STAGES

We're such an unfortunate family. Back when stages first started in the region, one of my great uncles drove a stage – very briefly. About his seventh day on the job, he had steadied the stage-horses for the long run up the hill before town when a man riding one horse and leading a saddled mount without a rider pulled up behind him. The spare mount moved up to one side of the stage, the rider swung his horse right up to the door on the other side, and before my great uncle could ask what was going on, it all began.

The rider leaned down, opened the door, jumped into the stage, crawled across the three passengers inside, swung out of the other door, and leapt astride his spare mount. He called to the first horse, and it galloped ahead to join him. My great uncle Matthew was annoyed. This man was a flashy-looking chap, with a brocade waistcoat, slicked down hair, and a fancy suit with pants' bottoms tucked into short boots and my great uncle disliked the look of him. Besides, two of the passengers were respectable ladies and they were complaining about a man they didn't know crawling all over them in a public conveyance, and he felt that all of this was quite irregular. So, he called out to the man who was about to ride away still smirking.

"Say, stranger, what was that all about?"

And in a very fancy accent, the dude called back. "Nothing at all, Mister. I'm an actor and that was just a stage I'm going through." Then he started laughing like a fool. Well, my great uncle didn't like that, and his passengers were still upset, so he up and shot the man, and once he got back to the depot he resigned. He said to the manager that a man had better things to do with his time than to provide a stage for bad actors.

ABOUT THE AUTHOR

Lyn McConchie started writing professionally in 1990, since then she has seen fifty-one of her books published and nearly four hundred short stories. She has written SF/F, but also true-life humor about her farm and animals (7 books known as the 'Daze' series), children's books, a YA quartet set in her own New Zealand, a western, a dozen Sherlock Holmes pastiches, half a dozen post-apocalyptics, and one non-fiction. Lyn says her imagination is related to the energizer bunny, and she hopes to be writing for years to come.